LOVE
in the time of
CORONA

First published 2021

Copyright © Kalyani Sandrapragas 2021

The right of Kalyani Sandrapragas to be identified as the author of this work has been asserted in accordance with the Copyright, Designs & Patents Act 1988.

All rights reserved. No part of this book may be reproduced, stored in a retrieval system, or transmitted in any form or by any means, electronic, electrostatic, magnetic tape, mechanical, photocopying, recording or otherwise, without the written permission of the copyright holder.

Published under licence by Brown Dog Books and
The Self-Publishing Partnership, 7 Green Park Station, Bath BA1 1JB

www.selfpublishingpartnership.co.uk

ISBN printed book: 978-1-83952-281-9
ISBN e-book: 978-1-83952-291-8

Cover design by Andrew Prescott
Internal design by Andrew Easton

Cover illustration 'Hope Rising' © Rana J Rodger, 1. p38 'Black Bird' © Trish Flynn, p213 'And a Black Cloud Came' © Darrie Payne

Printed and bound in the UK

This book is printed on FSC certified paper

LOVE
in the time of
CORONA

COVID CHRONICLES

EDITED BY
KALYANI SANDRAPRAGAS

CONTENTS

Dedication	8
Acknowledgements	9
Preface – My Story, Kalyani Sandrapragas, UK	11
1. Writing My Way to Calm and Connection, Sue Edge, UK	18
2. Breathing, Emily Hill, UK	22
3. For the Love of Telling Stories, Timothy Seekings, Taiwan	25
4. For the Love of Testy and Google, Kathy Fennel, UK	29
5. Lessons, Mina Cullimore, UK	31
6. Speaking of Light, Mehri Holliday, UK	36
7. Blackbird, Trish Flynn, UK	38
8. Not What Is, Rosie Gladwell, UK	41
9. Simone, Hilda Billy Todd, Italy	42
10. Unexpected Times, Marisol Vigor, Spain	45
11. Whatever the Times Bring, Josélon Gipsy Floyd, Spain	48
12. A Blessing in Disguise, Tara Esther Kleij, Spain	49
13. A New Sense of Time, Pete Lumb, Isle of Man	51
14. Island of Us, Louise Gabriel, UK	54
15. Positives and Negatives, Jolanda Van Denzen, Netherlands	56
16. Looking for Motherland, Cecilia Örtenheim, Sweden	58
17. The Upside of Lockdown, Stephen Bellm, USA	59
18. Watching Rosie Bloom, Ann Wilson, UK	62
19. Lockdown Love Story, Cathy Whitefield, Spain	66
20. Shining through the Pandemic Gloom, Raymond Yeung, Hong Kong	70

21. Circling the Fortress, Dawn Rees, UK	73
22. Could It Be That You've Always Lived Here? Fawzia, Switzerland	75
23. For the Love of Lavender, Athena Lambrinidou, New Zealand	77
24. Finding New Paths, Lucy Counsell, UK	79
25. Certainties in a Time of Uncertainty, Amanda Jane Gibbs, Spain	83
26. Lockdown, Josélon Gipsy Floyd, Spain	86
27. Notes to Self, Claudia Chapman, UK	87
28. Befriending Uncertainty in Our 'New Normal', Sue Edge, UK	91
29. A Love Story from a Century Ago, Roger Wilson, New Zealand	94
30. Corona Chronicles, Andrea Mcintosh, Germany	98
31. Compassion and Self-care, Sue Edge, UK	101
32. Feeling the Love through the Stillness of Life, Jaqui Pixi Rose, Spain	104
33. For the Love of Freedom, Susan McMackin, UK	107
34. For the Love of Small Things, Rebecca Heloise Faro, Spain	108
35. For the Love of Writing, Rose Wadham, UK	110
36. A Country Boy, Jonathan Barnard, UK	113
37. Green Rhapsody, Rachel Hutchings, UK	115
38. Laureate Box, Ginny Keith, UK	118
39. Painting My Way to Peace, Carol Miles, UK	120
40. Medway Dawning, Lesley Conquest, UK	123
41. Time It Is a Precious Thing, Shujata Luptajan, Spain	124
42. Morning Coffee, Mix Amylo, Spain	126
43. Taking One Step, One Breath, One Moment Along Our Path, Sue Edge, UK	129
44. The Alchemy Garden, Rana Rodger, France	133
45. The Peace of This Time, Sonaa Digby, UK	135

46. Garden Haven, Frances Moore, UK	136
47. So Lightly Here, Lisan Bremmers, Sweden	139
48. The Power of Connection and the Pain of Isolation of the Pandemic, Sue Edge, UK	141
49. Musical Notes and Favourite Quotes, Ebe Ghansat, UK	145
50. This Cloistered Life, Arpy Shively, Spain	147
51. Lockdown in the 12th Century Community of St John's Hospital, Eileen Routh, UK	151
52. Regeneration, Jeff Rees, Wales	154
53. A Return to Roots, Nicole Wilkinson, UK	156
54. On Reflection, Love Is All That Matters, John Richards, Spain	159
55. Melting Pot, Rebecca Heloise Faro, Spain	162
56. Our Shrinking World, Louise Gabriel, UK	164
57. Awakenings, Pamela Marianna Lassalle, UK	168
58. Lockdown in Aotearoa, Cindy Baxter, New Zealand	170
59. Something Lost, Something Found, Thuranie Aruliah, UK	175
60. Bearing Witness, Elizabeth Hill, UK	178
61. A Secret Garden, Topy Jewell, UK	180
62. The True Meaning of Life, José Florenza, Spain	181
63. The Blessing or the Curse, Bridie Jackson, Spain	182
64. Music Is My Medicine, Cara Jane Murphy, UK	184
65. For the Love of Flowers, Joanna Corcoran Wunsch, UK	189
66. Beauty Everywhere, Lorena Marchetti, Italy	192
67. An Earthly Love Story, Belen Alvarez Marin, Spain	194
68. The Milk of Human Kindness, Svetlana Vinogradova, Denmark	197
69. My Neighbours, Marc Joyeux, Italy	199

70. Getting Out: Reflections during Lockdown, Zoe White, UK	203
71. A Rhyme for Our Time, Shujata Luptajan, Spain	208
72. Live, Love, Eat – Amalia Yasmina Rasheed, Spain	211
73. Return to Self-Love, Veronika Poola, Spain	214
74. The Gift of Deep Connection, Giovanna Barker, UK	217
75. Trust and Surrender, Sarah Tilley, UK	220
76. A Different Kind of Seeing, Robin Davies, Hong Kong	224
77. 'Where Do I Come From?' Linda Sinclair, UK	230
78. What a Time to Become a Granny! Fiona Parker, UK	233
79. I Dream of Being What I Was, Joanna Crowson, Spain	235
80. Going Back to Normal? Kim Henry, USA	240
81. Like a Rock, Anna Begas, Spain	242
82. Expecting the Unexpected, Cathy Stanton, Spain	246
83. Love, Liberty and the Pursuit of Science, Charlie Griffiths, Spain	250
84. And A Black Cloud Came, Darrie Payne, UK	254
85. Translating Covidian, Arpy Shively, Spain	255
86. In the Light of Love, Antonio Perez, Spain	258
87. Sending Out an SOS to the World, Shujata Luptajan, Spain	262
88. One Year On ... How Much Longer Before It Ends? Sue Edge, UK	267
89. Embracing Hope, Kalyani Sandrapragas, UK	270
Your Covid Chronicle	275

Dedication

I dedicate this book to people all over the world who give love in all its miraculous and mundane manifestations.

And, especially, I dedicate it in profound love and gratitude to my mother Sharada, and my children Kamala, Kailas and Minakshi, my gifts from heaven.
Shortly before publishing this book I, asked my mother Sharada, aged 94, what Love is:

'Love is within us and all around us. It is not exclusive to the sentiments of love between people. Love is in a flower, a stone, a tree, the birds, the sky. Everything in nature is love. Love is kindness, duty, compassion. It is all embracing. God is love and love is God.'

> *'There is only one element in life which is worth having at any cost and it is love. Love immense and infinite, broad as the sky and deep as the ocean. This is the one great gain in life.'* Swami Vivekananda

Acknowledgements

This book would not have been published if not for the enthusiastic and generous response and participation of all the people who contributed their story to this project. I celebrate each and every one of you and offer you my heartfelt gratitude for joining me on this journey. My thanks also to my dear friends and family for simply being there for me!

More specifically I wish to thank the following people:
Jonathan Barnard for his unwavering support, encouragement and feedback from concept to completion, not forgetting his listening ear! He was the first person with whom I shared the seed of an idea that grew into a project, and nine months later was able to celebrate the birth of this book, which he has so neatly summarised on the back cover!

A special thanks to my amazing team of friends, Shujata Luptajan, Arpy Shively and Charlie Griffiths for stepping in at the eleventh hour to help edit the manuscript to ensure that the book steps out to the publishers on time. I thank you for your dedication, knowledge and support and for doing everything with love and passion.

Arpy Shively is a very skilled and versatile writer who contributes a range of content for websites, blogs, lifestyle and travel magazines. Her diligence, skills, enthusiasm and hours spent in front of the computer screen made the task of editing the manuscript so much easier. Working with her was a pleasure. Her informative and inspiring blog WomanWorks focuses on challenges and positive change for women worldwide. http://www.womanworks.org.uk
For more information https://spark.adobe.com/page/39KbCxzfQaNG1/

Shujata is priceless! Her talents countless, and if I were to list the innumerable ways in which she has supported me, I would not know where to begin! Shujata and Charlie between them are a rich library of knowledge and experience and their insight and feedback have been invaluable. Generous with their time, they were always available at the end of the phone to offer help and guidance. Their love and passion for almost anything they put their mind to is a gift and blessing to anyone who engages them in their story.

My thanks also to Sue Edge, who has kindly given permission to print some articles from her illuminating blog https://keepingcalmincoronatimes.blogspot.com Sue's interest in wellbeing, yoga and writing culminated in the creation of this blog in the spring of 2020, whilst taking a break from her job teaching literacy skills to disadvantaged children. In her blog, she shares her personal experiences and moments of wisdom, combined with her love of nature, yoga, travel and life by the sea.

Last but not least, my immense gratitude to Rana J. Rodger for granting me permission to reprint her beautiful painting, Hope Rising, for the front cover.
Rana's works are a wonderful combination of colour and form, spirituality and art. She draws her inspiration from Native American and Aboriginal indigenous art, culture and philosophy. In the Australian outback she created her own paints from pigments, experimenting with different media and textures, colours and hues. Her work is vibrant and rich in colour and texture, touching something universal and primal within us, to bring a sense of positivity and optimism to this world. Her paintings are milestones on her spiritual journey.
Rana lives in southwest France where she has her studio and holds creativity retreats at Alchemy Garden https://www.thealchemygarden.com/. To see her artwork and prints, visit her website at: https://www.ranapix.co.uk

Preface – My Story
Kalyani Sandrapragas, UK

'A journey of a thousand miles begins with a single step'
Lao Tzu

Looking back at the journey of this book, it was that single step I took in March 2020 when the world effectively was on 'lockdown'. Since then I have travelled many virtual miles reconnecting with friends and family dotted around the world, spanning almost a life time.

So how did this project begin? A random idea that gained momentum and took a life of its own. Before I knew it, I was being taken on a journey of which I had been unaware, culminating in this book.

No one could anticipate the devastating consequences of the coronavirus, the pandemic forcing many into financial hardship and loss of life. And for those who were already sick, homeless, stateless and penniless; untold suffering.

In the UK, Prime Minister Boris Johnson announces national lockdown restrictions to take effect on 26 March 2020. Figures put the death toll at 465 people with about 9,530 people infected. The number of people known to have been infected globally stands at more than 465,000.

The restrictions imposed on everyday life as a result of the pandemic highlighted the inequality in society, having different consequences for different people based on their material status and security. For some it was an inconvenience, for many, life changing. And for those of us who were able to manage the transition, the pandemic enabled us to take a glimpse into our own lives and come to the realisation that we were being presented with a unique opportunity to create a different society. The 'new' normal. More words and expressions to add to the dictionary following the pandemic.

The virus has forced us to re-evaluate life itself. Lockdown effectively 'unlocked' our minds, bodies and hearts, fine-tuning our sense of awareness. It was as if the curtains of perception were flung open and we finally began to take stock of our lives and environment. Permission was granted to stop in our tracks, put aside the life to which we were robotically entrenched and to step back, reflect. Our senses were heightened and our hearts opened still wider.

Lockdown brought blessings to our environment, with cities becoming less congested and polluted, and wildlife reclaiming spaces from which it had hitherto been excluded by the noise of human activity.

My lockdown journey began as it did for many people, seeking refuge in my home and nature with loved ones. Mindfulness and living in the moment became more real than ever. Plans were put on hold as we had only the 'present' moment. I felt blessed, privileged, that I had the means to sustain this journey. Surrender and gratitude became my mantra, the rudder and sails of my voyage across uncharted waters.

Before lockdown I spent half the week commuting by public transport to London from Kent to share in the care of my mother, who is now 94 years old. With advancing years, my mother required increasing care and support, and to this effect my brother Selva, took the meritorious step of moving into our mother's home; a steady and loving presence. My sister Larissa, who lives in Spain, would normally visit our mother at least every couple of months, but since the outbreak of the pandemic in Europe at the beginning of last year, her visits have been severely curtailed due to the restrictions and lockdowns imposed by each country at various times; sadly, for her and for us.

As the possibility of a lockdown loomed, my first thoughts were with my mother. How do I make that journey without risking her health? My own home that I share with my children is based in Kent. How can I safely navigate between both households where my heart belonged? Being a 'carer', I knew that I would be permitted to travel.

Thoughts drifted to the immediate practicalities of travel and within a few days of the seed being planted a solution arose – with the help of my friend

Emily, I was blessed with a car that enabled me to make the journeys safely and unimpeded by traffic.

The car was the first of the many gifts that flowed my way during lockdown. My friend Susan sold it at an affordable price, and managed to get it through the MOT on the last day, on the last appointment before lockdown. Gratitude was the order of the week! Now for the next challenge.

Facing my fears! For a number of years, I hadn't driven on the motorways after a bad experience that left me traumatised. And despite attempts at overcoming this fear, eight years after resolving never to drive on motorways, I had to face my fear once more. There was no choice in the matter now. If I was going to drive and navigate between the two households, what more perfect an opportunity than driving on relatively empty roads. So gradually working my way up from a modest and dangerous 50 mph I slowly revved up to 70 mph with confidence brimming! I am now a seasoned driver on the highways and byways.

'Come to the edge,' he said.
'We can't, we're afraid!' they responded.
'Come to the edge,' he said.
'We can't, We will fall!' they responded.
'Come to the edge,' he said.
And so they came.
And he pushed them.
And they flew.'
Guillaume Apollinaire

I couldn't help thinking how the pandemic helped me face my fears. I was flying! I added this to my gratitude list, that seemed to be growing ever longer.

So on a beautiful day in May, having taken myself on many walks and seeing the miracle of nature with new eyes, and using the cycles of nature as a metaphor for birth, death and renewal, I decided to walk the labyrinth.

This labyrinth lay near the footpath at Eliot College that links the University of Kent to Canterbury city centre. It is created from York stone and turf, based on a medieval design. Perched on the top of the hill, surrounded by trees, it offers wonderful views of the cathedral and the city below.

I had never walked a labyrinth before, so here was my opportunity! The weather was another gift; it was May and spring had arrived in true splendour. Everything around me seemed alive, full of inspirational messages from nature. Life seemed full in the emptiness of human activity.

I had no preconceived notion of how to walk a labyrinth. Theories bore me. Spontaneity and an open mind nourish me. Suffice to say, labyrinths have been used by various cultures and mystical and religious traditions as a form of centring. Like mandalas, representing the circles and cycles of life, they take you on a metaphysical journey inwards and then outwards, and back again *ad infinitum*.

It seemed the perfect moment to take time out to quieten the mind and open the heart. A moving meditation.

The labyrinth offers a single circular path that winds its way from the outside of the circle to the centre and back out again. There are no dead ends as in a maze, and no choices as to which way to turn. Walking 'forward' was the only choice being presented.

Walking a labyrinth is symbolic of the journey of life, which also contain twists and turns. The movement as you weave your way around the path is circumambulatory with no chance of getting lost. There is only one way in and one way out, so you don't need to think about where you're going.

So with no plan in mind I started my journey. As I stepped onto the path, I was overwhelmed by a deep sense of gratitude. Gratitude for the miracles in my life, however big or small. And as if it was what I was meant to do, I began to give thanks to everything that has met me on my path, despite the ups and downs, from childhood, through adolescence, into adulthood. And there was plenty to be grateful for, as life is a great teacher.

Now in the centre of this circle, without a moment's thought, I offered my prayers, beginning with the nearest and dearest, like ripples extending out to the world. And as I turned back to where I began, the journey outwards, I took these prayers and hopes back with me. It was a symbolic journey, powerful and wholesome. I returned home feeling at peace.

Social media, for those who have access to it, played an important role during this period of 'confinement'. Although physically confined, those who had access to the internet were able to socialise and work from home. I speak not for the many, but the few, who had the luxury of being able to stay in touch with friends and family and the wider world, through the power of technology. We were inundated with stories of how people's lives were transformed, living under the new constraints of lockdown. Stories within stories. In amongst them were also stories of love, creativity and connection. And, whilst I have my reservations about social media, when the constraints of lockdown became a household reality amidst the chaos and uncertainty, people began to open.

To be human is also to be vulnerable. And when change happens like a bolt of lightning from one day to the next, we have a remarkable capacity for resilience. And consciously or unconsciously tap into our inner reserves of creativity, to try and transform the negative to a positive, like alchemists.

'He said, "In the midst of hate, I found there was, within me, an invincible love. In the midst of tears, I found there was, within me, an invincible smile. In the midst of chaos, I found there was, within me, an invincible calm. I realised, through it all, that in the midst of winter, I found there was, within me, an invincible summer. And that makes me happy. For it says that no matter how hard the world pushes against me, within me, there's something stronger – something better, pushing right back."'

Albert Camus

As the weeks of May unfolded I witnessed the stories from within my circle – returning to family, gardens, homes, nature, forgotten hobbies and activities, rediscovering themselves and their lives – and one theme stood out. The power of love and connection. I thought how wonderful it would be to collect these stories.

I shared this idea with my friend Jonathan. Unequivocally he said 'Do it!' And then I shared the idea with other friends and they said, 'Do it.' Encouraged by friends, another journey presented itself out of the blue, under the beautiful untainted skies of lockdown in May.

I decided to call the project 'Love in the Time of Corona', inspired by the title of Gabriel García Márquez's iconic book, *Love in the Time of Cholera*. Different stories, but the title was 'apt'. *Love in the Time of Covid-19* did not have the same resonance.

And so the journey began as it did in the labyrinth. Lockdown had 'unlocked' potential in the here and now. I called this my 'project' as a book seemed a very long way away. I am not a writer and have never been published.

The seed being planted, I began the task of inviting my friends to contribute. And the response has culminated in this book, for which I am immensely grateful. More to add to the Gratitude list!

Looking back, I realise that this book is also about my journey with friends and family through decades.

So here is the essence of the invitation I eventually sent at the beginning of June 2020:

I am writing to invite you to make a contribution to a project very close to my heart, 'Love in the Time of Corona'.

In these strange and unprecedented times, everything about love is both extraordinary and precarious, miraculous and devastating, poignant and inspirational. A time of immense changes and adjustments, of beginnings and endings. Familiar routines have disappeared, plans cancelled, relationships changed.

We need love more than ever and consciously or unconsciously seek and discover it in the most unexpected of places. Creativity has flourished. Creative thinking, creative planning, creative living. The last few months have been replete with stories of how people's lives have changed and evolved. Their tribulations and blessings, their highs and lows.

But ultimately, as Philip Larkin has said, 'what will survive of us is love'. It would be wonderful to hear your story. your story from these times of Corona - something that has impacted you, something that you have experienced, seen or felt, your musings, your observations. Your story of love.

For the love of nature
For the love of humanity
For the love of children
For the love of parents
For the love of cooking
For the love of movement
For the love of music
For the love of work
For the love of community
For the love of solitude
For the love of animals
For the love of art and craft
For the love of your home
For the love of your garden
For the love of your life
For the love of You

Do any of these themes resonate with you? These are just a few ideas to inspire you.

By the end of August 2020, I had received eighty responses and realised that a book was in the making; one to celebrate all of us, on our journey. The majority of the stories in this anthology were between June and September 2020. Each one that was submitted has been published, as together we make the whole. Diversity makes for a rich tapestry.

'If history were taught in the form of stories, it would never be forgotten.'
Rudyard Kipling
I hope that you enjoy this piece of history.

Writing My Way to Calm and Connection through the Challenges of Corona Times

Sue Edge, UK

> 'Writing about upsetting things can influence our basic values, our daily thinking patterns and our feelings about ourselves. There appears to be a basic need to reveal ourselves to others'
>
> Dr James Pennebaker

While spring was slowly beginning to unfurl in March this last year, the sudden arrival of coronavirus shook the UK to its core. I was feeling a multitude of swirling emotions including fear and shock. If you had asked me then about the power of the heart to thrive in this impending crisis, I might have laughed in disbelief. Non-essential things such as creativity or love were the last things on my mind as I read copious scientific articles about pandemics and Covid-19.

As we began our lockdown, it was taking all my energy to deal with practicalities: obtaining enough food, cleaning, rearranging parts of my life onto Zoom and trying to relax enough to sleep through a night. It was as if we had been hit by a slow-moving tsunami, seen looming far away, that we thought would only trickle ashore. I longed to feel some calm, but mostly wanted to escape to somewhere free of coronavirus or lockdowns.

After a week of feeling like my life had been overtaken by coronavirus stress, I heard myself telling a neighbour (from a distance) that I was going to write a blog. The idea had come to me the night before, while awake again at 3 am, with thousands of thoughts flooding my mind trying to make sense of this overwhelming experience. I needed a way to lower my stress levels while being mostly stuck at home. I figured I wasn't the only one feeling like this, so if I wrote about becoming more relaxed I hoped it would not only help me, it could support others. Writing would give my mind a new focus, other than simply surviving another day without getting sick. I chose a quality for each week such as kindness, compassion, then gratitude, that could each be easily practised. This antidote to tension would follow my yoga teacher's advice to engage the 'heart chakra' as much as possible on the bumpy journey ahead.

Writing is something I've done intermittently as a hobby over the years, filling a small pile of dusty notebooks. I've found it therapeutic, but being a very private person, have rarely shared these personal words. Curiously, I'd noticed that I hadn't written much in the last couple of years since going through a tough period of multiple bereavements, redundancy and a health struggle. Life had felt too painful to write about, needing some skin to heal over the raw wounds that I was protecting. However, the enormous jolt that coronavirus caused as it crashed into our lives and communities was enough to reawaken my inner writer. Not only was I going to write regularly each week, I had committed to sharing my words. What was I thinking? Would anyone read it? Maybe that wouldn't even matter if it helped me to feel more balanced again.

My first week focused on kindness as this would become the all-embracing theme of the whole blog. To help deepen a sense of kindness, I chose two simple practices for the week. The first seemed effortless, but was to smile at people while out on my daily walk. Learning to navigate the new two-metre social distance felt initially awkward and unnatural. The simple act of smiling lifted my own soul and was usually reciprocated, bringing some warmth back into my heart. The second practice was to sit for five minutes each day and notice with kindness how I was feeling. I didn't want my blog to ignore the struggles and difficult emotions that would no doubt be present in these unprecedented times. By giving some kind attention and space to these exhausting feelings, they seemed easier to manage and accept. By the end of that week, I could already feel my body starting to uncurl its tense muscles and find its way back to some peace.

Sharing my writing with readers brought about its own sense of vulnerability and excitement in varying measures. A blog is different to more instant forms of social media as it requires the reader to stop, breathe and read slowly. I hoped the experience of reading would engender a feeling of reassurance or grounding. I often wrote in the garden, surrounded by the soothing sounds of birdsong and the rustling of trees. I imagined my writing coming from a steady oak tree, firmly rooted into the earth while the coronavirus storm raged over us. The comments I have received each week have built a web of connection that I was never expecting. While writing, I would often wonder, is it just me going through this? And after pressing 'publish' with some trepidation, I would always be relieved to read comments saying, 'I've just read this, I feel like that too.'

I initially set out to write until we were past the peak of our coronavirus curve and safely out of the woods. I hadn't expected that easing lockdown and adapting to our strange 'new normal' would be filled with an array of topics to journal about. During some weeks, a quote would come to mind which would become a starting point for my words. Brené Brown's teachings were the first to resonate as I wrote about the importance of human connection in relation to millions of people being ensconced in their homes. Eckhart Tolle's wisdom of staying in the present moment has echoed more strongly in recent weeks as it becomes clear that this really is a 'marathon, not a sprint'. As we have to dig into yet more reserves of energy to face the next phase of reopening our country, it has started to feel like a much longer marathon than I hoped for.

But while the pandemic is still unfolding, if you ask me now about the power of the heart in this crisis, I wouldn't laugh. I would nod quietly, with tears in my eyes, feeling gratitude for discovering my ability to write and connect during turbulent times. I wrote in my blog about a coronavirus 'cloud' that has been hovering over us for months, full of collective grief and uncertainty. And as the dark clouds part, rays of light stream through, radiating out hope, warmth and compassion. That has been the gift of writing, to bring a ray of light into the hard moments of the pandemic, reviving my flagging spirit and soothing my heart. And reassuring others that they are not alone.

http://keepingcalmincoronatimes.blogspot.com

Breathing
Emily Hill, UK

'You are a volume in the divine book.
A mirror to the power that created the universe.
Whatever you want, ask it of yourself.
Whatever you are looking for can only be found inside you'
Jalaluddin Rumi

There is a deep love within us all, often unspoken. I feel it for my daughter, I feel it for my mother, and I feel it for all living things, yet when I try to speak of it something inside me disappears. My voice sounds shrill and empty, words come out but I feel no one can hear them. I try to write about it and my language sounds trite. When I try to hug, my emotions feel trapped inside my body.

Somehow I fail to express my heartfelt love, my true self, and it and me, perhaps one and the same, dissipate silently. I feel lost and a sense of loss. I am in deep grief, as are many others, at what I can only describe as a profound disconnect. Any surges of feeling subside into shadow, and are quietly veiled for another time, reserved. So as I conceal, I withdraw back into a hollow, dark and familiar shell.

Even during this global crisis, if I am really honest, I feel little has touched me, and I haven't reached out. This is not to say I have not absorbed what has happened; I've cried at personal accounts of loss heard on the radio, empathised with the exhausted faces of key workers on TV, heard the rally of clattering pots in the air outside my house, but despite the global swathes of fear brought about by this pandemic, inside I remain unmoved. What I have slowly begun to realise is that I was already locked down. The only notable difference to my life was that my daughter was not going to school. My shock was at how little things changed about me rather than how much.

Although I am grateful that no one I know personally has died, thankful that friends of mine who have suffered have recovered, and relieved that my parents are still alive and well, I remain distant and out of touch, especially with relatives. I consider how little we care, how seldom we touch, how rarely we connect, or maybe it's just me. But here is the thing: somehow given the time alone with permission to stop, things have changed; I have begun to breathe deeply, I have started to care, and gradually I have reconnected, not so much with others, but with myself.

Stay still too long and the mind overwhelms, move the body and energy shifts. After my realisation, my response, like so many of us when feeling trapped, is to run. Now my eyes, mouth, and lungs are opening and my heart is unlocking; my senses awake and I see swifts, hedgehogs, hawk moths and toads. I smell bluebells, roses, sweet peas and lavender. My dog is my companion, and my daughter has become my heartbeat. I want to stay healthy so I live long enough to see her birth her own children, smell their hair and touch their skin.

I keep running, consistently throughout the pandemic, away from fear and towards a new sense of family, of babies yet to be born, of another world. I watch *Grayson Perry's Art Club* and my faith in life is restored; he gets it, and so does his observant wife, Philippa. All the contributors, their conversation, their art, amaze me; their efforts melt me and I long for my fully feeling artist tribe. I weep for a boy who lost his twin aged four, who pieced together his life in collage, literally putting people back together. Finally, I feel moved inside as well as out. I yearn to connect; yet still I make no art, I just hold my daughter quietly in a common sense of grief. I silence the very language I use and I mute the controls.

The only relief I find is to stick my fingers into soil and earth. This is what I do, and somehow this is enough. The garden receives a half-hearted makeover as my attention is still elsewhere, trying to connect, to find love, but I know not to look for it in others. So as a single mum in lockdown, I try not to shut down, and start to love from inside out; I stroke my cats and I start to serve, I give to strangers and protect my friends. I teach my child and we immerse ourselves in nature. We spend our days outside; we dig, plant, and go for walks in the orchards. We go with our own flow, and finally we honour our own rhythms. My world opens up and something shifts.

Love, I know love is within. For me no words, no sounds, no artwork comes close to expressing that which lies deep inside; no tiny fingers can reach it, no lover can really touch it, perhaps no one can truly share it, yet somehow, unspoken, it touches us all, seeping out of some damp inner chamber, some part of ourselves, from source. This sustaining life force finally fades for all of us, or perhaps it pulls us through as we 'pass over', but my inner source now nourishes me, as if wanting nothing suddenly attracts everything. And so on I go, surviving and reviving, regulating my heart rate, encouraging my blood to travel around my body, cleansing as I continue to move, breathe and love.

I know there is no cheering party at the end of this race, we die alone, and yet no other support system is more vital than our own. All we have to do, like an ancient trusted mantra to the divine, is surrender to the breath. In that act alone we exist fully, and there is nothing to connect to; the beginning and end of every flow is cyclical; even as we rest, we are retreating and returning only ever to ourselves.

For the Love of Telling Stories
Timothy Seekings, Taiwan

'The power of storytelling is exactly this: to bridge the gaps where everything else has crumbled.'
Paulo Coelho

Summary
We tell stories all the time, and we become involved in those of other people. Stories are powerful attractors with which we create our desired realities. The story of Covid-19, as of mid-2020, is rather frightening and disorienting. Fortunately, we are not compelled to indulge in it. We can and should write our own story. Thereby, whether we want to write a comedy, a tragedy, or a love story is up to us.

For the love of telling stories
Charles Eisenstein wrote a nice essay on Covid-19 quite early on. Inspired by the shape of the corona virus, he likened what was happening across the world to a coronation. The enlightened ones today waiting for the planetary shift in consciousness were given an inter-paradigmatic vehicle to transcend the old world of chaos and ascend to a new form of being, devoid of duality, compulsion, and other impediments to a spiritual and intentional existence built on love.

There is a point in being optimistic. It colours our thoughts and words, and what we produce then are positive attractors, energetic fields or whirlpools that pull us towards them and in that way help us manifest the world we want to create. Tom Atlee from the Co-Intelligence Institute writes about this in his theory of story fields. I fully subscribe to this idea.

An old Mauritian philosopher by the name of Jean Russell, who was my mentor for a while in London, used to say this: 'Words are like bees. They can sting you.' What he meant was to be careful and conscious in the choice of words and the telling of stories. I also learnt the power of words when I once wrote a text in a state of depression, in which I asked for the gates of hell to open and something of significance to happen to me to wake me up from the all-embracing sensory dullness I was drowning in. About a week later, my manic schizoid neighbour broke from his adjacent apartment through our bathroom wall and escaped through the kitchen window. It was no coincidence. It was frightening. It took a while, but I learnt that writing is powerful. Sometimes like a prayer, sometimes like a meditation, sometimes like medicine, and sometimes like a field that attracts things and people and ideas and all kinds of stuff.

Still, while I believe in the power of writing positive stories, I can only write what my soul whispers into my ear; or simply what I resonate with, the frequency I'm tuned in to. And while I'd like to be purely positive like Charles Eisenstein and so many others and do my part in ushering in a new era of elevated consciousness for humankind, I seem to resonate more with other stories. Case in point: *A New Dark Age* by James Bridle. I don't know. The mode of analysis or the language just resonates more with me. I'm still positive and optimistic, believe me. Life is good. Death is good. It's all a cosmic joke. Dead serious and comic relief at the same time. Laughing is good. Humour is as universal as love. The reason why angels can fly, G. K. Chesterton reminds us, is because they take themselves so lightly. The heavy sinks, the light ascends. The reason for being optimistic is not to be found at the end of the world or in the conclusion of a storyline, in some kind of accomplishment or resolution, but right here, right now; simply in experiencing a certain lightness of being, and in seeing the humour and irony that is part of existence.

Covid-19 as a story has mutated into a nightmarish whirlpool pulling everyone into its delirious and dystopian vortex. Fear has spread. Everyone is divided on the subject. People have been deprived of their freedoms. The world seems in great peril and nothing will ever be the way it was. We will all be vaccinated or else excluded from spheres of social life. Everyone is now a potential health risk. Mad conspiracy theories spread faster than the virus and, as in an episode of *The*

Twilight Zone, twist people's minds. We can't tell any more what is real and what is fake, and we have the uneasy feeling that the fear and confusion that are spreading are actually much more dangerous than the microbe.

What on earth is happening? Some really awful stories are being peddled. And the media has them on repeat, 24/7. Covid-19 is sucking not just people and communities into it, but entire societies. When this all began to unfold, at the beginning of 2020, an old friend came to visit – a friend of trees and a lucid dreamer. From the first conversation we had on the topic, she insisted she would not buy into any of it, not for one single moment. And she didn't.

OK, we had it easy here in Taiwan. No major lockdown, no curfew, no major inconveniences. No major public health crisis. People wear face masks quite readily anyway, so a period where everybody wore them in public was not overly taxing or weird. But the point is that, regardless, my friend would not indulge in the storytelling, because she knew instinctively that it was not healthy. You would only get lost in this story, because there was no way to ascertain truth. Whether the Covid-19 stories came from the mainstream media or the alternative social media was irrelevant. The point is that they would not contribute to a healthy spirit in the here and now. As such, they were not a desirable attractor towards the story of her own life at this point in time. Therefore, she opted simply to stay away from them. The point here is that you have a choice of stories.

There's this Woody Allen movie called *Melinda and Melinda*. It's such a good idea, I love it. It begins in a restaurant with a couple of friends out for dinner when they start arguing about whether life is a tragedy or a comedy. To put their disagreeing views to the test, they decide to sketch out the beginning of a story and then the two writers in the group proceed to tell their versions of the story, one being a tragedy and the other a comedy. And that's kind of the idea that I feel should be applied to the case of Covid-19. We are in charge of our own storytelling. If the current Covid-19 story field feels like a dark and unpleasant place, we should try and stay a safe distance from its gravitational field. Instead, we should meditate and activate the storyteller within us.

Take something as the starting point – the first news report you heard on the topic, the microbe, or an individual friend's story. Alternatively, begin before any news of Covid first surfaced. Then, tell a story. Tell your story. It's really up to you if you want to tell a tragedy, a comedy, a science-fiction story, a crime thriller, a period drama, or a love story, because, at the end of the day, you are your own storyteller. For my part, I'd suggest making it a love story or perhaps a romantic comedy, because, after all, your story is supposed to make you happy and healthy. As long as you can laugh and feel a certain kind of lightness in your being, you are probably on the right track. Then, you can go back to perceiving and appreciating all the love around you and begin developing a deep and lasting love for writing your own stories.

For the Love of Testy and Google
Kathy Fennel, UK

'Animals are such agreeable friends – they ask no questions; they pass no criticisms.'
George Eliot

I have two chickens. One is called Testy after a rather short-tempered friend of mine. The other is called Google because she is a search engine. They are old now and rarely lay eggs. Their friendship brings me delight especially on the days that I garden; they come up beside me and look at what I am doing, then turn their necks to look at me. 'What you doin'?' they cluck at me. 'What you doin'?' They 'help' by tearing at my precious plant roots in order to find grubs and then nest in the soil, so they can have a dirt bath. Recently worked beds where seeds have been sown are their favourite.

To protect my plants, I have, on occasion, put the girls in a fenced area. They are happy for an hour or two and then devise means to escape with a mission to head towards the house. In the house the dog's bowl sits temptingly, in the conservatory. Google is always the ringleader and silently enters the conservatory to avoid detection. Sadly, Testy is not so canny and announces her entrance by calling 'hello'. My dog, Enzo, usually comes to find me as if alerting me to the interlopers. He learned long ago, as a puppy, to let the chooks be and not chase them. Sometimes he sits there watching them eat his food and 'harrumphs' at their cheek.

If you have chickens, then you inevitably have rats … and foxes. Both animals are opportunists and will risk their luck for an easy meal. If the meal isn't too easy, then both will work at finding a way to get what they want. Never underestimate a fox – he can jump higher and further than you think; play with a latch, a lock, and burrow like a rabbit.

Consequently, my girls live in a Fort Knox of a coop! Reinforced wire mesh on all sides and underneath too. Hah! Take that Monsieur Reynard.

There is no such thing as a rat-proof chicken coop. During the lockdown I became somewhat obsessed with their existence in my garden. Now, rats are vermin, but they are also sweet, clever and incredibly funny. So, I struggle with this relationship, and occasionally relent in my quest to banish them. I refuse to introduce poison into their ecosystem and so have to resort to other methods of dissuasion.

One such method during the heatwaves was to sit in the garden with a hose gun and fire at them whenever I saw them. The babies would jump in the air and squeak ... then run away. Unfortunately, they came back for more (sigh). Also, this habit was becoming strangely addictive.

I put down pots of mint and peppermint along their 'runs', which is meant to dissuade them – does it heck. I blocked their runs and tunnels (that's meant to upset them – rats don't like change, apparently). Still no joy.

The only real way to lose the rats is to remove the food. So down came the bird feeders, no more crumbs put out for my little blackbird, and chicken food was firmly locked in the coop. In fact everything was going quite well, until the little blighters realised that I had tomatoes in the greenhouse. A stone flag floor and bolted door still didn't stop them climbing and trying to get into the vents. It occurs to me that if we could instil into children half the determination a rat demonstrates in seeking food, we might be onto something!

Until I lose my lovely girls, I shall probably always have a fox or a rat (family) lurking. Somehow though, lockdown has taken me through a cycle into having patience with my nemesis. Life is too short to spend it all eradicating another. When so many lives seem to have been lost already, I think I shall be content to just ... be.

Lessons
Mina Cullimore, UK

petals bloom and fade
birdsong fills garden and sky
lessons on love found

1
It was February.

Verdant energy, having retreated deep under the bark and soil due to dusky short days and northern winds, was tentatively rising and unfurling.

Slowly, as the early vernal winds shifted to the east, and the balancing of sun-filled days and star-filled nights returned, stories of the illness spread.

As people began to open to the fear, the borders closed.

I went back into my classroom in early June.

On the whiteboard was the last date that I had written for my last live lesson in this classroom – 20 March 2020. I have not yet wiped this day off its shiny surface; I am not ready to remove this marker in the trail. This date reminds me that the world which I had become accustomed to was to be transformed beyond recognition.

As I pack up my classroom and prepare for new adventures, this date remains on the board for a little while longer.

2
There was a quietness to those early days.

As my body began to slowly recover, I sat in the sunshine-filled garden reflecting upon the events that cast ripples swelling into tsunamis through so many lives.

The road across the fields fell silent; there was no rumble of tyres on tarmac, no growl of engines climbing the hills in and out of the vale.

The absence of planes allowed the sky to arch from horizon to horizon undisturbed.

We were all paused, hushed,

suspended in anticipation and unknowing.

In the quietness the conscious witnessing began ...

... the bees in the wild cherry blossom, eager to collect the bountiful sweetness

... the cracking of last summer's wisteria pods as the buds of this year's blooms swelled

... the rustle of the early leaves of beech and birch and oak and ash and laurel and willow and rowan as cooling dusk moved the warmed air

... the buzzard coasting on thermals, calling across the fields and hedgerows

... the nesting black-capped tits and wren in the ivy under the eaves

... the fledging thrush asking its parent for more seeds

... the lark ascending and hovering over ripening maize

... the snuffling of badgers as they move through the shadowed borders under a waxing moon.

And I was deeply moved, filled with love for all beings striving to nurture and endure.

3
I began to unpack the bags.

For many years, home had increasingly become a waystation, storing bags that were needed for the various tracks in my life.

A bag for each identity I carried, exchanged at intervals in the course of each day and week.

I was, and remained, at home. Emptying and folding each one away, I made space to accommodate the contents of these bags.

I listened to myself teaching in a new way. I listened to young people who logged into my online live lessons, seeking to gather threads of connection and continuity.

My voice responded to their 'chat'; we explored questions of life and truth and 'bliks'.

I listened to students in a new way – each task they completed reflecting time they had spent pondering this strange and unfamiliar world. Each message expressing a vulnerability, each comment revealing their determination to work through these new experiences.

Some came to lessons just to be present ... not wanting to respond in written dialogue.

I spent each day planning, preparing, guiding, joking, reassuring, and speaking of the past, present, and a future that was yet to unfold.

In quiet times I would be filled with tears, aware that in each encounter I carried a responsibility to bring calm and positive continuity in these months where most previous routines had been wiped away.

We were sharing this moment, this tide, this journey through uncharted waters.

We were all seeking calmer seas whilst the silent unseen storm spread.

4
I reflected upon fear.

I listened to two storytellers share a Grimms' fairy tale, steeped in murk, malevolence and malicious intent. I listened to updates on events around the world. I listened to lessons of life, death and hopes for renewal.

I spent many hours each day outside, never straying far from my cottage between two streams. One afternoon as I dug the garden, preparing the beds for beans and squash seedlings, my spade disturbed an ants' nest. My awareness of disrupting their home was raised by their stinging attacks on my ankle. I quickly stood away and watched this community. Deep under the soil, without me realising, these ants had been building and tending to the needs of their young. The cold metal and pressure of my clog had provoked rapid responses. Some frantically began to bring the eggs and young larvae to the surface to seek an alternative place of refuge to protect them. Others swarmed to find and attack the source of danger. Their sense of fear and confusion was apparent. I waited and watched; over time, they settled and reordered their nest once it was clear that there was no further or ongoing threat.

I listened to the voices of those who were suffering, those who were helping, those who were afraid, those who were filled with scepticism and those who appeared to misinform and mislead. In these past months of the coronavirus pandemic, we have witnessed stories of endurance, bravery, arrogance, ignorance, cruelty and selfishness. Profound questions we have had to explore are 'what kind of person are you?'... 'how do we survive?'... 'what distances us'... what do and can we share?'.

I now understand more clearly that causation, rather than being a linear chain of events, is a spiral of inter-relational strands.

These months have confirmed for me the enduring truth found in Donne's 'No man is an island'... we are all part of the continent, the main, sharing our fragile moments of existence on this precious earth.

5
Spaces emerged in the garden between my cottage and the stream.

Listening to the needs of flora and fauna alongside my vision in earth-crafting, I altered, dug, moved, removed, planted, harvested, dried, tasted and shared elements in the garden.

As my sense of smell returned, I breathed in the perfume of jasmine, nicotiana, rose, rain on soil, and the sun-sweet maize in the warm breeze.

The fallen and browned petals on the path, still fragrant, reminded me to respect that growth and transformation involve cycles of creation and destruction.

When hearing stories of loss and longing, I was grateful for and humbled by my privilege in having a safe home and garden in which I could find refuge.

These past months have reminded me that my control of events in this life that I cherish is limited.

6
Contrasting claims of 'truths' have, more than ever, brought to the surface the importance of striving for open communication.

The story of the blind men when each claimed they *knew* the concept of 'elephant' (from their limited experience of touching an ear, a tail, a leg) teaches us that not one person can have a complete 'handle' on truth. Working our way through understanding and responding compassionately to the challenges we face relies upon respecting this interdependency.

I have witnessed the final decades of the last 1000-year 'age' and the first decades of this new millennium. Momentous global changes have been formed and honed by local events.

Stories of courage and resilience when faced with disrespect, neglect and cruelty reveal that, even though we are fallible, we have the capacity to rise. When threatened, we are vulnerable to fear, anger, isolation and seeking to find someone/something to identify as being responsible for our experiences. We are all seeking sustained moments of harmony, shelter in storms, and a place to nurture and protect those we love. We can, through benevolent intention, effect change that ripples far beyond our immediate sphere of influence.

Experiences of tsunamis, Chernobyl, 9/11, armed conflicts and this pandemic carry a similar signature: the recoil, the shock, the witnessing of power unleashed, the wiping away of people's ways of life in moments stretching into hours, then days, months, years.

These current experiences are not a battle to be won; through these hardships we have the opportunity to learn, share, support and mindfully restructure.

Let not the discord and fear push away our compassion.

My role as an educator has involved exploring spans of time, shifting paradigms and sharing stories of human beliefs and interactions with younger minds. In the course of these dialogues, many questions as to 'how?' and 'why?' arise.

One thing that I now see clearly is that the tool by which to navigate through our varied and challenging journeys is this: *compassion is the key.*

Speaking of Light
Mehri Holliday, UK

*'What thanks sufficient or what recompense equal
have I to render thee, Divine Historian'*
John Milton, *Paradise Lost*

Deep in me there lives a spiral of despair. I feel and fear the dark yet I must speak of light.

The pandemic has come. My daughter is suffering from its symptoms. Her quarantine, the home-schooling of the two young children, and the extent of the day-to-day domesticity as well as working from home are overwhelming. I am asked to give a hand with art sessions.

I stack some books on the kitchen table and place my iPad on top and select images for discussion on my phone. I smile at my granddaughter Aara who is just nine and lives five hours away. 'In this first session we are going to think about Observational Drawing,' I say. 'Open a fresh page in your drawing pad and write this as the title with today's date.' She nods attentively and proceeds. I explain that observational drawing is about looking and looking; and looking again. I ask her to write this under the title. We then look at the image of a tulip from her garden sent to me by her mummy recently. We discuss what we can actually see. We establish no stem is in view, just soil beneath the flower head. We observe six rounded petals in bright yellow, rising and opening from a black centre with sharp edges. We look at her drawing. We discuss more images including David Hockney's recently released paintings of blossoms and daffodils. Thirty minutes already! We blow kisses, and Aara goes to her garden to observe and draw another tulip.

Adrian rushes into the kitchen and says, 'It's working beautifully, it's fantastic, thirty-one are attending, all these little squares, and suddenly one person moves, more like a shuffle, and a hand goes up with a question or comment ...' He has been working on finding the best online system to hold these three-hour research seminars. Seventy and never happier working; a drink of water and a piece of cheese in his mouth, he disappears down the corridor.

Time for my daily walk.

Out of the house, left and left again along the now quiet A257. It's a Roman road. Cross it and I am in the vast apple and pear orchards, eight fields and the woods beyond. I am grateful for the Right to Roam demanded and fought for by ordinary citizens one hundred years ago. I walk-run the gently sloped paths and nearing the end I hear a gentle quack ... quack.

I look up, anticipating a flock, but see just two mallards circling. Undisturbed by my presence, and the piercing sound of a shotgun from the farmer beyond to disperse crows and pigeons, the mallards gracefully land. The puddles in between the rows of apple trees shine and reflect all that is around. Captivated, I note the opalescent emerald green head of one, and the other's shades of brown. They are beautiful and small, never far from one another as if connected by an elastic band. With a gentle munching sound they feed, paddling, heads in the shallow water, heads up, walking and looking ...

And I think to myself: 'a loaf of bread beneath the bough and thou beside me in the wilderness', from *The Rubaiyat of Omar Khayam*.

Blackbird

Trish Flynn, UK

'How sweet the harmonies of the afternoon:
the blackbird sings along the sunny breeze
His ancient song of leaves and summer boon:
Rich breath of hayfields streams through whispering trees;
And birds of morning trim their bustling wings.
And listen fondly while the blackbird sings'
Frederick Tennyson

The first sound I remember in the beginning of my life was the clear melody of the blackbird song across a lawn in the dappled light somewhere.

The second sound that of a push lawnmower cutting the grass, and the third, tennis balls plopping on the courts nearby.

Darling blackbird

always there yet unnoticed by me as I entered the busy life of school, work and relationships.

So the years passed.

Suddenly I was middle-aged.

One day calling in at a farm shop returning from Ashford I triggered a security trap at ground level that looked like a house but then again like a cuckoo clock with two holes from which two mechanical alternating blackbirds sprang in turn singing, 'I'd like to build the world a home and furnish it with love , grow apple trees and honey bees...' etc, a song by the New Seekers that flew from their opening and shutting bright yellow beaks.

I bought it on the spot thinking it the funniest security trap I had ever seen! To this day it gives friends and visitors a laugh though the poor birds are now very tatty.

And then,

along came Covid 19. Worldwide pandemic that forced home isolation for the foreseeable future.

Our world became quiet

except that it didn't go quiet at all.

Lucky me to have a garden that I could step into and hear sounds that replaced the incessant din of motor vehicles and mechanical machines. Silent roads.

Now it is like the first time. Dawn chorusing chattering squawking and singing of the birds going about their life as they had done well before we came along, and I pray long after we are gone.

Blackbird, bright eye, yellow beak

sings his throat out marking his territory, merrily vandalising the new garden beds, yanking out anything that could reveal something of interest underneath.

I love him so.

Here is a line from a hymn:

>   Morning has broken
>   Like the first morning
>   Blackbird has spoken
>   Like the first bird
>   amen

Not What Is
Rosie Gladwell, UK

Not fear,
But joy, feeling the intensity of the air,
The silence of the wind,
The yellow dots
Against green.

Not confusion,
But clarity
The sun's pure light.

Not death,
But the springiness of nature,
All laughing,
All wakening.

Not sleep,
But a song of life.
All this, and more,
God's words to my upturned heart.

Simone

Hilda Billy Todd, Italy

'You never know how strong you are until being strong is the only choice you have.'
Bob Marley

February 2019 - Discovery

We've just discovered our 21-year-old son has a serious drug problem. We discovered it through a test on his hair after he was found in possession of hashish and his driving licence was suspended. Yes, we suspected the odd bit of joint smoking (didn't we all at 20?), but this was something else. Our world collapsed. You name the drug, it was there in his hair and had been taken in the previous six months, and it had all begun with hashish and progressed. How could we have been so blind? This young man who used to be so happy and full of life had become a sombre, taciturn recluse in his room (when he wasn't staying out all night and not answering his phone – I have lost count of the hours I stayed awake waiting to hear his key turning in the lock of the door). We had put all this down to late adolescence, but we were wrong and perhaps we had closed our eyes to the fact that there really was a problem. What parent ever wants to admit that their child has a drug problem?

March 2019 – What do we do?

In tears I telephoned San Patrignano rehab community in Rimini, Italy to ask for help. I had seen so much about this place over the years in the news, about how they were able to rehabilitate so many young people who had lost their way in life. When I called their helpline, they were so kind when confronted with this sobbing person over the phone and understood immediately. They directed me to one of their many associations throughout Italy, and Fausto and I started going to parents' meetings. Take the hard line with your son, they said – either he accepts the help he needs, or he has to go his own way. It didn't take us long to understand what we had to do, despite the fact it was enormously difficult and painful for us: we put him in front of this choice. In the end it was obvious what needed to be done, but hard to do. If you keep feeding and clothing him and giving him money, you are only helping him to take the wrong direction in life. It is time to say no. And in the end his parents are the only real reference point he has from which to start again.

April 2019 – December 2019 – The hardest time

Simone's choice was to leave home and to live more or less on the streets for eight months until he finally surrendered at Christmas (always a special time for us as a family) and came home. I can't begin to express how painful those eight months were, not knowing if he was dead or alive, but we were convinced that by making life difficult for him, it was the only way to really help him. When he came home on 23 December, he was painfully thin and emotionally fragile, but he was finally home and accepting he needed help. The first rules to follow were no phone, no internet, and he must never be left alone until he went to San Patrignano. The temptation to go back to where he was before would be just too great otherwise. He agreed and we began to prepare him (with the help of the San Patrignano association) to go to the community in the following weeks.

March 2020 – July 2020 – Lockdown

Lockdown is on and San Patrignano has closed its doors to protect the people in the community from the Covid-19 virus. But things at home have changed during these months! From the poor thin zombie that came home at Christmas, I have my lovely smiley intelligent son back (weighing 10 kilos more, too!). This lockdown has been an amazing opportunity for me and Fausto to rebuild our relationship with our son and not taking drugs has let his true personality gradually re-emerge, as if a sad mask has been pulled away to reveal a happy ray of sunshine.

16 July 2020 – San Patrignano

Now that the lockdown is easing, Simone was able to enter this wonderful place called San Patrignano (look it up online) that gives lost souls an opportunity to rebuild their lives. It will take at least three to four years but it's the best place for him to be and we love him so much that we are prepared not to see him at all for the first year as he starts rebuilding his life. We can only communicate by letter, which is wonderful, no more brief messages by SMS or WhatsApp, but words that come from the heart, and he manages to express himself so well in writing.

Although lockdown for so many has been a time of such tragedy, for us it has been a time of hope and rebirth.

Simone wrote this in his first letter to us: 'I know that hard times will come, and I feel that they will. But I know that I am now in the perfect place to be helped to face my difficulties and to make them part of my rebirth.'

Unexpected Times

Marisol Vigor, Spain

*'My house is in the mountains,
in the woods, rivers, lakes, beaches.
That's where I live
and there I express my love for you.'*
Baruch Spinoza, *About God*

On 8 March 2020, I said goodbye to my last guests in the cortijo before the confinement. Having that feeling of uncertainty with the Covid-19 news and the suspicion that something serious was going on, I decided not to go back to Granada for classes in university (which I love because besides the interesting subjects, it is an occasion to meet with my lovely friends). To avoid risks and as the news advanced on the state of the virus, I decided to stay in the Alpujarra mountains, here in the middle of the Barranco del Poqueira in Pampaneira. I raised my kids and I worked for over thirty years and enjoyed doing it, so rather than coming back to the city, a retreat at this time seemed the perfect option. There is a part of me that has developed in these mountains in solitude, and having the time to observe nature and quietness makes me extremely happy.

I have been in the rural tourism business for over thirty years and having nobody around for months has been a surprisingly luxurious feeling. No more work for a while, no need to please anyone, no waiting, no cleaning, no phone calls … Only my best guests and friends now will not be able to come this summer because of the quarantine, but … next year hopefully we'll meet again and make up for this summer I have missed them.

Every morning I woke up to the blissful sound of the waterfall running through the mountain gorge opposite my house and falling into the river Poqueira. It has been absolutely beautiful, lots of fast running water, loud, full of life, what a sensation of cleanness. Then the cat is waiting for her food at the kitchen window and after feeding her, I put the coffee pot on the fire and toast the bread while listening to the news on Radio Nacional. Very uncertain news and not at all optimistic, but then a routine seemed to be necessary after a few days of just festering by myself.

When it was cloudy and rainy, I seemed to live inside a cloud. Gathering firewood was another task and part of the morning routine.

I would light the fire after lunch and have a siesta with mama cat on the sofa. Then I would continue with my French course from Dave Languages. Then I might paint some more, listening to music until it was time for the evening meal. For days I fell into that routine. I had converted the living area into an improvised studio, and once I had finished the painting I reclaimed that space. That was the advantage of being alone, having all that space to use without annoying anybody.

As days passed, I fell into other routines. I drove to our nearest large town, Orgiva, maybe every 10 days or two weeks, saw nobody that I knew, and met very few cars on the road. Surely, some other way of life had arrived; How was it going to be?

I don´t know the answers yet, but I feel very privileged to be able to retire to such a beautiful place where I have decided to stay for the time being and where I feel easy and at peace. Solitude, loneliness, *'Soledad'*, (my Christian name), it all comes together to cover me in a layer of protection against these uncertain times.

As September [2020] comes around, the future still looks uncertain. Yet I feel there are a good few changes that we must adopt in this new way of life, experiments that hopefully are going to change our attitudes in a positive way and make a better world for the coming generations. The earth needs respect, love, appreciation. Hopefully this is the message that we are receiving from it. We must take the opportunity to learn from this situation. Maybe the virus is after all a lesson to us all to rethink what we are doing with our lives and what future we are going to leave to our descendants.

There is no light pollution here either, so watching the stars is a perfect way to finish my day. I have rediscovered a private little piece of paradise that I always had, but had forgotten to enjoy.

Of course I must acknowledge that these feelings come from me, somebody who has no relatives suffering from the virus. I truly respect the feelings of other people in all types of other situations, understanding that this strange period of quarantine has not been the same for lots of others. I wish and hope that something positive is going to come out of this.

Nature bloomed splendidly this spring, showing us it can recover without humans doing all the wrong things to it. We have had the opportunity to reflect, meditate and adopt a new way of thinking and acting. We have seen how badly we sometimes treat our environment and ourselves. So let's dream that a new world and a better one is possible. If we truly are bright, intelligent beings, let's demonstrate that. Our choices now can improve life for all human beings and help us to regain the balance that we have lost through thoughtless behaviours. Let's build something healthy and positive for the next generations based on respect for all forms of life. Without care and respect for the natural world we are a part of, we will continue to create negativity and disease on our beautiful planet.

We are so lucky to live in such a place, on such a marvellous planet. Let's protect it for the wellbeing of the whole world. Together with all other forms of life, we deserve to be happy. With a new conscience, I am sure it is possible.

Whatever the Times Bring
Joselón Gipsy Floyd, Spain

Grey clouds are shading out the light
but there is nothing we can't overcome
keeping the spirits high
in the sacred name of love.
Give me your hand and sing along with me.
Caring for each other, living in peace,
we will keep growing whatever the times bring
with love by our side, feeling free.

A Blessing in Disguise
Tara Esther Kleij, Spain

'Yoga does not just transform the way we see things;
it transforms the person who sees'
B K S Iyengar

What was happening?

I could not grasp or understand it but one thing was for sure, the world had suddenly changed. I felt fear and chaos surrounding us. It was March 2020 and we were travelling in India and Nepal when things were really starting to get heavy. Borders were closing around us and I felt a soft voice inside me telling me to get back to Europe as soon as possible.

So I followed that inner voice and the same evening we took the night bus from Pokhara back to Kathmandu and in the early morning flew back to Spain. The next day we heard that the borders to Spain had just closed that morning. We were so happy that we made it back in time!

During the period that followed, I was very aware of the news and sometimes felt fear creeping into my body. Luckily there was also this deep sense of trust and feeling of coming home, taking a rest. There was nowhere to go, and nothing to do.

We had to cancel my spring retreats so there was more time to create other things. I allowed myself to be in the flow ... Mother Nature opened her arms to me. We made beautiful gardens so we had enough fresh fruits and greens. Eating as much as possible from our garden was such a blessing. For me the fresher the food, the better it feels for my body. I can live just on smoothies and salads, honouring my body as my temple and our mother earth as our home.

I also decided to be careful of the news I took in, and to go out in nature whenever I could (sometimes I had to sneak out). I kept a strong meditation and yoga practice, which helped me stay grounded and find balance. For me yoga is not just physical exercise but a way to find inner stability, strength, and peace.

I kept trusting that behind all the fear and chaos that was surrounding us this was all happening for a reason and that maybe it was also a blessing in disguise. At least nature was flourishing again and people in highly polluted cities could breathe again, animals had more space and freedom and I could hear more birds and bees than ever.

I started to give online yoga classes because I felt I wanted to help people come back to themselves, help them relax and release fear and tension. I had always felt reluctant to teach yoga online but now I just had to do it, and a whole new doorway opened up for me. It was so beautiful to connect with old and new students all over the world and help them to find more security, trust and calmness in themselves, through yoga and meditation. I decided to give the classes in return for donations, so that everyone could join. It felt good to be of service, to feel the connection, and to earn a small living that kept us going during this difficult time.

Corona and the lockdown inspired me to find new ways to share my gift of yoga with the world. It also helped me to see how lucky I am, living with my partner and two sons, and how beneficial it is to live close to nature and grow your own food if you are able to. Covid-19 and the events that followed have brought me closer to myself and closer to the Earth Mother once more.

A New Sense of Time
Pete Lumb, Isle of Man

'Tra dy Lioor/Time is enough'
A saying from the Isle of Man

Living on an island as small as this, the sea is a constant presence, lending space and light to our perspective as we go about our daily lives. You come to revel in that untrammelled horizon, always on the edge of one's vision. No matter how constrained our lives may become on this tiny landmass, there is always that visual release to be experienced.

At first the virus was a curiosity, something for others to deal with in far-off countries. Then it took hold in one country after another, relentlessly marching our way. Still we thought our island nation would be safe. Surely they would close the borders soon? Not soon enough, it transpired.

Uncertainty drove us indoors, even before all the announcements. We read the news and asked, is this Armageddon? Fear of the unknown completely pervaded our daily routines and preoccupations, rendering them impotent and meaningless. Forget that Spanish holiday, bin that trip to see Mum, cancel that haircut. Do we have enough of this and sufficient of that? We became an island within an island, our horizons now tiny, and the sea reduced to an inch-wide strip visible only over trees from a high window.

During those first weeks we had to occasionally check with each other whether this was really happening. A war we could comprehend, or an economic crisis, but we had no experience of living within a science-fiction novel. Yet we surprised ourselves with how easily we passed the days without going beyond our small garden. In a way the pressure was off. No lingering work ethic to pander to, and no feverish consumerism to indulge in either. The world had indeed stopped, and we were now welcome to get off at our leisure. Time became a commodity we could spend extravagantly. All those little jobs got done, then the bigger ones which were always for some unspecified time in the future. Seeds which had sat for years in a packet were lovingly planted into improvised pots and meticulously watered. Even the shed was painted.

There was a week when my weekly scurry in mask and hooded anorak to the supermarket revealed many empty shelves. This was more due to problems with the ferry than to the virus, but it put us into a survivalist mindset. We devised new ways of eking out meals and researched recipes with minimal ingredients. One great success of the austerity drive was the discovery that wonderfully tasty Irish Potato Farls can be made with nothing more than flour and mashed potato. They can be heated without oil in a dry pan, and became a breakfast staple for much of the time.

As time slowed, my capacity to be absorbed by the mundane increased. I found that I could happily spend three hours a day painstakingly stripping paint off a bannister rail with nothing more sophisticated than a bush knife I had spent another half an hour sharpening. Not only that but I could continue further the next day and the next, gradually working through an entire three-storey staircase, post by post. I loved the grainy sheen of the timber revealed, knowing that it last saw the light in a previous century.

I have always been a keen guitarist and I took the time to learn a flamenco guitar technique that had always eluded me. Known as *Alzapua*, it involved using the thumb to play up and down very rapidly, and required hour after hour of repetition. In this soporific atmosphere this no longer seemed irksome, and I gradually began to make headway. After a month of daily practice, I could use it in pieces of music I had always faltered in. After another month I had more or less forgotten it again, as my meanderings in guitar playing returned me to Bach, the only music that seemed to truly make sense in these times. The sheer grace and momentum of his great big rambling 'Chaconne' endlessly fascinated me no matter how many times I played it. There always seemed more to unravel, new depths to perceive.

As the weeks went by, the daily coronavirus bulletin from the Isle of Man government became a crucial barometer of our hopes and fears. As the numbers rose, we worried all the more. After all, our Chief Minister is just a farmer and the Speaker of the House is our local chemist. I wondered whether they were simply out of their depth given the unprecedented nature of the crisis. Yet slowly I came to respect their honesty and sincerity. In dealing with the press they gave straight answers without obfuscation and bluster. They really did seem to be doing everything they could for the good of all. I had always thought the island a bit of a banana republic, drawing its government from a population of only 80,000, but when comparing the UK news with ours during lockdown I had to reconsider.

A day came with no new cases, followed by another. A week with none, followed by another, then a month. Gradually the restrictions eased, and we crept out into daylight, blinking and nervous. As of now life is pretty much back to normal, although we all know it's a fragile victory, and certainly not time to start crowing. For the time being we have been given back our distant horizons and our cloudscapes. We can wander wherever we wish and see whom we choose once more, yet there is a small part of me that feels just a little nostalgic for the sheer simplicity of those cloistered lockdown days.

Island of Us
Louise Gabriel – UK

'We are like islands in the sea, separate on the surface but connected in the deep'
William James

I would tell you everything but that would be too much, so let's water it down a bit.

Kettle drums of panic:

Boom! This virus is deadly.

Boom! Close your front door with the people you love, or choose to love, behind it.

Boom! Now stay put!

It started like any other strange day, a reminder to ration toilet paper, let's sit down at the table to eat, what was that film we watched ten years ago, the good one, with thingy in it? Not too much news eh …?

Perky optimism and shenanigans. Quirky selfies with knives and vodka bottles. Such larks!

The drawer rearranging took a while. Alphabetising certain books took himself half an hour. Important work, especially the pairing of socks! Phew! Then: 'It's only three o'clock … too early for wine?'

Reaching out with phones and modern stuff, to our loves, behind their own battened hatches, in other lands or nearby streets. Making their own confined whoopee.

What now?!

Ha-ha – let's make for the garden, see what survived this winter of negligence … four not very green thumbs poking around in the earth's business. That keeps us going for a while, only to find the garden had survived despite us.

Sex? Why not?! We've seen that film before, at least ten years ago. Oh, I'd forgotten you like that, I'd forgotten I do too! Physical archaeology. Some time passed behind politely drawn blinds.

But work carries on! Off you go then! Out there! Mine is from home, emails, zooming and teaming (except for one day every three weeks on a stupendously limited timetable). When you are gone, when you are out there, placing each foot, like Armstrong, onto a deserted Covid landscape, I am fearful. When I am waiting patiently in a silent, distanced line outside some supermarket, I am anxious, despite the book I have thought to bring. When we are reunited far earlier than is usual, such relief! Sharing stories of seeing someone other than ourselves, but barely speaking to them. Oh, and the aggressiveness of seagulls at the duckpond where I'd taken the stale bread (I said we'd bought too much).

I cry on the back step while having a cigarette, when the deaths reach nearly a thousand in a single day. Not from war or the usual disasters, but under the hooves of another horseman. Looking up to the stars, hoping their souls can navigate the way. Too much, too many.

Best not dwell, so I come to the silverest lining; finding what we hadn't lost, behind the kettle, or the gardening and the 'what shall we watch then?'. Happening on our love, robust and resplendent! This could have been a domestic disaster but ...

No corners for spiders or broken moths. Our bed unmade. The distance between our notes. A pause in your thoughts. Rubbing cream on mosquito bites. Something of nothing. Your smile in the sunshine. Turning to see you. Words in the dark. A picnic of pebbles. The front door opening, there we are, home.

Positives and Negatives
Jolanda Van Denzen, Netherlands

*'You can't plan life. Because no matter how perfect your plan is,
life has a way to rearrange it.'*
Mina Deanna

In June my boyfriend and I took the train to Limburg in the south of the Netherlands, and went on a cycling holiday there. Covid-19 infections had peaked in this area at the beginning of the coronavirus crisis. I had developed a slight cough, but nothing out of the ordinary.

The holiday went well. But once we were back home I felt some discomfort while breathing, but again, nothing too serious. My boyfriend had also started complaining about his lungs not working very well, a couple of weeks before. He has asthma so I was keeping an eye on him.

Later that week I decided that it was probably a good idea to do a test since he is in a risk group. So I called and made an appointment for the following Monday. Since it was only to make sure we didn't have it, I wasn't really worried. We went and had the test – it is a nasty one – and my boyfriend went to work and I worked from home that day. The next day I went to work. I didn't feel well, coughing and feeling overheated.

We got the results and my boyfriend sent me a message to say he'd tested negative – what a relief. Then they called me to say I had tested positive. I was upset; how could that be? We are always together! Now we had to deal with all the business of listing contacts and giving information to others about my infection. It was a real hassle, but worse was to come: my colleagues were upset that I had come in to work before getting the result, and of course they were right.

They felt I was being irresponsible and that was tough for me to hear.

I stayed at home and my boyfriend and I were isolated from each other for a fortnight. Not great for our relationship and very inconvenient. In the end no one else got infected. In fact, some of my colleagues and friends doubt if I even had it.

My opinion? Of course it's a serious virus and of course we need to be careful. But I really doubt if the current rules are in line with the actual danger. An ordinary flu takes lives too, but we haven't killed our economy in the way we do now ... I can tell lots more about what I think but I don't think it adds to the story.

There is a brief epilogue: I was asked to return to work in the middle of May, so I did. But when I got ill, I wasn't welcome because colleagues thought I was still a danger. So my boss decided it was best for me to return to the office only after my holidays. I emailed my colleagues with apologies and said that they were free to share their grievances with me. Two people took that opportunity. One email I could understand. The other person sent me an email ten paragraphs long! In the email she listed all the things she had missed out on because of my infection, and thanks to me, she had to go into quarantine herself.

Looking for Motherland
Cecilia Örtenheim, Sweden

'We are fragile creatures, and it is from this weakness, not despite it, that we discover the possibility of true joy.'
Archbishop Desmond Tutu

My main reaction to the pandemic was anger and confusion. Why isn't Sweden, where I live, applying the same strategy as the rest of the world!? So many old people in residential homes are infected! Are we just going to let them die without taking any extra precautions to protect them?

Here, precautions such as quarantine and wearing masks are voluntary. It's up to each individual to take responsibility. But do the old and weak, who are dependent on others, have a choice? How can they protect themselves?

I go out on the street. Fear grabs me. Everybody out there feels like a potential threat. It's difficult to keep a distance in shops and on public transport. I can't even hug my friends and family members. To show love is to keep a distance. How unreal and unpleasant!

In the forest I feel safe. She is the embracing mother. A friend who is always welcoming me. Life is now, now, now! More time for introspection and reflection. What is really important? Everything is so uncertain, except that our life is fragile and finite. That is very clear.

I long to go visit my mum, but cannot enter Denmark because of our strategy. Who knows what will turn out to be the right path in the end? I do hope and believe that we will all have learned something about what really matters, though. To me it is to love and respect myself, others and Mother Earth more than ever.

The Upside of Lockdown
Stephen Bellm, USA

'I think people are learning to enjoy what is right in front of them instead of worrying about the future.'
Stephen Bellm

Life changed drastically on 15 March 2020. My daily routines and those of my children and friends died on that day and a whole new way of living was born. For many, quarantine became a time of retreat, of dealing with a smaller existence and government restrictions and hardships. Some people lost their jobs, children no longer had a school to go to and the elderly no longer had visitors coming around to check in. For sure, our society took it on the chin and a lot of victims were created.

On 15 March, the public schools here in North Carolina where I live closed down. I am a private music teacher with over thirty-five students coming to my door each week. I follow the public school calendar; when they close school I close. Before this date, my daily routine was as it has always been for the last ten years of living here in the States. I would wake up, work on my online business in the morning and then start welcoming students from 2pm through to 7pm. That was a lot of foot traffic in my house each day, over 100 people per week on average. All of a sudden, my business was dead. I did not want to take any risks – a piano is a perfect conduit for Covid.

Luckily my online business started to thrive, as more people were forced inside, creating a huge boom for online retail. I spent the next few months focusing on my business and improving the website and the listings. The added income easily covered my piano teaching losses, so it kind of felt like I was on a vacation.

Teaching really took a lot of energy and now I could enjoy my afternoons, go to the beach or exercise. And that is exactly what I did.

My friend Eduardo is a schoolteacher. He is also the singer in my reggae band, so we are old friends. We decided to play tennis every day. We had met on the occasional weekend to play, but now we had our mornings free to play. We stuck to it like personal trainers, holding each other accountable. We not only got better at playing the sport, we also transformed our bodies. We both lost over twenty pounds playing in the humid Carolina spring and summer. Having the regimen brought peace to my day, starting each morning sweating and laughing and running. The mental wellness I experience now is incredible. I feel peace after exercise. Our love of tennis has created the perfect balance in my life.

Our band gigs for the year were all cancelled, due to the bars and venues being closed and no gatherings allowed. However, I did commit to playing as a duo with my keyboard player. I switched over from bass to electric guitar and we started getting booked as soon as restaurants were allowed to open up again. Here in the south, the locals are rebels, they do not want to be told what to do. Any bar that served food was allowed to open at 50 per cent capacity. A local bar on the beach had just opened an upstairs outdoor restaurant looking out over the white sand and Atlantic Ocean. We were their favourite band, so they hired us to play every weekend. We are still playing there, sometimes twice a week, performing Roots Reggae for a local tribe of fans and the tourists that pile into our beach town each week. The music has brought out the best in people. They all seem to really appreciate live music, since it is so rare these days. We have people getting out of their chairs and dancing and leaving generous tips. The reaction has been great, so much more than when we played out pre-Covid. It is incredible what a difference it has made. I think people are learning to enjoy what is right in front of them instead of worrying about the future.

Tennis in the morning, running my thriving business by day and gigging on the ocean in the evening. Life feels like a permanent vacation, it feels in balance and I have never felt better. For now, my kids are also going to have to navigate this crazy world without my guidance, since this sort of pandemic has never happened. I feel sorry that their old way of life has died. Both of them were already free of the system. Jaya had graduated early from high school and Kashi was home-schooled with an online programme. They hardly felt the shift. But now their future is up in the air, we don't know how many changes this society will face in the coming years. Entire industries will shut down and our way of life will change forever. Maybe! Jaya is still wondering what a college education will look like. Kashi meanwhile has become a surfer dude. He is out on the waves every day and I encourage him to follow his passion. Surfing the world doesn't sound like a bad career choice at this point.

Luckily for us, we are not in a lockdown at all. This town is a tourist beach town and the beaches are open, the restaurants are open and our southern rebel neighbours don't want to be stuck in their houses. It seems the local authority agrees and I have not seen any type of enforcement. I am glad we don't live in a place that has us jailed in our homes!

Watching Rosie Bloom
Ann Wilson, UK

'You are the bows from which your children as living arrows are sent forth'
Kahlil Gibran

Rosie came into my life in 2012 when she was four years old. No one can really prepare an adopter for the challenges they are likely to face. Children who come from the care system often have some form of additional need due to past trauma; Rosie has attachment disorder and unspecified global development delay. These are known as 'hidden disabilities' because she doesn't look or sound different to any other child but her behaviour is very different.

School has always been a challenge for Rosie; she struggles academically and has to try to fit in with other children. But she has always loved school and it has helped with her development and social skills. In 2014 I started a relationship with a man from my youth, who later became my husband. He couldn't move to live with us as he couldn't be far away from his children, so we had to move 100 miles north. Rosie was now nine and I was very worried about moving her school, but fortunately she had a fantastic teacher at her new school who really helped with the transition.

Rosie moved from primary to secondary school in September 2019. We had chosen to live in a village that had a very small secondary school, where I was sure that Rosie could cope. She settled in well, getting to know her way around, getting used to moving classrooms, accepting she would have to try to play games like volleyball and rugby.

Then in early March 2020 there began to be rumours about schools closing due to Covid-19. On Friday 23 March Rosie had her last day at school, and it was reported in the media that this would be until September. I was horrified! I would have no respite, no break at all from Rosie, for six months! Rosie would have no routines that helped to keep her calm and even-tempered; I couldn't imagine how we were going to cope. As a Children's Services Key Worker, I had to continue working. I could ask for a school place for Rosie, but none of her friends would be there and it would all be different, so how would that be for her? And there was a risk to her health.

I made the very difficult decision to keep Rosie at home during lockdown. Rosie doesn't read well yet and is predicted to get all Grade 1s at GCSE. She hadn't completed much homework at primary school but it had to be done at secondary school. We had struggled over every single homework assignment set, and I realised early on at that it wasn't helpful for me to do too much for her, it had to be her work at her level. But now students were expected to complete work at home by reading emails from their teachers! They were expected to undertake tasks in each subject without any teaching assistants to help. Rosie stumbled at the first hurdle; she can't read emails. I could have tried to become her teaching assistant, I could have fought and struggled with her every day to get some academic work completed and emailed to her teachers. That would have made me feel like a good mum to the teachers but it would have been hell. I made a decision during the first week of lockdown that we would only focus on her reading; we would read four pages of a book together every day. I decided we wouldn't go into battle to get work completed that was beyond her academic ability anyway.

I worried and lost sleep over what life might be like. I imagined every day would have arguments and temper tantrums as she vied for my attention and became bored and emotionally dysregulated.

But it turned out be so different from everything I had imagined. Every day during lockdown Rosie woke up at around eight, with my husband and I already trying to share a work space at the kitchen table. She would plonk herself down on the sofa and pick up her phone and tablet, while I delivered some breakfast to her. We would have a brief chat about how she had slept or what she might want for lunch later. She would sit and scroll through her phone and her tablet until midmorning. Rosie then spent most of the rest of the day creating videos. These were often very technical with dolls looking like they were riding horses and seamless changes of her outfits. She asked for Japanese anime wigs and make-up, which she wanted to use to make her films. She carefully styled the wigs, created make-up designs and used her books, dolls and other toys to create imaginative stories.

Rosie joined in on some social media chats with her friends during lockdown but found it difficult due to her reading and writing skills being at a lower level. She Face-Timed one or two of her best friends but was mostly quite content with her own company, being creative, making her films. She became totally absorbed by her newfound love for making videos. She loved to show me the clips and I praised all the different techniques used.

My husband and I were working from home but for the short time I left the house for an hour or so to get food and supplies, I would call her from my car. Once when I asked what she had been doing she said, 'Making videos with the guinea pigs in the garden,' which made me laugh out loud. Before lockdown I had very much restricted her screen time but while trying to work at home I had to allow her more freedom. She used that time to be her most creative. I was amazed by the ideas she developed, the love of Japanese anime she discovered, and the way she became much more introspective and independent.

I worked in substance misuse rehabilitation units for 15 years and saw people struggling with drug and alcohol dependency who had to learn to be quiet and spend time alone during their recovery. They had to learn not to crave drama, attention and validation from others. There are also statistically high numbers of people with addiction problems who have experienced childhood trauma and/or the care system. Due to my past work, in the back of my mind I worried about my beautiful little girl growing up and developing substance misuse problems. For lockdown to give me the gift of seeing her enjoying her own company, being creative just for her own pleasure, is something I will always treasure.

Lockdown really taught me not to worry about Rosie and her future. I learned to love her deeply, to trust her and let her live the life that she wants. She may not fit into the 'normal' development patterns, she may not pass her GCSEs, she may not go to university, but she is a very creative, funny, inquisitive, self-reliant young person, and I now know in my heart that she will succeed in whatever she chooses to do.

Lockdown Love Story
Cathy Whitefield, Spain

'It doesn't interest me how old you are
I want to know if you will risk
Looking like a fool for love
For your dream
For the adventure of being alive'
Oriah Mountain Dreamer

On 5 March 2020, I stood waiting expectantly for an old friend at a bus stop in the small town of Orgiva, in the foothills of the Sierra Nevada mountains. I had lived here alone for most of the five years since my husband, Patrick, died. Having just hit my seventies, I was coming to terms with the possibility of being alone for the rest of my life.

I first met Rich and his girlfriend Carol in 1979, in a little stone cottage in Wiltshire, where they lived with miscellaneous hippies, no mains water, no electricity or car, and a few goats, pigs and chickens. They were escapees from London who wanted to live the self-sufficiency dream, whereas I had just escaped London where I had been in hospital for nine months with bone TB, after a two-year overland trip to India and the Far East. The 'sixties and seventies' dream was not so different from the dream of many younger friends living in this alternative Spanish community now, I mused, as the bus arrived.

Rich climbed down carrying a small rucksack and gave me a brief warm hug. Tall and slender, in blue jeans and a casual jacket, with the body of a youth, his age was only belied by the sensitive lines etched around his refined features. He was cheerful and full of tales of his two-day adventure in Granada, but looked pale, with haunted eyes. I drove him back to my sweet casita where he immediately stroked my little shaggy dog Luna, always a good sign in a house guest.

That evening we shared deeply. He had lived a quiet, somewhat circumscribed life in the same cottage for forty years with his wife, who grew and sold organic vegetables, while he became a teacher and art therapist. Meanwhile I had had several different careers, from yoga teacher to group facilitator, several relationships and had lived in too many rented houses, before settling in Glastonbury with my husband of the last twenty-five years. We had kept in touch intermittently throughout this time, making a happy foursome, until Patrick died. Then last year his beautiful wife suddenly suffered from an anxiety disorder and unimaginably took her own life.

The day after he arrived, I took Rich up to Capiliera, a pretty village in the hills, where he recalled a sudden brake failure when his car toppled down these same mountains thirty-five years ago. 'That was a car crash I survived almost unscathed,' he recounted animatedly, as we sat eating tapas and drinking grape juice, gazing at the distant snow-covered peaks. My heart ached for him as I thought about the emotional wreckage he was now navigating.

That night we sat outside on my patio by the light of the moon and I suddenly found myself standing up and acting out prayers and incantations like a Greek priestess. He intended to stay with me for a couple of weeks, to have a holiday walking in the mountains and to escape his grief. Little did we know how brief our assumed freedom would be, before we were locked down in a pandemic nightmare, as the coronavirus escalated exponentially. Suddenly we were only allowed out individually, to shop or to walk Luna nearby. Rich railed against this misfortune. 'My whole life has been shattered with death and now the whole world is being shattered with this virus and I can't even have a holiday,' he complained sadly.

However, we both soon contrived a somewhat desperate humour, where we found ourselves behaving like a comedy act, making banana bread, laughing hysterically at the absurdity of lockdown life, as we decontaminated shopping, sterilised kitchen surfaces and washed our hands obsessively. Not only did we have the same whacky sense of humour, but found we were on a similar, eclectic, spiritual path of non-duality. We cried with Cat Stephens's wistful songs, bemoaned the loss of our sixties' dreams and began to understand each other's emotional landscapes.

In April Rich found solace in wandering out with Luna, taking photos of the moody clouds hanging over the mountains, while I attended Zoom meetings and meditations. Our most precious moments were had in nature, when we visited a nearby meadow to collect kindling for the fire and to lie in the spring sunshine amidst wild flowers, listening to the distant murmur of the river Guadalfeo. Rich helped me recognise different birdsongs as he took photos, whilst I became inspired to write poetry fuelled by our shared time in the elements.

A month had passed and we were still physically distancing from friends when I was beginning to miss all the hugs and emotional intimacy with my women friends. Rich and I had the routine of a quick evening hug as we disappeared into our separate rooms, neither of us admitting to the strong physical attraction that was growing between us. I was longing for more contact, but respected that with his bereavement he needed space. However, one day I braved my needs and asked for a longer hug. Instead of the rejection I half expected, Rich jumped at the suggestion and started kissing me passionately! I was astonished, until he explained that he had been really attracted to me from the beginning, but felt he needed to tread carefully, in case an intimate relationship didn't work out and with lockdown there would be no escape!

It was the first day of May, a traditional Celtic celebration of spring, when we watched the waxing moon rise over the mountains and celebrated our new union. At last we could snuggle down entwined in each other's arms in the evenings and openly share our feelings. One day we spent a magical hour lying together under an azure sky, listening to nightingales singing in the river valley, amidst a coppice of poplar. By mid-May we were allowed to drive out and enjoyed our first romantic meal together in a restaurant. Gone were the complaints of limitation and lockdown, because life had become beautiful again.

In June, with yet more freedom, we celebrated Rich's birthday, enjoyed our first meal out with friends and skinny-dipped in mountain waterfalls. We visited

Granada like two young lovers, whilst the city appeared subdued, with everyone wearing masks.

All too soon, four full moons had passed and Rich started talking of returning to England to sell his house and land. 'And what about our relationship?' I asked, preparing myself for my old story of abandonment.

'I will come back when I have sold my house and we can live together here,' he replied, taking my hand.

'Do you think we are ready for that?' I asked, suddenly feeling nervous.

'Well, we have already lived together happily for four months. Why not?'

Why not indeed, I asked myself. 'Let's tell our friends and celebrate lockdown love!'

Shining through the Pandemic Gloom
Raymond Yeung, Hong Kong

'In the midst of darkness, light persists'
Mahatma Gandhi

The last twelve months have been a rollercoaster of highs and lows for me. On one level it's been a struggle, particularly because Hong Kong has been going through a lot of changes. Furthermore, launching a film during the coronavirus pandemic has certainly proved to be very challenging. On the other hand, the success of *Suk Suk,* my third feature film, has taken me on an incredible journey.

Suk Suk completed post-production in August 2019 and soon after, we were invited to have our World Premiere at the prestigious Busan International Film Festival (BIFF), where we had originally pitched our project to potential investors at the 2017 Asian Project Market.*

Our next big surprise was an invitation from the Berlinale International Film Festival to be part of their Panorama program. Subsequently, *Suk Suk* became the only Hong Kong feature that was screened at Berlinale 2020 and nominated for the Teddy Award, winning accolades from leading film critics.

We had been scheduled to screen at many film festivals throughout the spring and summer. Unfortunately, the pandemic exploded in Europe soon after Berlinale, forcing many film festivals to cancel their events. The world went into lockdown and everything stood still. Nevertheless, the trajectory of our film continued. The pride and joy this created for our team helped us greatly to combat the never-ending gloom of the Covid-19 crisis that was engulfing the world.

By April 2020, the pandemic continued to spread, but things seemed to be under control in Hong Kong when cinemas reopened with socially distanced seating. *Suk Suk* opened in 60 theatres across Hong Kong, quite a milestone for an independent film with a LGBT theme featuring seniors. The film played in cinemas for seven weeks until a third spike of cases in Hong Kong caused cinemas to close again. We hope when the cinemas reopen we will continue to play in selected venues and finish our run.**

Over the past few months I spent more time staying at home due to the semi-lockdown in Hong Kong. I decided this would be a good opportunity to catch up on watching old movie classics, which I had always wanted to do but never had the time. This turned out to be a wonderful decision and confirms for me that movies are truly magical.

Films are like time machines with many windows to the world. A film could take you somewhere far away in time and place, and provide insights through another person who might not even be the same gender or the same age as you.

There are movie moments, which are as emotional as one's own memories. Scenes such as Jeanne Moreau walking down the streets at night to the jazz score of Miles Davies in *Elevator to the Gallows*; or Alain Delon gazing at his own reflection longingly in *Purple Noon*; or Anouk Aimee dancing and flirting with a top hat in *Lola*; or Anna Magnani running to her lover just before being shot by the Nazis in *Rome, Open City*; or the Japanese army singing before their defeat in *The Burmese Harp*. These magnificent movie moments are forever imprinted in one's mind.

Here is a list of films I watched recently. Each is brilliant in its own way:

When a Woman Ascends the Stairs	Mikio Naruse	Japan 1960
Elevator to the Gallows	Louis Malle	France 1958
Il Vitelloni	Federico Fellini	Italy 1953
The Hero (Nayak)	Satyajit Ray	India 1966
Il Posto	Ermanno Olmi	Italy 1961
The Burmese Harp	Kon Ichikawa	Japan 1956
The Fireman's Ball	Milos Foreman	Czech. 1967
Belle de Jour	Luis Bunuel	France 1967
Playtime	Jacques Tati	France 1967

An Actor's Revenge	Kon Ichikawa	Japan 1963
Purple Noon	Rene Clement	France 1960
Apur Sansar (The World of Apu)	Satyajit Ray	India 1959
Lola	Jacques Demy	France 1961
The Sun's Burial	Nagisa Oshima	Japan 1960
Wild Strawberries	Ingmar Bergman	Sweden 1957
Aguirre, the Wrath of God	Werner Herzog	Germany 1972
The Rules of the Game	Jean Renoir	France 1939
Loves of a Blonde	Milos Forman	Czech. 1965
Magnet of Doom	Jean-Pierre Melville	France 1963
Journey to Italy	Roberto Rossellini	Italy 1954
Bay of Angels	Jacques Demy	France 1963
The Mirror	Jafar Panahi	Iran 1997
Rome, Open City	Roberto Rossellini	Italy 1945
M	Fritz Lang	Germany 1931
Germany Year Zero	Roberto Rossellini	Italy 1948
The Fiancés (I Fidanzati)	Ermanno Olmi	Italy 1963
Late Chrysanthemums	Mikio Naruse	Japan 1954
That Obscure Object of Desire	Luis Bunuel	France 1977

*Taiwan's Golden Horse Awards nominated *Suk Suk* for five awards including Best Actor for both leads Tai Bo and Ben Yuen, Best Supporting Actress for Patra Ga-Man Au, Best Screenplay and Best Narrative Feature.

**We were nominated for nine Hong Kong Film Awards, and another eight nominations from HK Film Directors Guild, HK Screenwriters Guild and the HK Film Critics Association. We eventually won seven awards including Best Film from the HK Film Critics Association, Best Screenplay from the HK Screenwriters Guild and our lead Tai Bo won Best Actor from all the above-mentioned organisations.

Circling the Fortress
Dawn Rees, UK

'Dance me to your beauty with a burning violin
Dance me through the panic till I'm gathered safely in
Touch me with your naked hand or touch me with your glove
Dance me to the end of love'
Leonard Cohen

There was a time when what is happening now was beyond my understanding. I was well defended – stuck there on a rise in the land, my ammunition loaded against the pointed barbs of words. I was lonely. Alone. Only me – the last bastion of hope against oblivion.

For years a part of me stayed over there, beyond the hill. Beyond your sight. I existed in my fortress of fear, not knowing where I was and why I was there.

The only thing I revealed to the world was my energy. The energy that kept my world turning. I was the weaver of magic around every opportunity. The darner in threads that fell loose. The patcher of impossible dreams. I remade my world so that I could live in it.

At night, alone and in darkness, I laid out all those skeins of memory; picking them over, delicately lifting the gossamer-thin veil and letting it fall again. Because everything looked better that way, clouded from view by the criss-cross weave. I was fearful of examining those strange shapes beneath.

Then you appeared. With your eyes and your kindness. You sought to find the flesh beneath the skin. My thin skin. You sought the shape of me. Bit by bit. Patient. Cautious. Acknowledging your own margins as well as mine. It felt right. Tentative. Dancing. Like a quadrille – touching fingertips. Pacing. Watching. Waiting.

Our dance has lasted for decades and now we have learned our steps, the dance moves on. Through the dance we learned how to open a space so the other could live. We checked and cross-checked as we paced the dance-floor. As we've grown older, we have traced the ghosts of those steps inside our heads. We've danced and travelled, we've read and shared music and art and our thoughts. Silence has become our friend, no longer the void that ached to be filled. Year on year the layers have unfolded and now we are bare. Naked to one another. There is no place to hide because there can only be truth. It is this we have been seeking.

Once it seemed as if the only task was to follow the footsteps on the floor and live within their pattern. In finding and acknowledging silence and truth we can be vulnerable, and weak, and we can fall. Because it is part of the pattern. It was always going to be the pattern. It was never about being invincible, it was always about exploring and being ourselves. Together. In that discovery, I found you and then I found me. How does that happen?

Now, in the time of lockdown, it feels like the whole of our life together had been shifting, year by year, towards this point. We can be together and separate, simultaneously. Our lives have worked in reverse. We started – desperately seeking contact, as a couple, then as a family; we hurtled into careers and out the other side. Many times, we circled the reality of our life, failing to acknowledge the single truth that binds us. But now we have time.

And what truth do I know?

I know you are mine and I am yours. I know I can forget the world when I am with you – just for a moment. With love, we are different and I am glad of it. But, in love, we are the same. It is like I've always known you and now I cannot forget you.

There was a time when what is happening now would have been beyond my understanding. But knowing that I have a fixed point in my world, I no longer need to seek out the truth of the whole world. I just need this and to dance with you.

Could It Be That You Have Always Lived Here?
Fawzia, Switzerland

*'See how nature – trees, flowers, grass – grow in silence;
see the stars, the moon and the sun, how they move in silence.
We need silence to be able to touch souls'*
Mother Teresa

You might always have been here but I never noticed. I'm glad I've been able to stop and spend some time here myself – it's been a while and it's beautiful.

I see that you know your way around. So much so, that at first, I felt myself the intruder. But you do not seem to mind me; for that, I really am grateful. Thank you for staying when I appear and for carrying on as you do. If you look at me directly, I might not be able to help whispering a quiet 'hello'. But that's it. There's something magical about both of us being here, pottering around, each with our own thoughts – sharing the same space in peace and in silence.

Yesterday felt different. I understood – I think – that you have a partner and that she is a she! She seems timid and I don't think I've seen her before. I wonder if she is busier than you? Preoccupied elsewhere? With the family – even? The delights of sharing your presence increased as I imagined the possibility of your family out there somewhere and that, if I'm patient, I might be rewarded with a glance!

You've made me glad I fought to keep those Tilias and planted the trees I have – you clearly enjoy their shade and know them intimately. I'm particularly glad you've discovered the cherries. It's odd, but I do not mind sharing them with you one bit. They seem more rightfully yours than mine. When I watch you nimbly dart below the canopy, landing on invisible branches, sensing cherries, which I can only barely see – they surely belong to you. You nip, then peck, then swallow them whole. For all I know, you may be responsible for the two new cherry trees I discovered, just alongside the one I originally planted.

I imagine you think of me as friendly – if not a friend; otherwise, surely you would take off at the very sight of me. That you remain is in itself an honour.

It's been good to stop time and be with you. Do know that I'd like you and yours, to stay. And thrive. This is our home. In fact, it would greatly sadden me to see you go.

For the Love of Lavender

Athena Lambrinidou, New Zealand

'Love is the flower of life and blooms unexpectedly and without law'
D.H. Lawrence

On average I think I have approached most relationships in my life as a sort of Mowgli who decided to leave the jungle to check out the mesmerising human village, only to rush back completely perplexed to live with Bagheera and Baloo.

Men I have been with have tended to characterise me as more of a wild horse than a human woman. I cannot say that I have resented that label.

Existentially exhausted after 30 years of doing everything I possibly could to reverse the absurd and criminal international environmental crisis we all seemed passionately committed to not solving, there were two things I felt I now wanted to do in order to grow old as happy as possible. One was to become an elementary-school bus driver. The other was to be surrounded by lavender.

On the summer of my return to New Zealand, I heard of a man who had decided to leave the big city to go live in the countryside, close to the ocean, and start a small lavender farm whilst serving coffees at an ocean beach café. He was a friend of friends. As soon as the summer season was over we arranged for me to drive up to his newly acquired small farm to look at his dream from up close.

Total lockdown was announced on my way to driving up to visit. He suggested I stay.

I would not be able to gallop to absolutely anywhere except the empty ocean beach for six weeks. The sound of the wild ocean close by was both beckoning and taming.

I had arrived at the beautiful small farm of an almost stranger and yet I decided to stay.

Under normal circumstances my wild horse-ness would have galloped away in wild abandon at the first opportunity into the sense of freedom and safety of the wild-flower fields on the horizon. We had been stopped. We had been locked in.

We spent the next six weeks sharing stories lots, reading the news lots, philosophising lots, weeding the overgrown farm lots, feeding the two inherited grandmother chooks lots, sharing our life stories lots, being silent lots, reading lots, dreaming lots. Attached to the main house is a small, beautiful, empty, horse stable. It is right there by the veggie garden and the field of lavender to be.

Finding New Paths
Lucy Counsell, UK

'In family life, love is the oil that eases friction, the cement that binds closer together and the music that brings harmony'
Friedrich Nietzsche

Lockdown for Lily, Charlie and me began a little earlier than most. On 18 March Charlie and I drove to Leeds hospital for a liver scan, to check that his liver was still working properly. He suffers from ARPKD, a genetic condition that is characterised by the growth of cysts in the kidneys (which lead to kidney failure) and liver and problems in other organs, such as the blood vessels in the brain and heart.

I was in two minds about going as it's a large hospital and there could be people there who actually had Covid. But I was sure Charlie's doctor wouldn't have sent for us to attend if it wasn't safe. I work at my children's school as a one-to-one teaching assistant, so I was already feeling nervous. The atmosphere in school was each day becoming heavier with fear. The adults were trying to keep calm and be reassuring, but everything was so unclear and scary, it was a totally new situation that nobody could really understand or control. Inevitably, the children started to get a little crazy; tensions were high at home and in school. I'd been at work all day on the 17th, which was a Monday. It was to be my last day at work for six months, Charlie's last day of year four and Lily's last day of primary school.

Charlie's scan was good, his liver showed no signs of damage and was working well, which was amazing news, although a scan of his kidneys a month earlier showed many cysts. He has 75 per cent kidney function which is good but any damage from a nasty virus could reduce that and cause all sorts of lasting damage. I asked his doctor's advice about taking him out of school, and she agreed it would be wise. I was petrified that if he was to become ill with Covid there might not be a bed for him in hospital or I wouldn't be allowed to see him. The news was conflicting and everyone was scared and confused about what to do. It was becoming increasingly clear that this horrible, life-threatening virus was starting to pick up pace and anyone could have it. It was a strange, terrifying feeling: trust nobody, keep your distance; even friends could be carrying it.

So we drove home, collected Lily and, after getting a few supplies, went in to lockdown. My boss (headteacher) was totally understanding and supportive, so I was lucky that I was still being paid.

Spain had already been in lockdown for a few weeks and this meant Lily and Charlie's dad was stuck, unable to travel over to see them; he said he was being looked after by the local shop, they were delivering his shopping, and he lives in a secluded rural area so at least he could get outdoors and stretch his legs, unlike many others.

I was also worried about my parents. I couldn't see them or do their shopping; they were as vulnerable as Charlie so I felt helpless.

By Friday 21st all schools had closed. Because I work in school it was easy for me to chat to my children's teachers as we are a team, so I was able to access work for them both; having experienced four years of teaching in primary, working with many children of different ages meant I could support them with confidence. That I was grateful for, but although Charlie plods along with life and is just happy to be with me, Lily was missing out on her last few months of primary school, a time of hard work building up to SATS, then relaxing and enjoying time with her peers: parties, school plays, her final year assembly and signing of shirts. They had worked so hard and it was looking like they would never return. Lily was sad and I felt for her.

The first few days were surreal; we watched the news for updates, did home-schooling and went out for exercise in our local car park. We took bikes and a football and played for an hour each day. On 24 March it was Lily's eleventh birthday. She didn't have the sleepover we'd planned, but my sister had bought her a mini portal which meant we could have group chats, so we just had to make the most of it.

I think my worst experience in those first few weeks was not being able to shop or get a delivery, people were panic buying and our main supermarket just couldn't handle the pressure. They never really sorted it out. The first delivery I managed to get, after days of trying to grab a slot, arrived with none of the meat I'd ordered, and there wasn't any pasta to be had. All the essential stuff was missing. I was worrying about feeding my family. Luckily, I do have good friends who made shop visits for me and picked up Charlie's meds from the pharmacy, otherwise we would have been stuck. I also knew there would be people and families far worse off than us and that brought lots of emotions to the surface. I know it was the least of some people's worries. We were lucky we had each other and enjoyed spending lots of time together, although even that starts to wear thin after weeks and weeks of being stuck in the same house.

By the third week we'd had enough of playing footy and biking around the big overflow car park next to us so we decided to start walking and biking along a track that runs behind our house, with a variety of routes. Charlie learned to ride his bike, and after a nervous start, over the next few months he became a strong, competent rider. As we strolled, ran and biked, we would pass (at a two-metre distance) many other families doing the same thing. I used to run the tracks regularly and hardly ever passed a soul!

Our daily exercise would take us through fields, woods and country lanes. I remember in early April how the wheat was beginning to grow and by June it looked like an ocean, the wind rippling through it like waves; the trees became lush and green and buds grew, we heard woodpeckers and spotted lots of amazing wildlife. We did the same route for a few months and watched as the wildlife around us changed with the seasons. It was the highlight of my day to get out; my children did get a bit bored eventually of doing the same trail but while it lasted, we made the most of it.

However, by the second month I was starting to crave adult conversation and company, and started to feel really down. There were OK days and bad days. I think if the weather had been horrendous and it had all happened a few months earlier it would have been a different story for most. So I made the most of our tiny garden and the sunshine. Lily was missing her friends and there were a few silly arguments, and Charlie just wanted to be with me all the time. I think he only slept in his own bed twice in the whole lockdown period.

When we were told we could form a bubble, we were a little apprehensive but at the same time the feeling was amazing. My next-door neighbour and I share a garden; it belongs to my house really but they only have a garage on their bit and in the past we just shared mine as we are close friends. We had chatted during those months whilst clapping for the NHS on our doorstep but it wasn't the same as sharing a bottle of ice-cold wine in the sunshine and putting the world to rights. We formed a bubble and I was able to relax a little.

I think things will take a long time to go back to normal, if ever. Lockdown brought many emotions with it and although I'm looking forward to getting back to work in three weeks, it's going to be really tough and different. Charlie is still vulnerable, which is my biggest worry, but we need some normality and routine back in our lives. Luckily Lily is itching to get to secondary school. She's confident and capable, which makes me proud, as she's had no transition time, just a FaceTime with her new teacher and a virtual tour of her new school. At times it was a struggle, hours melted into days and days into weeks at the beginning, but we managed to pull together.

Certainties in a Time of Uncertainty
Amanda Jane Gibbs, Spain

'Something inside so strong...'
Labi Siffre

I think it's an inspiring idea to bring people's stories together; just to sit down and reflect on the last few months has been good for the soul.

Our finca, Las Plumas, is tucked away in a valley on its own with running water meandering through the *rambla* (water course) below the house. We have always felt lucky living in this unique spot though as with most *campo* (Spanish countryside) living, my partner Andy and I call it the 'tough paradise'. People don't drop in and we catch the odd hiker looking for the nearest village. We welcome any surprise visitors who have braved the track and not got lost. We don't have a TV and only one of us keeps track of the news through social media. To help us with our tribe of animals – horses, dogs and cats – and our farm, we have been fortunate to meet Brie and Stu through HelpX.

So now that I've set the scene at home, we fast forward to the day 'lockdown' started.

We were enjoying a few days away in nearby Gaucin from 12 March when it dawned on us, old and new friends, that things had really escalated. Two of us had travelled from the Alpujarras, two from London and two from South Africa. The conversations started with serious thoughts on the situation and our individual states of health but we naturally moved on to focus on each other's company. We cooked good food together and laughed a lot. Unbeknown to us this was to be our way in the coming months.

Our helpers, Brie and Stu, did not want to leave our farm and we agreed we would stay together and take care of each other and the animals.

We got together most days before lunch and practised yoga, tai chi or qigong, finishing with a meditation to help us focus on what really mattered to us as a group. There were days that we got into serious conversations and shared concerns for what was going on with our friends and families. There were days we disagreed with each other's opinions. We came back to taking care of each other and being kind despite our differences.

We began to realise that we had more time for each other and our animals. We took care of the horses' feet ourselves and learned to barefoot trim through an online hoof school that another friend had created so he could continue to work.

There are people living around us without vehicles or with very little money and we would shop for them and take them extra things that they needed. We are blessed with three cooks amongst us, and we lovingly created and enjoyed good food together. We created the biggest vegetable garden since we have lived here and watched it flourish and provide us with organic food.

Our dogs welcomed more attention, especially our eldest who was showing signs of leaving us. We spent time with her, changed her diet and encouraged her to come on short walks. She is still with us now and is walking 40 minutes a day and barking at the wild boar again.

In the evenings, Stu played his divine homemade flute, often perched on a rock somewhere in the grounds. We had a couple of music nights where we all had a go at playing something. We contacted our families and friends more regularly and gave thanks for the wonders of technology.

There were moments of frustration when we realised that there would be no visiting family and friends wherever they lived. Feelings of sadness for those trapped in an apartment, especially children, and for those perhaps struggling to take care of their families and learning to be in a different way, with no time to really prepare.

From 'lockdown' to the 'new normal', whatever that means! This was a much more testing time. Finding out what is expected of us, reading many theories about the direction this virus will take us. Realising that more than ever, key people are making decisions that affect our lives greatly. Reading how others feel about what has happened and is happening. Being saddened by arguments that only prolong confusion and unkindness. People losing lifelong friends over a difference in opinion.

During this time, we attended a wake and a wedding and despite the challenges we were able to be together. Sure, it wasn't great to feel like you could not hug anyone but wrongly or rightly I did.

I recently lost my uncle. Trying to be there in the UK to support my aunt, who is in isolation, was complicated. I was made aware that my presence coming from Spain would cause great alarm. The friends and family involved over there are truly doing their best.

For me personally my love of animals and nature has helped me a lot to deal with this year so far. Animals accept you as you are and live quietly wanting to be loved and cared for. Isn't that what we all want? I ask myself.

Maintaining the peace that we experienced during 'lockdown' is my mantra. Enjoy the company of those around you, welcome others, especially those who are struggling, keep in touch with your family, write a letter to those who have no mobile phone or computer.

I want to find a way to turn this crisis into an opportunity to change and grow and help others to do the same. I am truly grateful and appreciative of the life I have, and enjoy sharing what we as a couple have, with others, and no virus or other threat will undermine that feeling for me.

As the singer Labi Siffre says, it's 'Something inside so strong'.

Lockdown

Joselón Gipsy Floyd, Spain

This lockdown has opened two doors.
One has allowed me to see within myself.
The other has allowed me to see what is happening outside.
Inside I have found calm above all.
Outside I have seen accepted inconsistencies.
Inside is the desire to hug everyone.
Outside, fear is your only friend.
Inside, love continues to grow.
Outside, humanity sleeps confidently

Confinamiento

Este confinamiento ha abierto dos puertas.
Una me ha permitido ver dentro de mi ser.
La otra me ha permitido ver lo que pasa fuera.
Dentro he encontrado calma ante todo.
Fuera he visto incongruencias aceptadas.
Dentro hay el deseo de abrazar a todas.
Fuera, el miedo es tu único amigo.
Dentro, sigue creciendo el amor.
Fuera, la humanidad duerme confiada.

Notes to Self
Claudia Chapman, UK

Lockdown …
Isolation …
Stay safe …
Stay at home …
Stay alert …
Use your intuition … like this one!

Jeez …
Where to start …
Fear bubbles up from the earth …
Should my kids be at school? …
When will they shut down? …
We're all home …
I feel safer …
Now what? …

Realisation that my family are home with me for the next few weeks …
How will I cope? …
I know … I'll set them all work stations … starting with my husband's new office …
That didn't go down too well …
He's refusing to be locked away …
Home education … I don't fancy that! …

I know ...
I'll start digging a veggie patch and baking cakes ...
Oh dear ...
I'm eating too much sugar ...
On my yoga mat ... that's better ...
I can cope now! ...

Days pass ...
We organise a schedule ...
home school,
lunch and walk the neighbour's dog! ...
We pick up rubbish in the woods ...
My neighbour and her dog are our saviours ...
We have our favourite tree ...
We put the worlds to rights ...
The kids climb trees and splash in the brook ...

I call my light worker friends ...
Did we make this happen? ...
Did drumming in Trafalgar Square last year really make this happen? ...
We wanted a climate change right? ...
I remember a guy from France talking about a climate pause on the XR Rebellion Facebook page ... I felt a surge of euphoria fill my gut and I knew this was the answer!
I felt sure! ...
Pay off ... Here comes the angel of death! ...
I feel overwhelmed! ...

My first Goddess retreat might still happen ...
but it didn't ...
Oh well it'll be even better next year ...

Should I send the kids back to school? ...

Might be best to keep them home until September ...

Oh well school didn't open anyway ...

Oh god six months at home with all the family ...

Our self-sufficiency bubble has burst! ...

Breakdown ...

I want out! ...

Preferably off the planet ...

Husband leaves ...

I face my shadow ...

Husband returns ...

I face my shadow ...

It's going to be fine ... Breakthrough ...

Realisation! ...

A new age is dawning and time to embrace the future ...

Not sure what it will look like or who will be in our bubbles? ...

The Awakening of a new world is dawning ...

The Age of Aquarius and the Divine Feminine is rising ...

The planet has been so kind ...

My life amongst the trees has been nourishing ...

My skin has been in the sun ...

I've seen nature flourish ...

I've taken my vitamin C ...

I've taken care of my family ...

I've zoomed my clients ...

I've started to study the Kabbalah after thirty years of wanting to ...

I'm showing up live on Facebook every day, connecting through Chakra and

Goddess cards …
I'm helping my daughter to raise money for charities by dancing online …
She's danced at a care home …
Gratitude …
We've collected clothes and items for the homeless …
We've bonded as mother and daughter and found a common ground in helping others together …

Now life is opening up again and our schedule is changing and we're adjusting to this 'new normal' …
This time has been a great magnifier over us …
It's highlighted my fears and made me face myself up close and personal …
Into the future I go …
Being rather than doing …
Who knows the next step? …
I am more aware of the fragility of my existence …

I have found a renewed respect for Mother Gaia and our Planet.

Befriending Uncertainty in Our 'New Normal'

Sue Edge, UK

'If you're invested in security and certainty, you are on the wrong planet'
Pema Chodron

17 June 2020

We've reached a milestone here in the UK in dealing with coronavirus. We have passed the end of the 12-week period since the first day of lockdown. By then I figured we'd be over the worst and nearly back to normal. Friends that were 'shielding' had been told that they needed to stay at home for this length of time. Even Boris Johnson said that in those twelve weeks we could 'turn the tide of this disease and send coronavirus packing in this country'.

We have turned the tide, thankfully. The rate of infection appears to be slowly reducing each week in most areas. I can feel my shoulders relaxing a little more as I see the numbers finally coming down. The dreadful peak with all the tragic losses has indeed passed. The weather is gloriously sunny and we are able to enjoy it now in our small groups of up to six people. EasyJet has just taken its first flight in 11 weeks on Monday from Gatwick to Glasgow with 51 passengers. As more things are opening up, I can feel myself almost being swept along (although I'm not about to queue up for Primark).

But I still find myself checking data and reading articles fairly regularly. While celebrating these tentative steps towards returning to normal that are happening around us, I simultaneously feel uncertain. Like everyone I speak to, there's a shared uncertainty of what will happen to the spread of the virus as we ease restrictions. On the one hand, I can now go to FatFace and try on some jeans. And at the same time, the WHO is telling the UK not to ease up much more as it remains in a 'very active phase of the pandemic'.

Our conversations seem to now revolve around the crucial word 'when'. When will we be able to get our hair cut? When will we be able to sit inside a friend's house if it is raining? When will my dentist be able to replace a filling that needs fixing (not yet, no fillings allowed)? When can I go to a yoga class with actual people not on Zoom? The list goes on and on. We each have our own personal list of when will …? But underneath lies the actual question that I would like the answer to:

'When will this all end?' An actual date when we have an effective vaccine, successful treatment and/or no cases? When will we be able to properly get back to normal? When will we be able to carry on with our lives without thinking about coronavirus? We are not at the beginning of the pandemic here in the UK, nor are we close to the end. Instead, we have rolled into the 'seemingly interminable middle' as I heard it described recently. And in this middle phase, we each live with a plethora of uncertainties.

I have been wondering what the antidote to uncertainty is? I struggle with uncertainty and find it uncomfortable to sit with. One way that I deal with uncertainty is to gather information. Which explains my carefully rationed habit of checking statistics and reading the latest scientific information. It helps to some extent; my brain can start to make some sense of this ongoing pandemic. However, even with this research, there are no simple answers. Just a lot of small steps and reviewing, which feels a lot more like trial and error than I would like!

Maybe you have all figured this out already, but uncertainty seems to be part of the landscape at the moment. Information can only help to some degree to reduce the unknown. So I am wondering if it is possible to befriend uncertainty rather than trying to outrun it? The more enlightened question could be 'How can I become more comfortable with uncertainty?' rather than 'When will it end?' Rather than resisting uncertainty, could I accept that it is going to walk quietly next to us for a while to come?

Pema Chodron (Buddhist nun and author) writes frequently about uncertainty and she says:

'What if rather than being disheartened by the ambiguity, the uncertainty of life, we accepted it and relaxed into it?'

It sounds like a sensible approach, but maybe not so easy to do. How do I relax and accept uncertainty rather than spend an hour on the computer or eating dark chocolate (my other tendency)? It comes back to living as much as possible in the present moment; for example, as I write, as I wash the dishes and as I walk outside along the beach. Rather than mulling over the latest changes as I walk, I make a point of looking at the sky, hearing the waves or listening out for varied birdsong. And when I do come back to the present moment, I feel more accepting of uncertainty. It's OK, we are all feeling it. And in this moment, I am OK.

But what about making plans and looking ahead? Well, we can try to take some tentative steps knowing that there is still an unclear path ahead. When a neighbour asked me the other day if I would fly to Spain soon, all I could do was look confused as different uncertainties ran through my mind. Before coronavirus, I could never have imagined that flying to Spain for a nourishing yoga retreat could be difficult. It won't always be like this, but for now I'm accepting that uncertainty is here.

http://keepingcalmincoronatimes.blogspot.com

A Love Story from a Century Ago
Roger Wilson, New Zealand

'You live as long as you are remembered.'
Russian Proverb

I adored my grandmother, Dorothy Melville. As a child, I used to visit her in Auckland during the school holidays and built a strong bond with her; I also developed a strong relationship with Auckland that endures to this day.

Dorothy was born in Dunedin, New Zealand, in May 1893. Her father, Charles Hale, was a local jeweller who had migrated as a twelve-year-old from the Midlands in England, with his family. Her mother Mary-Jane was born in Kent, though her family roots lay in Exeter. They married in Dunedin in 1889, and soon had two children, Dorothy and her brother Norman, three years older than her.

Dorothy's paternal grandfather died before she was born, her maternal grandfather died when she was only a month old, and her father died when she was eighteen months old. She grew up never knowing any of the significant men in her family. Dorothy, Norman, and their widowed mother and grandmother moved north to Auckland, and eventually settled in Remuera, where they lived in a house that remained in the family until I was a young adult.

From about the age of fifty, Dorothy lived on her own, until she became blind and moved into a rest home in her eighties. During the many years I lived abroad I would always prioritise visiting her on trips home, and our bond grew stronger and stronger. In the mid-1990s, she agreed for me to record her voice and her memories for posterity and I somewhat inexpertly interviewed her with my newly acquired Dictaphone. The first interview was in June 1994, when she was 101 years old, and the second two years later in April 1996, when she was nearly 103 years old.

The recordings were transferred to audio cassettes, and there they remained for more than twenty years in a dusty corner. When I rediscovered the cassettes, years later, I found I no longer had anything to play them on. During the Covid-19 lockdown, I finally found the motivation and organised the technology to convert the by now more than twenty-five-year-old interviews into digital format. As a lockdown treat, for the first time in decades I listened to the voice of my grandmother.

Though I already knew something of Dorothy's life, I especially wanted to learn about life as a young person in the first decades of the twentieth century. She told me that in her teens, she was part of a group of about eight who used to socialise together. Around 1910, this meant going on picnics (Milford beach was a favourite spot), playing tennis, going to the theatre, going to dances and playing music (her brother Norman was a good violinist).

Randall 'Mel' Melville (no one called him Randall) was the son of Scottish immigrant Alexander Melville and Eliza Fogarty, born in Melbourne but also of Scottish ancestry. Mel was initially brought up in rural Northland, but his family moved to Auckland so that he and two of his academically inclined siblings could attend secondary school. He went on to university and on graduation joined the *New Zealand Herald* as a journalist.

Mel was one of Dorothy's social group. She was around seventeen when they met, he was three years older. She had had one or two 'slight romances' before, but she and Mel were attracted from the start. Neither was very communicative on an emotional level, but an understanding gradually developed that they were a couple. The barrier to taking the relationship further, however, was Dorothy's diabetes.

Little was known about diabetes in those days, other than that it could be a death sentence. It was known that it could be inherited from a parent, and Dorothy was adamant that it would be wrong to marry and have children if they too might inherit the disease. She and Mel continued to grow fonder of each other, and surely would have married had it not been for her diabetes. And then came the First World War.

Two weeks after the war began, Mel signed up. He was assigned to the New

Zealand Expeditionary Force and sailed for Egypt in late 1914 to train for an assault on the Gallipoli peninsula in Turkey. He took part in the first assault on Gallipoli on 25 April 1915, a revered date now permanently etched in the history of both Australia and New Zealand as 'Anzac Day', the day on which the two nations truly came of age.

Mel wrote letters home about his experiences of war. He wrote of the first assault on the morning of 25 April:

> Dashing out of their boats they drove the Turks helter-skelter up the cliffs at the point of the bayonet, when by all rules of war they ought themselves to have been annihilated ... Our men stand tenaciously holding their ground, at death grips with the enemy, and undismayed by the horrors of modern war ...

After five weeks and two days of the horrors of Gallipoli, Mel was injured when a piece of shrapnel passed clean through his shoulder. He was evacuated to Egypt, from where he wrote home to reassure Dorothy and his family:

> I heard the shell burst, and then felt as if a ton of bricks had hit me on the shoulder ... I have seen artillery duels, aeroplane manoeuvres, warships in action, a battleship, the *Triumph*, torpedoed and sunk by a submarine, have been under shell and rifle fire, have experienced an armistice, and have generally run through the whole gamut of experiences.

Mel was repatriated to New Zealand to convalesce, and was discharged in November 1916. Mel and Dorothy resumed their relationship, but initially saw little of each other as Mel was posted to Wellington as the *Herald*'s parliamentary correspondent. It was understood that they would marry if they could – but diabetes still stood in their way.

Desperate to find a cure, Dorothy visited many doctors, even giving up her teaching job to go to a doctor in Nelson, where she stayed a year. During another holiday she went to a doctor in Napier. She told Mel he should not wait for her to find a cure, and that he should move on. But he didn't. Then she found a doctor who told her that sugar in the urine was not on its own a positive indicator of diabetes, and asked her if she had ever had a blood test. After six months of regular blood tests he confirmed that she did not have and had never had diabetes.

After considering themselves a couple for around fifteen years, Mel and Dorothy finally felt free to marry in 1925 when she was 32 and he 35. Unfortunately, they were not destined to enjoy a long and happy marriage, as Mel was unexpectedly struck down by a heart attack in 1944, leaving Dorothy on her own with two children, just as her mother had been.

Hearing my dearly loved grandmother's voice from the past, telling her own love story, tinged with sadness and lost opportunities, brought tears to my eyes. Thanks to my foresight in interviewing her all those years ago, and to the Covid-19 pandemic, I can now hear her voice, and her story, whenever I want to remember her.

Corona Chronicles
Andrea McIntosh, Germany

> 'The sweet spring day is ending, the sun is sinking low,
> we children homewards wending are singing as we go,
> the butterfly is swinging his way through warming air
> the angels aloft are singing and beauty is everywhere.'
> Author unknown

I meant to start a diary to document my experiences at the height of the corona pandemic. Me, a child of the Caribbean living in Germany. I never did put pen to paper, so I will now have to draw on my memories, which are already fading. It was so surreal what was happening. What started out as something in a distant Asia, something that should not affect us in Europe, let alone the entire world, came to dictate a new way of life for us.

For me it was a beautiful time even though I feared in the beginning that I had caught the virus. I had stood long hours in the rain and cold at the Berlinale film festival in February – still winter – trying to get tickets and caught a harmless cold, it seemed. Three weeks later in mid-March, the media was only talking about this killer virus, people began to get scared and here I was at home with a cold. No fever, no aches, just sniffles. And just as measures to mitigate the spread of the virus were being debated, I developed chest pains and shortness of breath.

I thought maybe I should get tested for the virus but testing was only available to people returning from high-risk countries like Italy or China. Doctors' offices hadn't yet established a protocol for dealing with the disease so you were asked not to come into the practice if you thought you might be infected. It was a feeling of total abandonment, angst and confusion. Where to turn for help or more information? My good neighbour, a general practitioner, came by, listened to my lungs and declared they were clear (no indication of pneumonia) but should I have trouble breathing I should use my asthma inhaler.

To be honest, in retrospect, I am not sure how serious my upper respiratory problems were. Was I panicking or overreacting because of the constant bombardment of Covid news, messages, jokes? I worry that I might have used the inhaler too much and too often. My stomach burned. The doctor never gave me a diagnosis but he discontinued his usual jogging with my husband. His wife, a close friend, did not return my telephone calls or messages and stopped enquiring about my health. By this time I was beginning to feel somewhat like a pariah. Then came the lockdown.

But in all of this craziness and confusion, there was a silver lining. I got to know a new side to my husband and together we discovered new pastimes. He started to cook, something which he had never done before, and together we cooked the most complicated of delicious meals. He went shopping, sometimes twice a day, he took out the garbage and cleaned up the kitchen. He never flinched from my side all the time I felt ill and kept me optimistic and buoyant when I feared that I might be carrying the virus. The chest issues began to wane after seven to ten days (I can't remember any more but at the time it seemed way too long) and although I was definitely experiencing a shortness of breath with the slightest exertion, I was determined to build up stamina by exercising my lung muscles more.

And then began the most wonderful hiking experiences. I wasn't a hiker so I am still amazed that I found the will to take this on. Every day we hiked for hours in the woods, every day we took a different path and allowed ourselves to get lost and find our way back. Sometimes it was not fun because it took too long and I was way too exhausted. I wondered if people could get heart failure from such exhaustion. But we found our way home eventually every time and I was alive.

I never knew the forest could be so enchanting, that the colour green existed in so many hues. I downloaded an app called iNaturalist (thanks *New York Times*) that helped me to identify some of the wildlife and flowers that we would encounter on our walks – like cuckoo flowers and knapweed to name two. Looking down at the Neckar from 200 metres high up in the woods, we could see that the river water had changed in colour from its usual dull or muddy brown to a crystal blue. Amazing. There was also this stillness, this quietness to be heard about us. Only the chirping of birds or the hammering of a woodpecker in the trees interrupted the tranquillity.

When we descended back to the town the usual noise of traffic from the streets was no longer to be heard, there was hardly a soul out, shops were closed, commercial activities were at a standstill, no trams, no cars, no buses – a strange new life had enveloped us. Although livelihoods were threatened by the new status quo, I had the feeling that many had come to appreciate this halt in time. Nature could breathe again, people could slow down and step off the hamster wheel of life which had now stopped turning.

Even now, after the easing of lockdown restrictions, I do not yet miss meeting up or seeing friends. We check in with each other via social media and remote conferencing. That suffices for me right now. I feel fulfilled having a partner with whom I can share daily walks and cook and eat together, as well as pursuing our individual interests in our own time. (At one stage during the lockdown I was doing a 1000-piece puzzle of central Paris and he was peer-reviewing a scientific article for publication.)

After 27 years together, my marriage was never this harmonious. For most of the years it was quite the contrary actually. Covid-19 changed a lot for us and I am thankful for that. I am hoping that post-Covid, we will continue to pursue and develop this love of nature, and do more to protect this gift that up till now, most of us have taken for granted.

Interestingly, when I finally got a chance, I tested negative for SARS-CoV-2 antibodies.

Compassion and Self-Care

Can I notice my own 'small' moments of struggle when *there is so much REAL suffering going on right now?*

Sue Edge, UK

'The surest way to ensure you have a reserve of compassion and empathy for others is to attend to your own feelings.'
Brené Brown

'I'm coping' or 'I'm enjoying the bird song and sunshine!' are my standard replies to anyone asking how I'm doing in lockdown. Is it just me giving this kind of fairly bland answer? The conversation often moves quickly to sharing how lucky we are to live by the sea in these times. The most revealing answer I've given (and this is to close friends) is 'Pretty okay, a few ups and downs.' What on earth is happening to my power of communication?

Ah yes, the pandemic. I'm so aware that all of us are experiencing lockdown with its own struggles that I don't want to burden anyone with more details. Or I'm mindful that as soon as I might try to reveal a concern the gratitude conversation will return – 'How lucky we are to be healthy and how much worse it could be.' As someone who recently spent a week writing about gratitude, I get this. I enjoy heart-warming conversations about the abundance of nature, or having more time with family. There's much to appreciate.

Since the start of the pandemic, my compassion levels have been operating on full and directed outwards to all the affected people. We sadly have far too many people being affected by coronavirus in such a short space of time, plus thousands of families coping with bereavement. Each day I am fully aware of how lucky I am to be in the 'well' category and that is all that really matters. While remaining healthy, our job is to remain steady and supportive to those who are affected.

In the meantime, I have kept myself pretty busy, which is a great way to not notice how I'm feeling. Normally at 3 am or before bed (or even in the bathroom) I find tears down my cheeks most days. Why do I not share how I feel? Because we are all in it and maybe we just assume that it can be hard at times? Or that my own small struggles just don't matter in the scale of the worldwide problem. The wise words of Brené Brown have helped me explain this pattern of not sharing or even recognising our personal feelings right now. It has to do with the process of 'comparative suffering'. Which basically means that we are selective in what we share because we know that others have it worse right now.

'Even our fears and pain are not immune to being assessed and ranked ... without thinking we start to rank order our suffering and use it to deny or give ourselves permission to feel.' (Brené Brown).

So I don't share my struggle of not having any alone time at home, because I know many single friends are having far too much time alone. I don't share that my back pain is difficult right now because on the scale of health, this isn't serious. I don't share that I feel emotionally exhausted a lot of the time because friends with children at home are even more exhausted. Why should I even be sad that I can't go to Spain (or a nice café) at the moment, because I am virus free? And so it goes on.

Yet what happens when we deny our tiny (or large) moments of emotional struggle or pain. Do they go away? No, they just sit and wait for our attention, often piling up so that one small thing can feel like a last straw. Having done this a lot of my life, I realise that stockpiling emotions takes a lot of energy.

And the gift of compassion is that it is infinite. Just because there is 'big' suffering going on that needs a lot of compassion, there is still some left for these 'little' fears, pains, concerns and struggles. We can all have compassion. And ironically, the more we give compassion to ourselves, the more recharged and able to help others we will be. I had forgotten that we need to fill up our own reserves of energy, otherwise we will be literally running on empty. And when we keep hearing that this is a marathon, not a sprint, we definitely need to give ourselves some compassion to keep going.

http://keepingcalmincoronatimes.blogspot.com

Feeling the Love through the Stillness of Life

Jacqui Pixi Rose, Spain

'So the darkness shall be light, and the stillness the dancing'
T. S Eliot

Once the rushing about getting prepared had finished and the initial shock, disbelief and fear had subsided, for me the first days of lockdown felt like life had simply settled into a peace, deeper and quieter than I had ever experienced before. It was like life had become a meditation.

One of the most precious moments I experienced was when I went to join my horse who was dozing and warming his bones in the March morning sunshine in his paddock. We have been working together to help him come through a period of severe anxiety due to previous experiences before he came to me and so being calm and letting him release is a big part of this. Not so easy to do because his anxiety usually meant he was very fidgety and unable to keep still. On this morning, I stood in front of him and did some deep breathing, while he brushed his nose so softly on my face almost like butterfly kisses. He started to breathe in my breath and I could feel his breath on my cheeks and forehead.

There was a stillness to the day with no wind and a quietness with no sounds of cars in the distance and no sounds of land-maintenance machines, just the birds singing and the sounds of nature. Sometimes I closed my eyes and he kept his head perfectly still just a whisper away from mine and we stood together and shared this mesmerising moment for about forty minutes. The feeling of timelessness without any reason to have to be anywhere or do anything else was pure bliss.

When we came out of this communication, I felt like I had done the deepest meditation and the connection between us felt so strong. It felt like he knew how much I wanted to help him and also, having experienced severe anxiety myself, that I wanted to release as well. It was the first turning point on our journey together to bring calmness, ease and joy into both our lives. And of course, for me, my love for this beautiful sentient being just filled my heart. These weeks of lockdown have given me the time and space to really work on our connection together, which is helping both of us enjoy the feelings of calmness and trust.

This calmness and awareness were also shared with my beloved husband because we both had all the time in the world to be together and share the happy life we have created together. We worked on our land and completed some projects that had been in our minds for a while. We even managed to hatch some peachick eggs, which needed so much caring and nurturing. It seems that nature flourished in front of our eyes and we had time to really notice.

Personally, I am completely blessed to have a wonderful life and to live in a beautiful place with stunning nature and surrounded by lots of amazing people. I have never taken any of it for granted and have always regularly given thanks for all. However, the pace of life still seems to have slowly gained momentum over the past years without really being noticeable, so the sudden stopping of so many elements was striking. I feel deeply grateful for all that I have but am also aware that there are many far less fortunate than myself and very conscious of the need to help others where I can.

At the beginning of lockdown many hours were spent chatting with close family and many friends through social media and sometimes even reconnecting with others with whom there had been little contact for a long time. It felt so important to feel the love of all with the reminder that anything can happen. As the lockdown restrictions started to lift, I started to have some physical contact with some of my closer friends as we all celebrated Love and Life. We wanted to hug, laugh, share amazing food and dance together.

Sadly, I haven´t been able to visit my family yet because we are all spread out around the world, but I have really felt the connection in my heart for all of them.

I keep getting these feelings of bursting with the love I now have time to really feel. I truly hope to remember the gift of these messages shown to us during these special times of challenge: that it is so important for us to take time to appreciate the Stillness of Life.

For the Love of Freedom
Susan McMackin, UK

'It is during the darkest moments that we must focus to see the light'
Aristotle

In the most perilous of times, while a nasty enemy lurks amongst us, we confront an unresolvable injustice: our fear of one another. Warned of the dangers of meeting, touching and hugging friends and family, we find ourselves opening the door to a world where basic human instincts are shattered and personal freedom revoked. The familiar company of loved ones, a usual source of comfort, is transformed into an impending threat and their companionship an offence.

And yet in the darkness and loneliness of this new age, an unexpected light appears. The feeling of imprisonment described by many is experienced as sanctuary, and lockdown on daily life, my liberty.

This new world with its toxic origin offers me choices I have never known. I find myself basking in the guilty pleasure of freedom: waking when I want, and navigating my day as I please. I have the luxury of time to feather my nest, renovating tattered interiors, discovering locked-away treasures, and creating new culinary delights and disasters. I explore the beauty of local landscapes, connect with long-lost friends, and experience new imaginary worlds and adventures in novels.

The juxtaposition of my experience within a world of fear and suffering leaves me confused and my reluctance to revisit what I knew leaves me baffled. The irony is stark: in this strange landscape of lockdown, I have discovered my freedom.

For the Love of Small Things
Rebecca Heloise Faro, Spain

I love the dappled light
dancing on my belly
the hunger for life
coursing through my veins
the sense of longing at dusk
the hum of loss
the tiny pause
between breath
the tear escaping
unnoticed
I love
the darkness of your skin
on mine lily white
the way lips part
the sense of arriving
lace on velvet
eyes that question
my face being stroked
the smell of musk

on wet skin
the tenderness
my children bring
I love
wiping dust from old books
asking strangers why
that fragile hand
clasped in mine
flying through dreamscapes
sumptuously feasting
with friends
watching as stories unfold
gazing into the dawn
as it spreads
like a sweet low purr
into another
forgiving day

For the Love of Writing
Rose Wadham, UK

'Follow your inner moonlight, don't hide the madness.'
Allen Ginsburg

When I was five years old, I wrote a letter to Jesus. It said: 'Deer Jesus, thenk yoo for the trees an flawrs. pleez mayk me a riyter so i can tell funy storees' and Jesus (who moves in mysterious ways) responded by making me a company director.

But through the years, my love of letter writing never wavered. Even as a teen I found time to dash off reams of Basildon Bond, in particular to those I was sleeping with. 'I ache for the tang of your teasing tongue' went to Mr Phelps, my history teacher (who left suddenly to build wells in Cambodia) and 'Why the hell did you throw my cactus out of the window? Can't you see that my wearing no knickers to the party was AN ACCIDENT???' went to Joe, my long-suffering Marxist-Leninist boyfriend.

One recipient who I wasn't sleeping with said:

'You should write.'

'I can't do that!' I said, horrified at the thought.

'Why not?'

'Well. Because ... Lucy's the writer.'

You see, I come from a family of five daughters. From a young age each was allocated a role, and woe betide any daughter who questioned that role. Thus, the *dramatis personae* went like this:

Louise – the responsible one.

Catherine – the compassionate one.

Amynta – the analytical one.

Lucy – the brainy one.

Rose (that's me) – the flibbertigibbet.

Being a good little girl at heart I never challenged my role and as a result, I have an impressive career portfolio that includes roller-skating waitress, cage dancer, zoo keeper, actor, yoga teacher and – for one disgusting afternoon – dental nurse.

But then lockdown happened and I had two choices. I could either spend my confinement balling socks and loading and unloading the dishwasher, crying 'Why Lord Why?' or I could challenge my inner flibbertigibbet and actually finish the writing projects I've toyed with over the years but subsequently – like an Instagram influencer with ADHD – abandoned.

A pile of seventeen odd socks made the decision for me and the next morning I scampered across the lawn in my nightie and disappeared into the garden shed as if into the arms of an old boyfriend in a cheap hotel in Bayswater.

Once inside the shed, I drew up a folding chair, opened my laptop and gazed lovingly at my poor abandoned babies – a TV script, a radio series, a blog and a character comedy show. And then they all started at once: 'Wah, waaah, waaaaaaaah!!!' and my inner flibbertigibbet began to panic.

'Breathe,' said a voice from deep within me. 'Just pick one, start tapping and go with the flow.'

Now if this were TV, there would be a montage scored with a schmaltzy track like 'Lovely Day' by Bill Withers, so would you please, dear reader, indulge me by humming that tune whilst picturing the following images:

1. A woman with terrible hair in a Marmite-stained nightie tapping away furiously whilst squinting into the screen.
2. The same woman with her feet up enjoying a cuppa.
3. A teenage boy opening the door and receiving a death stare.
4. The woman laughing uproariously at her own work.
5. The woman dancing joyously around the shed (though restricted in her movement due to bunions).

And so it has been for four luxurious months. Wake up, kiss the old man, feed the dog, cat n' kids and then chuck a Madame Bovary.

My family do their best to reclaim me. 'Mum, what's for lunch?' 'Mum, I need new hair straighteners!' 'Darling, I can't find the TV remote thingy' but I've already left, on a voyage round my head, exploring a kaleidoscope of different scenes: Two punks throwing a neo-Nazi skinhead into a fountain. Sylvester Stallone emptying a bottle of Krug over my head at a Sydney nightclub. A trans woman spraying Febreze at a Trump supporter. Boris Johnson's long-lost twin sister, homeopath Dr Faith Nettlebed, arguing that drinking one's own pee will provide immunity to Covid-19.

Then, last week, Lucy rang me.

'What are you doing?' she asked in that scarily seductive tone of hers.

Pause. 'Nothing.'

'Nothing? You must be doing something, I haven't spoken to you for ages.'

OK ... deep breath ... now or never.

'Um ... well, actually, I've been writing.'

'WRITING?'

Tiny voice. 'Yes.'

Long pause.

'Really?'

'Yes.'

'That's terrific, darling! And about time too. You were born to write!'

So there you go. And let that be a lesson to you. The stuff that you think is in other people's heads is almost always in your own.

© Rose Wadham 2020

A Country Boy
Jonathan Barnard, UK

'Nature I loved and, next to Nature, Art.'
Walter Savage Landor

One never knows when the ghosts may come.

Lockdown had brought a slowing down to our usually too-fast-paced lives and I was enjoying the concomitant peace of a city free from traffic.

The weather had been too good for the time of year and drew me down to the river, which I followed on foot for a while and further still with my eyes, before settling, legs hanging towards the gently flowing water, opposite a small, sunlit grassy opening in the woods of the far bank.

With nothing particular in my mind, I watched first chub, then eel and perch make their way slowly upstream. A movement opposite, in a patch of tangled vegetation, caught my eye. Birds move foliage in a different way from mammals. These plants moved in the way a walking mammal stirs the undergrowth. I sat motionless. As I watched, the vegetation moved again and slowly, cautiously, a fox appeared from it, followed by a smaller one. A vixen, still with her last year's cub.

The vixen sat in the sun, the youngster lay next to her. To be more comfortable, I moved my head slowly, as my neck was cricked. That was enough to alert them to my presence – the vixen turned slightly towards me and the young fox raised his head from its grassy pillow. And there we sat, none of us moving, just looking at each other across the water.

Then, in that moment, I was a boy of twelve again, in woods far distant from these in miles and years. I sat then, on a late summer evening, not wanting to return home, not wanting to give up the woods for a house. A half-wild country boy who loved the woods, but loved them unknowingly, never having given conscious thought to that feeling. The woods were just a part of me, as I was part of them. Then too, that evening, a fox had come; came slowly out of the bracken and stood not eight feet away. Our eyes met at about the same level across the forest floor; and so we stayed for a time that wrote itself into my memory. Then, as quietly as it had appeared, the fox turned and was gone again into the bracken.

I looked up from my past into today's woods – the foxes had slipped away, unnoticed.

Green Rhapsody
Rachel Hutchings, UK

'Plants are doing meditation all the time.
They simply surrender themselves and accept
the sunlight and the raindrops. They contemplate the rainbow.
They feel joy with the wind and the feelings from the earth.'
Arjun Das

I have loved houseplants since being a child. My mum's rubber plant left an early impression on me. I remember liking it very much and feeling sad when we gave it away to a primary school because it had grown too big for our house.

My teenage vision was to fill my bedroom with luscious green plants. I began making this a reality on my fourteenth birthday when my best friend's mother said I could choose a houseplant as a birthday present. I chose what I think is an umbrella plant and named it 'Roberto' after the boy I loved (adding an 'o' on the end for subtlety and secrecy!). That was exactly forty years ago this May and Roberto is still alive and well, reaching almost to the ceiling. Though partly old wood and somewhat scrawnier in leafage, Roberto's presence is still one of peace and silent wisdom. He is my oldest plant friend and I hope he lives as long as I do, because it is thanks to Roberto that at age twenty-seven, I had an enlightening experience.

I had been trying out meditation and one morning whilst my baby daughter was napping, I sat down to meditate next to Roberto. I was practising letting go of thoughts as they passed through my mind – observing and letting go … Then a thought guided me into imagining I was a leaf on Roberto; just a leaf like all his other leaves … lightly sitting there attached to a stem, observing sensations – no thought, no analysis – just allowing the inside and outside to pass through me in pure plant-like simplicity and peace. Well, for me, becoming leaf-like was a mysterious and magical formula that brought me to a feeling I can only describe as otherworldly bliss. Many years later I read about a Tibetan Master called Tilopa who taught an enlightening meditation technique by which one imagines oneself as a hollow bamboo. I think being a leaf on Roberto has a similar effect.

Our house is full of houseplants. I have another called 'Alexander (the Great)', now five foot in height and twenty-six years old. He came as part of a decorative plant display in a gift basket, given to me at the birth of my second daughter. Alexander was only about fifteen centimetres in height but I remember exclaiming 'Wow, that looks like a baby palm tree!' I subsequently nurtured him on a very long journey of survival. Alexander's stem was extremely weak and spindly at its base. It grew thicker and stronger as it reached the leaves at its top, making me compare Alexander to the legs of the horse and elephants in Salvador Dali's painting, *The Temptation of St. Anthony*. Alexander is a bit surreal as plants go! I'm surprised he survived, to be honest, but I could never give up on him. I even took him to my dark dingy mobile classroom when I was a French teacher in a secondary school and he survived that onslaught too. In 2020 he stands tall and handsome – a giant palm frond being the only way I can describe this plant – a true survivor who lives up to his name, Alexander – because he is truly Great!

Zoe is a 'ZZ Plant' or *Zamioculcus Zamifolia* to be precise. I gave her to my neighbours eighteen years ago as a green gift for their new conservatory. Zoe, however, ended up back with me when they moved away and has since grown into a stunning showpiece, filling an eighteen-inch diameter pot with her three-foot tall structural fronds of beauteous waxy foliage. You may be impressed by her Latin name but I cannot boast knowing the genus of all my houseplants, and Joey Jester is one such to join Alexander in that respect. He is a recent acquisition from my mum who could keep him no longer when she downsized. Joey has leaves like a medieval Jester's hat, hanging eccentrically all the way down a long central stalk. I may not know Joey's genus but sense in him a carefree joviality. I only have to look at Joey to smile!

Like many of us, I had a 'lockdown' birthday this year. It was hot and sunny so my husband and I ventured to a garden centre to purchase new pots for our houseplant family. Gorgeous terracotta pots were fortuitously on offer so we came home with fifteen of them (and a *Pilea Peperomioide* that I simply couldn't resist). All our houseplants are now upgraded into bigger, better pots and it has dawned on me that my teenage vision has been more than realised: our whole house is full of lush, green plants. Around their stems are pebbles and shells from Whitstable beach and stolen stones from the Pyrenees. The Pyrenean beauties are giant creamy-grey pebbles embellished with stripes of white quartz. I have a similar passion for my collection of stones, pebbles and crystals but that's another story.

You may be wondering why I have chosen to write about my houseplants for this collection of writings about 'Love in the Time of Covid' and my reason is that nothing dramatic or life-changing happened for my husband and I during the strict period of lockdown. We count our blessings and feel thankful. My job continued but I worked from home. My husband, a gardener, also managed to continue his work and got to drive around in the peace and quiet of surreally empty roads. We missed not seeing our family and friends but thanks to modern technology enjoyed Zoom get-togethers and keeping in touch by phone and FaceTime.

My green family was a comfort as I sat rooted to my computer station during lockdown – a constant friendly presence, reminding me to tap into their tranquil energy whenever I needed it. I feel a special affinity with my plants and am very appreciative of the silent wisdom they emit. People often comment on the lovely feeling in our home and I know our plants are silent contributors to this. I have a lot to thank my still, green friends for, ever exuding their harmonious vibes. I feel joy with the sprouting of each new leaf and every time I water them, replenishment is mutual. The silent song of plants speaks volumes within our walls. I call it Green Rhapsody.

Laureate Box
Ginny Keith, UK

'Painting is poetry that is seen rather than felt, and poetry is painting that is felt rather than seen.'
Leonardo da Vinci

I work as a multi-disciplinary printmaker. In 2019, as part of my MA degree, I created a 'Laureate Box'; a repurposed vintage 35mm slide box refilled with 125 handmade mixed-media tiles bearing nouns, verbs, adverbs and prepositions. I invited friends and fellow printmakers to randomly select a handful of tiles to create instant lines of poetry. The resulting poems were collated in an edition of tiny, clothbound concertina pages, entitled: *A Leaning Towards Bees*. The book features thirteen short poems. The book's title reflected the fact that, despite there being 100 tiles available for selection, it was the Bee Tile that was repeatedly chosen.

When we first went into lockdown in the spring of 2020, our conversations and dialogue shifted and changed. Using words gathered from these new conversations, and words selected by friends to describe their feelings about the new conditions, I created a second Box ('the Lockdown edition') with a new set of wooden word tiles.

Via Instagram, I asked friends and followers to send me five to seven numbers between one and sixty, which prompted me to pick the corresponding tiles from the box. I had intended to produce a second anthology of short poems, but in the Covid climate it seemed more appropriate to combine the individual lines to create a single poem from one collective voice. This poem was therefore built collaboratively, each line created remotely and randomly by friends I connected with between March and May 2020:

Words breathe slowly

Moods collide, words breathe slowly;
routine connects hope.
Days promise bliss –
thoughts spin silently towards home,
Days drag softly.
Slowly somehow, thoughts fold inside words –
walk dreamily over fields.
Days drag, words breathe slowly.

Painting My Way to Peace
Carol Miles, UK

'Art washes away from the soul the dust of everyday life.'
Pablo Picasso

'January 1, 2020. Hooray! It's going to be a good year.'

That's what I thought anyway. After far too many years of personal tragedies and disasters, this was the year when the tide would turn. If I think it, it will happen. Yes?

Well no, not exactly.

So this is where I was back then:

My beloved little sister and only sibling had been given an extended prognosis. This meant we could look forward to that family holiday in the spring after all.

I could finally get 'retirement/new life' off the starting blocks. Art and moving to Kent top of the NYRs.

And I was untypically so organised!! The diary was packed with stuff to do up until at least the summer.

February 13 2020, 10:00am: Started a refresher etching course – absolutely brilliant and all part of the plan to build up a portfolio of art work.

February 13, 12:30pm: Missed all the messages on my phone – had it on silent. Left the course and headed to the Midlands.

February 13 – March 3 2020: What sort of cruel world is it that decided my sister would get secondary breast cancer in addition to her other disabilities? The last three years had been hell for her and Paul, all but a brief remission. So glad we had that holiday in Whitstable last year while she was well. We were with her when she passed away on March 3. At least we were with her …

March 23 2020: LOCKDOWN

March 30 2020, 3:30pm: The week before the now restricted funeral, I wondered what to do. I had a sore throat. I had mixed with people before the lockdown. Would I end up making my elderly parents poorly? Would I come back and make my husband (with lung condition) poorly?

This layered on top of the grief.

I didn't go. It was early days, I think it was the right decision.

Instead I watched on the laptop. It broke my heart.

I wonder if I will ever get over this? Did I do the right thing?

I walked by the sea, crying. I made some food, crying, I went to bed, crying. My poor parents there without me, Paul isolated, without his soul mate, consumed by grief …

April 1 2020: Nothing more to be done. Couldn't go anywhere. No one could.

I spent more time on the telephone talking, talking, talking. Couldn't help, couldn't console.

Had to distract myself …

From that point onwards, I immersed myself in activity. I ran, walked, cleaned, decorated, gardened and tried to get a grip.

Then I noticed.

The world was silent. Except for the birds and the trees in the wind.

The beaches were empty and the weather and sunsets were glorious. I took the paints out …

You know when sometimes you say 'Stop the world, I want to get off.' Well, it actually happened. The hospitals and medical staff were on the front line and thousands of people were sick, everyone was panicking – yet the most beautiful moment was unfurling.

I've tried to sum up why, when I was already so sad, when everything was unpredictable and scary, why did I feel at my most peaceful, blissful, contented and creative?

This contrast between potential global catastrophe and a personal silent space was profound. I'm not sure that anyone will be able to grasp or properly explain it for years; already the memory of the sensation is slipping away like a dream. A new kind of (apprehensive) normal service is resuming, life is busy again.

During the lockdown period, I painted over forty paintings – nearly all of sunsets, each with their own special identity.

They will for ever serve to remind me of that silence, that moment when time stood still and sadness had the space to heal.

Medway Dawning

Lesley Conquest, UK

Morning draws near, and the water is cloaked in grey.
Soft mist clings to the river banks,
Tendrils spiralling around roots and rushes
And cobwebs drape the brambles and the hedgerows,
Setting them a-glitter with lozenges of dewy-glass.
The land around me is empty and filled with secrets, hidden in fog.
I see no one and nothing moves save a boat
With a swollen sail and a gull with a cry from another plane.
I can no longer see the truth of where I have been
Nor where I am going.
The future seemed to stretch ahead, but now it can't be seen.
The moisture in the air feels like tears shed for all mankind.
And yet there is a desolate beauty here
And a peace and a quietness which tells me that
The world is a fine place to be and all around me things are healing.
I sense a betterness on the horizon
And I walk towards it happily

Time It Is a Precious Thing
Shujata Luptajan, Spain

'Before us stands yesterday'
Ted Hughes

He was sitting on the edge of the bed with his back to her, faintly illuminated by the light of the Kindle on his lap. The glowing red numbers of the digital clock showed 3.30 am.

'What are you reading?' she said.

'Just a thriller,' he replied.

'I thought you were reading *Evolutionary Psychology?*' she said.

'I was. I am. But this is a thriller.'

'Is it any good?'

'No, it's rubbish. Pure escapism,' he said.

'What are you escaping from?' she asked.

He sighed and switched off his Kindle.

'Are you finding it hard, the lockdown?' she asked. 'It's funny. It seems like it's been forever but it's only six weeks. I can't remember what life was like before. Where did it go?'

He lay down on the bed beside her. They lay in silence a while. Then she reached in the dark for her mobile on the bedside table and searched on YouTube. 'Who knows where the time goes', the plangent strains of Sandy Denny's singing haunted the darkness.

'Across the evening sky

All the birds are leaving ...'

They lay there remembering the days of childhood, remembering the parents who had gone. It was all so far away, so long ago, and yet so present.

'Sad deserted shore, your fickle friends are leaving ...'

Their minds turned to things gone by, things beyond repair, beyond redemption. They thought of people alone in their beds this night. Alone in their days. She played it again while they lay together in the darkness with tears wetting their faces.

She played the song three times while they lay in silence. They did not count the time; they had no fear of time. Her voice telling, compelling, images of loss floating in the space between them.

'And I'm not alone when my love is near me ...' she sings. The eerie beauty of Sandy's voice filled the stillness. And finally, quiet acceptance, of the certainty of renewal after a long winter. And Sandy herself so young and long gone. Occasionally they held each other's hands. And eventually one fell asleep, and then the other.

'I know it will be so until it's time to go ...'

(Sandy Denny: Who Knows Where the Time Goes: https://youtube/5oBMDcLf6WA)

Morning Coffee
Mix Amylo, Spain

*'For small creatures such as we,
the vastness is bearable only through love.'*
Carl Sagan

Yes. It was this. Most mornings. Morning coffee, soft taste of Arabica, a wondering: will he answer, did he sleep well, is he more or less worried than yesterday? The dialling, the relief when he picks up with his familiar warmth, the loving greeting. This person, this constant in my life, is OK, is still on the other end of the phone. Still with me. With us. A deluded assumption of forever nestles confidently within me. It overpowers logic. It threatens to punch any part of my mind that dares to imagine that bond ever being broken.

That bond. It has grown, jumping from childhood neediness over the gap where I found my own path, to land on a couple of decades of something truly special. And that bond has tightened during these strange times, its knots rewound into new configurations, holding firm all that was, that is.

Conversations about nothing much become the everything. The weather is first on the agenda, to my amusement and incredulity that it is always the answer to 'How are you?': how warm or mild it is, how sunny these last days, we've been so lucky here in England since it happened, how is it there, oh, raining, really?

The weather is just the entrée. We delve into other subjects after that's been taken care of. Some days he is upbeat, chuckling about his cats or mine, engrossed in a new painting, boosted by hearing the voices of those close to him more often than usual, at least down the airwaves if not in the same room. Surprised at how little time he has to do all the things he wants to do every day, even though he can't go out. A sentiment shared by most people on the planet right now. On other days he is uneasy, quietly stressed, mildly depressed, again like us all, as the unknown stalks us. I try to make light of things, though I can't see the light that clearly, chat about people we know, dream of futures. 'When ...'

How important it is. How vital, this calling during morning coffee, its aroma mingling with our chat and filling the spring air, hearing him say hold on, let me just have a sip of my drink, listening to his slurp and his pleased 'mmm' as he swallows. Touching minds, checking in, reconfirming. Hoping. Hoping for an end to this enforced game of solitaire. Never much to tell, but we tell it anyway. Many times, in varying formations. And so. And so it goes on, a daily reaching out, through half of March and nearly all of April. I am comforted, as is he, by knowing the other is there. Making this moment feel better. Making our –

But. Then. The end comes suddenly. The start of the end during morning coffee, soft taste turning bitter, my throat burning, the handle of the mug freezing. I don't know that yet. That it is the end. Yet. I am afraid. The voice I have known. Known and heard since birth is. Is wrong. Its tone is odd, its pace slower, its. Its vocabulary confused. Slurred. It was. It was the last sighting of its sound for me. I think I. I think I told him I loved him, after asking him to call 111. I hope I did. I –

The slow confusion gradually. Stills. And. Only hours after. After the smell of Arabica leaves the room the voice stops. The silence. The silence shifts our world. Across land and seas, two thousand kilometres away from me, it stops. The voice that spoke five languages. Just. Stops. Just –

Over the next few days the diagnosis, also confused at first, clarifies. That brain. That brain that wove the twelve notes into piano sonatas and string quartets, that could tell you how many letters were in a word immediately after you said it, that brain that still loved to learn, that wanted to add a sixth language to its roster and new painting skills to its palette, that knew the birth and death dates of all the classical composers, that loved wordplay and Monet and food and Chopin and gardens and cryptic crosswords and colour and us, his family, most of –

Achingly, impossibly, that brain is – Isn't. Can't. Won't ever. The machine keeping his. Keeping his body turning is taken away, and. His physical self breathes unaided for. For one final day. The last. The last conversation we have is not a conversation What do you. What do you say, as a phone is pressed to an ear that can't hear? To someone who is not. Not there. Not them. But maybe. Maybe there is a sense of. A pulsing, a warming of your. Some vibration of something reaching inside their. And the actual words don't. Don't really matter anyway. Only the –

He. He was there. Now. I still drink my morning coffee, but. He won't. He won't answer his phone. I cling to the imprint in the air around me of his voice, the echo of our time following me like a persistent puppy, pulling at my trouser leg to remember. I will never not remember, I tell the echo. It's not. It's not possible to forget. The pieces. The pieces of me are held together by different webs of string, in. In many colours. Each one is the. Is the presence and the legacy of someone who is part of me, who has made me who I am. His string is bright red. He leaves it woven tight, even though. For him, because of him, to honour him and his love, I must not unravel. I will not, not too much. I sip my coffee and –

Taking One Step, One Breath, One Moment Along Our Path ...

Sue Edge, UK

> *'The place of true healing is a fierce place. It's a giant place, it's a place of monstrous beauty and endless dark and glimmering light'*
> Cheryl Strayed

Recently, I have become an armchair traveller. The travel books I am reading remind me of trips unaffected by coronavirus. While it remains difficult to consider venturing abroad at the moment, I can imagine varied landscapes of olive groves and mountain villages. During the last two years, I have been fortunate to spend a few months in Spain. It has been a very necessary tonic to help recover from a challenging patch of life marred by multiple bereavements, redundancy and my own health struggle. I had been knocked sideways and was unsure how to get up again, let alone recover fully. Would I feel crumpled and sore for ever? All I knew was that I was craving sunshine and quiet to help heal and thankfully Spain was providing this in abundance.

Life since coronavirus emerged has obviously been different. I initially felt the loss of my precious trips to Spain that helped my soul feel alive again. So now, instead of actually packing my suitcase, I am reading travelogues about walking the Camino de Santiago in Spain. This has become a well-known long-distance footpath, even a pilgrimage for some. I have not walked it myself but now and then wonder about doing something like this? An escape, a challenge and a dose of healing rolled into one. Reading about other people's losses and journeys has helped me not to feel so alone on this long road of healing.

The path most often walked on the Camino is a staggering 800km, running from a small town in France, over the Pyrenees into Spain and finishing in Santiago de Compostela. Something about the familiarity of walking each day for six weeks surrounded by raw, dramatic scenery appeals. As I read, I am filled with awe at the sheer energy and stamina that is needed each day. Within the first week of the trail, you are traversing the steep, rocky paths of the Pyrenees, often in lashing rain. Some guidebooks warn that this initial section, with its steep inclines and rugged descents, is the most physically challenging of the whole path.

Maybe I can use the metaphor of walking this long-distance path to help understand our route through a pandemic. Like the walkers, there is an amount of stamina required to get through week after week of uncertainty. We have painfully and tragically climbed the steep peak of the pandemic curve and are a good way in walking down the other side. This in itself has used up a lot of our energy supplies but a long stretch ahead remains. Now we have reached what reminds me of the section of the walk called the Meseta.

The Meseta is known as the mentally toughest part of the 800km walk, which has surprised me until now. The Meseta is the name given to the large and expansive flat plains of central Spain (translated as plateau). The path continues for 220 km through this flat, empty and tediously similar landscape. It has such a difficult reputation that some walkers even skip this section and take the bus! Why on earth wouldn't they enjoy a break from all the difficult mountain paths? I imagined it would feel amazing to stride out each day on an unchanging path without needing maps or raincoats.

But now I get it; flat and empty landscapes without any break from the scorching sunshine or change in scenery are tough going. No pretty villages to look forward to or delicious walker's suppers prepared for you at a mountain lodge. Isolated and alone with another day of the same ahead is hard. And especially challenging when you are already tired from weeks of walking, with raw blisters and aching muscles.

As we enter our 'pandemic meseta' I am not struggling with blisters but with the sameness of my life that is still mostly based at home. I haven't left our little seaside town since March except for a few inland walks nearby. Although I am grateful to live somewhere with wide open space around me, I am starting to crave a glimpse of somewhere different. I am tired of thinking about what to cook yet again that is interesting, healthy and using what we have in our kitchen. None of it is difficult but it requires a mindset of keeping going and finding pleasurable moments in what feels like a similar landscape week after week.

This 'meseta' section also reminds me of the grief journey I have been through. The initial peaks and troughs of shock and emotional pain at the start were tough, especially when one bereavement became three followed by a series of smaller ones. But at least it was obvious that I needed support and extra care for this emotional section. And then it all went quiet, the phone stopped ringing and people stopped asking. Within a few months it felt like the grief had been forgotten and I should be 'back to normal'. But of course the grief hadn't gone and I had only just begun to go through the healing needed. In that 'meseta' phase, I felt alone yet kept showing the world I was coping and fine.

In our 'pandemic meseta', it is beginning to remind me of that forgotten and alone phase of grief. Suddenly we are being encouraged to go shopping and have barbecues on beaches while I am still deeply aware of all the bereaved families and those in hospital with coronavirus. We still have a thousand new cases each day in the UK. Has this become normal, something we tune out from or pretend is no longer an issue? Are we supposed to shrug off the hundreds of people still dying in this country from Covid-19 each week? When I hear regular reports of care homes with coronavirus, I continue to think of my father, who is my last remaining older relative. I don't know how to just get back to normal when this is all simmering in the background.

But if I approach this phase of the pandemic as I would a long-distance footpath, the way is clearer. Each day, I just have to take the steps needed and follow the path ahead. The best thing about walking is its constant reminder to stay in the present moment and not plan weeks or months ahead. When it is scorching hot, I will need to rest in some shade a little more than usual. If my body is feeling tired or my back is sore, I need to take things a bit slower than I might wish to. And why rush? There is nowhere else to be except exactly here, where I am. This is my life right now, why would I want to try and be anywhere else?

If the last few years have taught me anything, I've learned that sometimes we can't control the exact plan of our lives. None of us would have chosen to live through a pandemic. But we can do everything possible to take care of ourselves and to enjoy the moments that are with us. And yes, it is going to feel hard at times, we are on a long path. But we can do it, just one more step, one breath ...

'*No matter how long your journey appears to be, there is never more than this: one step, one breath, one moment ... Now.*' **Eckhart Tolle.**

http://keepingcalmincoronatimes.blogspot.com

The Alchemy Garden

Rana Rodger, France

'Help us to be ever faithful gardeners of the spirit, who know that without darkness nothing comes to birth, and without light nothing flowers'
May Sarton

How was my time during lockdown?

Before the lockdown I used to find it hard if I didn't see friends for a few days. I live alone in an isolated part of France but was amazed that I spent two months without seeing another person and without any problem. Instead my connection to nature was enhanced enormously.

I'm lucky to live in a nature sanctuary called The Alchemy Garden and what I experienced during that time was pure alchemy.

I befriended a nature spirit called Melchior who is one of the main guardians of the property, and spent glorious days with the sun on my back landscaping and planting a garden of herbs and wildflowers around his little house.

Before the lockdown I had also managed to get some willow cuttings and during the two months I was amazed at how fast they grew. I created a living willow structure and willow fencing and arches.

I had time without pressure. Time to play and to do things I had always wanted to do – but never had the time.

I usually run nature retreats and art holidays but as all my bookings were cancelled due to the coronavirus, I was gifted with endless days to fill.

I had time to paint and found myself experimenting with new and different techniques. I expressed my feelings about the lockdown in a series of paintings and sketches. I had no idea what would emerge and was amazed at what started speaking to me. Symbols and forms would appear. A whole new world was opening up.

I've never felt so moved by the birdsong as I was during those two months. It is as if all my senses had been magnified: the sound of the cuckoo, the haunting sound of the woodpecker in the woods, the first nightingale.

And the scents: the scent of wild lilac blossoms after a soft rain, the scent of the pine tree in the sunshine.

I only ventured out twice to the shops during that time. I had no need. It was as if I were being showered with abundance from nature. I foraged for wild asparagus tips and *respounchous,* found edible shoots, grew vegetables in my garden and feasted off a carpet of wild strawberries.

Another thing was happening to me that took me by surprise: true, I was initially in shock as a lot of us were about the reality of the virus and all the implications, but I found it easier to turn my attention from the fear and to focus on the present moment and all the miracles that lay hiding there.

I was aware also how quiet it had become. No planes flew across the skies. No sounds of any cars in the distance. It was as if Mother Nature had time to breathe again and to cleanse from our human abuse. Nature doesn't need us humans. We think we are so important to this planet but what have we done to her?

I hope this *time out* will enable us to rethink some very vital matters.

The Peace of This Time
Sonaa Digby, UK

For me the peace of this time has been healing
spiritually emotionally physically

I feel the deep peace of this time
with love from the universe
the blue waves of colour turning to yellow during this time in my garden

I love that I am present in this time
prepared in a way that I have been guided to be
perfect in all ways in my city haven
wildlife garden

I see the beauty of life and all that surrounds me
and am filled with gratitude for the
changing times

Time for us to love this world and
all we have in it
Time for nature to return and be valued
Time for reflection

I love the diversity of bumblebee life
in my garden
I love Plot 14 with all the earthiness and magic
of the soil
Grounded in life
my life of love

Garden Haven

Frances Moore, UK

'All gardening is Landscape'
Alexander Pope

I believe that space to move, embracing nature and a purpose are essential for maintaining good thoughts and health during such a difficult time.
Nature is the only thing that makes any real sense. My job is in horticulture. The joy of understanding is paramount and the propensity never to stop learning or experiencing how it all works (or not) is my key to coping.

I feel lucky to be in an industry that is beneficial in enhancing our surroundings. During lockdown when the front door remained firmly shut, the space out back became a haven. It stretched skills and imagination and helped maintain a sense of physical and mental wellbeing. I love gardening.

Summer, 6 am is the best.

Any later and humanity disturbs. Wildlife is freer to go about its business with less interference. It is their domain. Except for me, of course, but I do make abject apologies for being there. Freddie and The Ginger One watch and wait; as cats, that is what they do, but they have been well fed. And it is their garden too.

I make my way to the chair under the apple tree opposite the *Ribes sanguineum*. The flowering redcurrant is as tough as anything and has a pungent smell. But it does have lovely dangling racemes of pinkish red flowers that have a resinous smell which is a more polite term than its common descriptive name 'the cat-pee plant'. The bees and all manner of buzzy creatures go wild for the rich nectar produced by those dangling blooms. Later the birds feast on the dark purple oval berries. It spreads across an old brick wall and is complemented by the *Cotoneaster bullatus* and the *Berberis darwinii* that over time have been tweaked to extend across the space creating a filtered lit alcove; a perfect oasis for the mass of tough, elegant snowdrops that push through frozen ground at the beginning of the year. Awash with these delicate yet determined little white flowers, full of strength and confidence, pushing through the frozen ground, hopeful and mindful that spring will come. It is so fitting that ants help to spread these perfect little flowers. Synchronicity.

The Arcadian apse, verdant, cacophonous and frantic, shelters the wildlife, and those birds make a mess! The blue tit mum works ceaselessly to feed the fledglings and I work overtime refilling the feeders and the birdbath.

Freddie crouches watching, just out of sight, he thinks. I am on to him, though. I screech 'Cat. Cat. Cat.' in a high fluting tone, thinking it might sound like a bird alarm call. Probably not!

The fence on the other side collapsed the other night. It was particularly windy and the old ivy did not help. It had taken over and had become a lot tougher than the fence. Hence it keeled over, leaving a yawning gap, much to the delight of the furry devils.

I decide to fill the space with the very large *Trachelospermum jasminoides*. This evergreen jasmine has highly fragrant flowers and is another insect haven. Hailing from Japan and the Far East, it is also known as 'Chinese Jasmine' or 'Trader's Compass'.

It sits in situ in its black plastic pot and looks happy enough. It could stay quite comfortably potted, but I want it to spread the length of the boundary and be knocked out by the perfume when I sit nearby with my early morning coffee. It will be a peaceful retreat into an innocent world that just is; without subterfuge.

A job needs doing, it has a purpose, I embrace the whole, and I understand what needs to be done. So I get down to the coaxing and encouraging and before I know it, it has got dark and I am in need of a cup of tea. Nature makes sense. The cats understand it, albeit destructively sometimes, but they use the garden and neighbouring gardens because there lie endless stimulus and opportunity. I remain contemplating the work required in my space.

I call the boys for dinner. The two of them, tails aloft, stalk like proud lions down the path. The path works now. It curves a little and appears to shoot off to one side then the other. The path has been altered over the years and I laid every brick in it. The bricks are not the right kind. Recycled bricks mostly, and not really robust enough. But do I care? The act of working out how to fit these oddments of bricks became an obsession, total absorption. I marvelled at how a rectangular solid object can appear to curve. The warmth and irregularities confusing the senses – that brick path has always been there, it seems. I am not really into New Age sensibilities, but I understand the mindfulness of bricklaying. It is a meditation.

We did not have a conventional area to sit in so, OK, I thought, I'll fix that. I'll do it my way, it is my garden. So the grassy oasis moved and I mindfully bricked away. I realised that I know every tree, shrub and perennial in that garden. I have worked out every angle of view and every potted shrub is moved to show the best side. I know how the sun moves round the garden and I know what works. I know this because I observe. It is a process of learning as you go over the long term. Work with the seasons is just what has to be done. And that is exciting.

So Lightly Here

Lisan Bremmers, Sweden

'Lightly child, lightly. Learn to do everything lightly.
Yes, feel lightly even though you are feeling deeply.
Just lightly let things happen and lightly cope with them...
walk so lightly, lightly my darling.'
Aldous Huxley

I miss my beautiful 89-year old mum. Since we moved to Sweden fifteen years ago, she has visited us every year. We always assumed that it would be old age that would stop her from making the journey one day. Now the pandemic has stopped her and so many others in their tracks. We've made new plans to visit in September, but all of a sudden, a plan is nothing more than a plan, and one with an uncertain outcome.

Something has changed for all of us. I think the world as we knew it has gone. We have no idea what the future holds for us. Of course, we never did, but up to now it's been easy to pretend otherwise, at least in this part of the world. Yet here we are. We are finding ourselves united with all of humanity, connected through an unstoppable virus that can impact anyone regardless of age, race or gender, showing us that we are not separate from one another. Turns out that we're all equally vulnerable at our core and that at any point in time, all of our lives can get interrupted in one way or another.

We've seen people around us showing up in new ways. We may not have been able to touch each other so much physically but many of us started to touch upon each other's lives in other ways. With our attention, our care, our deeds, our hearts ... have our hearts perhaps opened up a little more? Have we had the courage to befriend our vulnerability? Enough so that we cannot go back to the way things were? I think I have. I don't know to what extent, but I somehow do feel changed by the events of these past few months; exactly how much will show in my behaviour and future deeds.

I do not find life particularly easy but I do love my precious life on this beautiful earth and hope we will shape the future more wisely. But I am not naïve. We were stopped in our stride by stronger forces than our own and we will be stopped again. We needed to be stopped.

It won't surprise me if Covid-19 is the start of a whole new era. Climate change is already affecting many, but soon it will affect all of us. Sometimes I get scared or overwhelmed and I withdraw. Most of the time I feel inspired to do my practice, to show up, to be present, to move more slowly and listen more closely to the strong whispers of the earth ... to prepare myself for the even deeper lessons on love. Because I want to. Because there is no one to blame. Because this is my moment in time, at exactly this point of our evolution. Not to hang on to at any cost, but for the sheer love of it. A love that gets stronger and more tender as I get older. As in the words of Leonard Cohen: 'We are so lightly here. It is in love that we are made. In love we disappear.'

The Power of Connection and the Painful Isolation of the Pandemic

A monumental moment seeing my father
after four months of isolation in a care home

Sue Edge, UK

*'Love recognises no barriers, it jumps hurdles, leaps fences,
penetrates walls to arrive at its destination full of hope.'*
Maya Angelou

Social isolation is difficult. Sometimes I think our coronavirus pandemic is not only a disease of the body but also of community and relationships. The idea of loved ones or ourselves becoming seriously ill and needing to be isolated is unthinkable but has become painfully true for thousands of people. On a far less serious level, I never thought I could manage being at home for two months during lockdown separated from everyone I know except my partner. I have missed the sense of community that I took for granted pre-coronavirus such as being able to go to a yoga class, music event or my local café. I have missed normal things like being able to cook for friends and relax around a table.

But I'm surprised that I have found a sense of connection through the world of Zoom. I have done yoga classes with wonderful teachers I know from retreats in Spain. I have sung peaceful songs of hope with Deva Premal in the lush tropics of Costa Rica. Incredibly, I have also connected with Oprah Winfrey in her homely kitchen in California to talk about how to cope in a pandemic (alongside 40,000 others!). I would still say that online connection isn't as good as real human contact, but it has been a worthy substitute. It has shown me that we are able to connect through our hearts even when separated by physical space and in some cases across continents.

Now that we can meet up with friends in person outdoors, I have almost forgotten how isolated lockdown really felt. After two months of not seeing friends, I had started to wonder if I had lost the skill of having long conversations. Would it feel strange to see a friend outdoors with a two-metre gap between us? So I was relieved to find that my connection to friends feels just as strong as normal, maybe even more so for sharing such an unprecedented time. Even out on a blustery beach without hugs, my heart has received a little dose of warmth and contact each time.

But in stark contrast to the easing of lockdown for many of us, care homes remain closed for any visitors. In my father's nursing home, the only social contact he has had since March is with the caring and familiar nursing staff. He has to eat his meals on his own in his room rather than the dining room. He hasn't been able to use Zoom to connect to others round the world. Nor has he ever mastered using a mobile phone unless a nurse dials the numbers for him. How on earth is he coping, I have wondered many times. All I've done until now is phone, send greeting cards regularly and hope that the home remains unaffected.

This Sunday, we were granted permission by the Matron to make an exceptional visit while sticking to their rules of no visitors on their premises. This would mean being outdoors with extra social distance while we stand outside the boundary of their long garden. The visit took many hours of agonising over whether it was safe to see him like this and on a practical note, how to find a toilet somewhere 'safe' on the long journey. In the end, my gut instinct was to go but with extreme caution and care. It felt even more monumental as it was our first journey out of our seaside town since March, now travelling with face masks, disposable gloves and hand sanitiser packed in this 'new normal'.

Thankfully, the nursing home is located in a beautiful village right on a picturesque river. Our meeting place was nestled between huge ancient willow trees with the relaxing sound of the river flowing behind us. We stood waiting behind a wide brick wall, thankfully only waist height, for him to appear. As I saw him being wheeled out by a nurse, I wanted to simultaneously clap, cry and hug him. The moment I almost feared might never happen, did. His home so far has remained coronavirus free and it means that I can finally see him after three months of tension in my stomach hoping he stays well.

The nurse parked his wheelchair at the end of his path in the nursing-home gardens, while we stood the other side of the wall three metres away. It was almost comical, trying to converse at this distance while he juggled a huge umbrella and gusty winds made it hard to hear. He looked surprisingly well, stoically talking as if we'd only visited a week ago and not in these difficult circumstances. In answer to my question of how has he coped, his answer was predictably 'fine'. Did he miss having visitors? I asked, but he evaded the question by reassuring us that there was lots going on in the home.

My deep longing for an emotional response from my father always goes unmet. Even in a pandemic, it has not made him suddenly burst out of the nursing-home walls with tender words of connection. When my mother died a few years ago, he consistently remained unemotional telling me that he didn't miss her that much really, even though they were married for fifty years. The solid, wide brick wall between us today is normally there in spirit, with him feeling emotionally far out of reach. I've managed to cross it in the latter years by small physical gestures such as wheeling his chair or helping him to stand up. Stuck behind a physical wall on this visit, the emotional distance felt more acutely present.

In desperation to try to connect with him, I tried his favourite topic of conversation, the wildlife from his window. For the first time in the visit his face lit up fully. He told me about the hoopoe that he had seen recently, a bird I had never heard of. And in that moment came a strand of connection as I pictured my father in his room spotting various birds with delight. While he might be hidden behind emotional walls, he loves seeing birds as much as I do. And now when I wonder how he has coped on his own during these times, I remember that the birds and wildlife have happily kept him company just as they have done for me.

After he is wheeled back to the nursing home, we stay for a while so that I can soak up the nature that he sees from his window by the river. I look out for a rare sighting of a hoopoe, but instead see a lone swan and mallards. As I listen to the breeze through the trees, I know that this is the same sound he hears from his window each day. My heart feels full, in deep gratitude for seeing him and knowing that his care home has so far been spared from coronavirus.

I wish my father could share his heart with me in words, but I have to believe that love can travel over the wall of the nursing home, through the silence in our conversations and among the birds that we both watch with joy.

Back at home, my bird book tells me how rare sightings of the hoopoe are in the UK, as it normally migrates from Africa or Asia to warmer parts of Southern Europe. Somehow this unique, colourful bird can overshoot its journey and land on grassy patches of southern England before turning back.

If a tiny bird can travel thousands of miles to sit beneath my father's window, then it gives me hope that love too can travel even when we are physically separated. In some cultures, the hoopoe can apparently symbolise survival over long, challenging journeys. As we face further months of this pandemic, I will think of the hoopoe's long, brave journey flying across continents. I now know for sure that love too can travel great distances, even in these extreme times of separation.

http://keepingcalmincoronatimes.blogspot.com

Musical Notes and Favourite Quotes
Ebe Ghansat, UK

'My music will tell you more about me than I ever will.'
Ebe Ghansat

While the pandemic has disrupted our lives in a major way, it has also provided us all with an opportunity to reflect on our lives.

I don't read books and I hardly watch TV, so my world can be found in music and quotes – why reinvent the wheel? Quotes are my mentors, music is my counsellor; as I like to say: 'Music is my life, the lyrics are just my story.'

The purpose of this reflection with respect to the pandemic is to face reality and to evaluate my role as an individual, and also as a team player on Planet Earth. I am not scared of the virus for myself. Overthinking and worrying too much is not good. Life needs to go on, and in my opinion, music is a great vehicle for getting through the day.

I am concerned about what the coronavirus pandemic has done to people, especially those living in ghettos around the world who have little access to help or guidance. I'm sad for those people who have died in a hospital with nobody there to hold their hand and smile at them. But this pandemic has reinforced my belief than I can adapt and persevere in challenging circumstances.

People in all walks of life look to me as a mentor, and I have learned new things about myself, my family and friends. In fact, the situation has challenged me to consider my priorities. Apart from my mother I do not have anyone who calls me just to see if I am OK, so the lockdown has prompted me to identify opportunities for self-assessment.

Technology will never replace the human touch but it can be a great medium for intimacy. 'When passion rises, your nerves will fade away.' Technology has allowed me to connect with people and it has allowed me to recognise those who really care – and those who take me for granted.

Most importantly, the lockdown has challenged my very existence as a person by making me think about myself, my purpose, my activities and my relationships with other people. I'm thinking especially of those people who are too busy to say hello and with whom communication is a one-way street because they are busy. 'Don't make time for people who make no time for you' is a wise saying. We are all busy, but there are 86,400 seconds in a day. A text takes just a few seconds to create and send. Luckily when I send one out, the lovely people from my past do get in touch.

As an introvert nothing has changed that much for me. I often work from home and I am my own boss. Most of my friends are very strong females who don't play the victim card and go about life with a strong passion. Social media, particularly Facebook, has allowed me to make sure that they are OK without being intrusive. American author and columnist Lois Wyse got it right: 'A good friend is a connection to life – a tie to the past, a road to the future, the key to sanity in a totally insane world.'

I believe we all spend too much time doing things, and not enough time thinking about things. This is probably because we are all part of the culture of being busy, so we never have to make time to think and reflect on our lives. Another quote, from author and speaker Zig Ziglar: 'I realise that I have too many flaws to be perfect, but I have too many blessings to be ungrateful.' And to my children I say, 'I make mistakes. I am not perfect. I won't always give you your way. But I love you with everything I have. I have worked hard my entire life to be able to provide you with the best life possible.'

One day, when all of this is over and if we are still around, we can share more of our experiences. I'll finish with yet another quote, from an anonymous author: 'Knowing a person is like music. What attracts us to them is their melody, and as we get to know who they are we learn their lyrics.' I am content with where I am and with my connection to those in my inner circle.

This Cloistered Life

Arpy Shively, Spain

'For in this Rose contained was / heaven and earth in little space.'
Mediaeval Carol

Today, as for the past fifty days, I am sitting in the bright ringing silence of our dining room in this town flat, where I also work and write. Lunch is over, work becalmed, there is nowhere to go and no one can visit.

Day after day, my husband and I observe the ceremonies of breakfast, lunch, tea and dinner; go out separately for short walks with the dog, and watch a film or TV series at night. Twice a week, I carry out a masked raid on the nearest small supermarket. In our small mountain town south of Granada in Andalucia, we feel quite safe. But out in the street, we all avoid meeting each other's eyes, as if even a glance might be contagious.

Yet I'm not unhappy. And I'm not alone in this feeling. Several family members and friends admit to finding this new, more limited life not only bearable, but in some ways preferable.

'We don't have to give or accept invitations to lunch or dinner.'

'We're saving a lot of money, the days have more space for things we want to do, a rhythm and peace.'

'No one else is doing anything exciting or going anywhere "awesome", any more than we are.' (No mo' FOMO)

'I can watch Holby City in peace and without feeling guilty ...'

I am finding the reduced demands on my time, attention, energy and money surprisingly liberating. I feel protected from the many calls the outside world made on these commodities – I feel cloistered.

The Order of St. Clare ('the Poor Clares') was founded in 1212. Inspired by the preaching of St Francis, Clare of Assisi, an aristocratic young woman, refused the marriage planned by her parents and embraced a life of poverty, seclusion and contemplation.

The Poor Clares are members of the strictest order of cloistered life, the Papal Cloister. Here, 'the presence of strangers can be admitted only in case of necessity … it must be a space of silence and recollection, facilitated by the absence of external works …'

Clare's rules for nuns have come down through the centuries unchanged: 'once her hair has been cut off round her head and her secular dress set aside, she is to be allowed three tunics and a mantle … she may not go outside the monastery except for some useful, reasonable, evident, and approved purpose'.

Now my hair is growing out a fine penitential grey, and Clare's 'three tunics and a mantle' have been transmuted into three interchangeable tee-shirts and two pairs of jeans. As for 'going outside the monastery', my husband and I only emerge for the 'evident and approved purpose' of taking our dog on a toilet run, or buying ever stranger combinations of ingredients with which to conjure up cheering meals. Our days are bounded by customs that have become traditions, in a cycle as sacred as the canonical hours.

In ordinary times, so much resource goes into how I look to the outside world. I am amazed at how well I can live without all the stuff – clothes and cosmetics; particular brands and types of food and drink; travel and entertainment choices – all the things I thought were the minimum for the good life, before coronavirus captivity both narrowed and expanded my views.

I'm looking at photographs on a website called Cloistered Life. The nuns appear to live exclusively in 'the Eternal Sunshine of the Spotless Mind'. In her whitewashed room, a Sister kneels beside her narrow bed with its drab wool blanket, to pray. Above her, blessed light pours in through white-curtained windows. It is a modernised scene from a mediaeval Book of Hours. A nun sits on a dark wooden bench, in a garden carpeted with lawn and furnished with flowers. Sunshine tints the mellow stone wall behind her copper-gold. Tranquillity breathes from the very photos. Here in their different silences, in the 'Vultum Dei Quaerere', they 'seek the face of God'. Reading this in the quiet of a warm-day siesta hour, I glimpse the healing force of peace and contemplation.

Back to the real (surreal) world, where to date nearly 3.5 million people have been diagnosed with Covid-19 and more than a quarter of a million have died. There is grief, anger and worse to come. Yet fragile but positive outcomes are also emerging. For the first time in thirty years, it is possible for the people of the Punjab to see the peaks of the Himalayas, over 100 miles away. Up to 100,000 deaths could now be prevented if China's slowdown continues to clear away the deadly smog hovering over its industrial regions.

Towns and cities all over the world – even some banks and businesses – have breathed life on the embers of community spirit and some are practising practical compassion for vulnerable individuals. Hard-pressed workers are catching up on sleep, regular meals and family life. Yet I and everyone I know talks about 'getting back to normal', as soon as may be.

I long for Spain's *'estado de alarma'* to pass. I envisage a fresh morning and *café con leche* by the fountain in the plaza, our streets full of familiar faces again, the shops full of exciting ingredients. People smiling again, shouting greetings across the road, kids playing, dogs walking their people into town. And perhaps one day, I will have a good laugh with my brother and sister once more, us triplets all sitting together in a favourite London bar.

But behind this healthy wish, I harbour a shadow desire – that things will never 'go back to normal'. Greed of gain of those already drowning in wealth; politicians mouthing dangerous platitudes to hang on to power and governments that have been hijacked by corporate interests; health care that is more ailing than the patients who need it; a new cohort of slave-labour emerging from a numberless desperation; travel anywhere, everywhere and for no good purpose. The resumption of the oblivious rush to the deeper doom of accelerating climate change.

'All of humanity's problems stem from man's inability to sit quietly in a room alone,' wrote French philosopher Blaise Pascal (1623-1662). However that may be, I hope that when I emerge, when we all emerge from the 'war on Covid-19', that 'peace' and its attendant unleashing of appetites and activities, does not turn out to be the more dangerous outcome after all.

One of the Poor Clare's four vows is the vow of poverty: 'we are emptied of things to be filled with eternal riches; we are set free from slavery to materialism, secularism, and consumerism'. Denied the happy distractions of getting and spending, I have found the past few weeks to be surprisingly rich in moments of joy. Forced to turn inwards, I have found, at times, a 'heaven and earth in little space'.

Lockdown in the 12th Century Community of St John's Hospital, Canterbury

Eileen Routh, UK

> *'In every community, there is work to be done.*
> *In every nation, there are wounds to heal.*
> *In every heart, there is the power to do it.'*
> Marianne Williamson

During lockdown I was fortunate to be living at St John's Hospital. This is an ancient Community dating back to the 12th Century. Over the centuries it has developed so that residents now live independently in small flats. It is a beautiful environment full of trees, lawns and gardens. During lockdown the residents, guided by the Trustees, agreed to voluntarily isolate so that we were all protected.

After a couple of weeks of strict isolation of the whole community we were able to meet each other. We kept two metres distancing and the skeleton staff protected us by keeping the hallways in each block spotlessly clean. We residents used hand sanitiser whenever we went out of our flats and washed our hands regularly. These precautions meant that we could see and talk to each other, which meant that we did not feel too isolated. Within this context we began to create ways of enjoying community life.

Worship continued each Sunday when the weather was fine, by having a service in the garden with all the chairs spaced two metres apart. Because it was late spring the birds seemed to enjoy these times too and their singing was beautiful!

A short midday prayer time under the trees (weather permitting) was started and is continuing for those who find that helpful.

One group began to play croquet and a competitive edge soon crept into the game.

Individuals could be seen walking or striding around the inside edge of the perimeter; some walking freely, some with sticks and one with a walking frame. I walked regularly, but in the end found that even this became rather boring. I therefore changed to 'timing' myself round a large area of grass which acted like a running track, then trying to beat my time! We all knew that exercising was important.

As a community we found ways of celebrating birthdays with wine and cake in the garden – with every one socially distanced, of course.

We were also able to have a kind of socially distanced party to celebrate the big VE day with Vera Lynn and other war songs as a background.

On a practical day-to-day level, families got shopping for their locked-in relatives whenever possible, bringing the bags to the outside gate and dropping them there while waiting at a distance for their relative to pick up. Mobile phones were invaluable for these collections. It was also lovely to 'SEE' someone we loved, but like everyone else, we missed the proper meeting and hugs. Those who had no relatives to do this had their shopping done by the Chaplain, who had an arrangement with Sainsbury's. This included a trolley he could keep sanitised at St John's! Each block of flats had a day allocated when the residents could order food.

Individually people found ways of being creative or useful. Personally, I started relearning to play the piano on an electric piano in the common room, which was not open for communal use. I started a very gentle exercise group in the garden for interested people. The oldest person who came was 90+.

A photo of a sunset over the sea at Whitstable encouraged me to try a pastel picture of it. I then decided to learn more about pastels and practise with some new pictures.

I've also been reading more, and have become increasingly addicted to BBC Radio 4 during the day and Classic FM at night!

For the first time, I'm using WhatsApp more because of the lovely photos and videos of Cosmo my first great grandchild, and the lovely meditative words and videos that have been sent to me, especially by my daughter – though I still prefer talking on the phone to the constant text messaging that the younger generation seem to love.

I enjoyed getting together a collection of my own photos of flowers and trees and turning them into cards, as well as sorting through the thousands of family photos to distribute, keep or destroy. I made my first knitted jumper in probably thirty years, for a charity my friend supports. My neighbour and I then started making face masks to raise money for St Martin's Hospital Mental Health Charity and this is continuing now.

The Community as a whole has also donated a substantial sum from chapel collections to support homeless charities in Canterbury and we've enjoyed coming out into the central grass area each Thursday at 8 pm to clap or bang saucepans for the NHS!

On the whole our lockdown has probably been as good as it could have been anywhere in the country, and we have all felt very blessed by being in a Community such as this, supported by a dedicated, scaled-down and very hardworking staff, with the kind of freedom that few have been able to enjoy during this difficult period. The time has also allowed residents to get to know each other and (for better or worse) this is a good thing to have happened. Like everyone else though, not even all these good things compensate for what we love and miss most … our families … the hugs and kisses and simply seeing faces which are not on a screen!

Eileen Routh
Resident of St John's Hospital
Mother, grandmother and great-grandmother
(and retired Anglican Parish priest)

Regeneration
Jeff Rees, Wales

*'True love is eternal, infinite, and always like itself. It is equal and pure.
It is seen with white hairs and is always young in the heart.'*
Honoré de Balzac

I have been asked by my daughter's dear friend to write down my thoughts of how I am coping with this blasted lockdown and how love from others has helped me cope at this time. Well as there is nothing I can do about, I have to follow the advice of the 'SCIENTISTS' and stay put, as best I can, in this state of limbo. Fortunately, I have good friends, neighbours and a wonderful family. I also have an excellent phone line at my disposal which reminds me I'm NOT alone in all this and along with my great faith, I can cope.

My beloved wife Sheilah and mother to Sian was so cruelly taken away from us twenty-two years ago at the young age of fifty-eight and I miss her so very much. Strangely though, her spirit is in every nook and cranny of our home and I speak with her all the time; always saying good morning and goodnight to my sweetheart. My love for her has never waned and we still have our lovely Sian, granddaughters Lisa and Laura and great-grandchildren Brandon, Imogen and Oliver, whose help and love in all this has been absolutely marvellous, 'God Bless 'em'. I have to say also that I count Sian's beloved friend Kaly amongst those that have helped me, with cheerful phone calls on a lonely day.

I am not able to do the things I love any more, due to arthritic hands and feet. I loved long walks, gardening, playing the classical guitar and piano, to name but four I miss so much. Never mind, I have 'MANY' lovely books I enjoy, particularly Dylan Thomas and Charles Dickens and, of course, music. I love music.

How do I feel about it all now? In a word 'LOVE' and perhaps a little poem I wrote for my wife Sheilah on our twenty-fifth wedding anniversary. (We got married on Boxing Day 1959.) It can explain all my feelings just now. Here then are my thoughts 'THEN and NOW' engraved in my heart.

Here goes ...

This blessed anniversary of thoughts,
this Christmas time; our time.
Twenty-five short years of memories
evolve into love's tale of old and
treasured messages, resounding like
echoes through a thousand years

Life's bell chimes silently in our hearts;
As old but not forgotten fires
Comfort with evergreen warmth.
New light and love extend their powers:
This year's end is new again
For love is born once more

Jeff Rees
Circa 1970

A Return to Roots
Nicole Wilkinson, UK

'Wind, sun and earth remain
The birds sing still
When we are old, are old ...'
Rupert Brooke, *The Hill*

I have lived fifty-six years on this planet Earth. I was born by the River Thames, at the water's edge of a metropolis that never sleeps. Even though I came into this world on a Sunday, during an age when these days were sacred for rest, a chance to appreciate a springtime stroll perhaps, London folk would be preparing for the start of the ceaseless daily grind on Monday. Endless, relentless toil. This was the early shoots of post-war 'enlightenment' where the push was not to reconnect with the wisdom of our ancestors or find beauty in peace but to create a bubble in which we strive for possessions and to climb a ladder of status.

It was a time of birthing alone still. My dad didn't witness my grand entry. He wasn't allowed. My mum entrusted me, her first child, into hands she didn't know. She remains unconnected to the details of my birth but remembers there was a TV the night before and an unfamiliar programme called *Doctor Who*.

My dad drove his lorry into the cobbled streets of Covent Garden market the following day, to be amongst the fruit, vegetables and flowers of his livelihood, trailing a pink ribbon to announce to associate hawkers, pedlars and porters that I had indeed at last arrived.

He had hope for me. In his heart he carried the treasures of another life. Away from the clawing, scraping, binding poverty of London that generations of my family had endured. Away from the choking pollution and uncertainty of life. His head was filled with panoramic fields of gold and the azure heavens of Somerset, the warmth of Nancy, the loyalty of Patsy and the thrill of the jackdaw that sat upon his shoulder and brought him gifts of shiny paper. The war ended but Dad clung on to the tall grasses and let his feet touch the homely soil and dived from mossy banks into cool verdant waters. He wanted to remain the child. HIs encyclopaedic mind had blossomed with nature and all things rural; tuned to the stirrings of the air, the vibrations of birdsong and scents untainted by the onslaught of chemical alterations of the post-war apocalypse. But London city's fingers sought him out and enveloped him and he was drawn back to the granite and the edifices in the business of creating another kind of wealth, one that did nothing to nurture and comfort. A smoky turmoil to begin his adulthood.

When he could he took out a sketchbook and painted his childhood. He painted the peace. He painted an ease of mind. A longing. A belonging. An understanding. My mum hands me this sketchbook on the first visit I pay her after the virus lockdown. She has been reminiscing and turning up the past because of her imposed confinement. I have a vague memory of the book in our old house in London. She gives it over to me like she has no need for landscapes and aged dreams. Her life is closing certain rooms. Dad has passed nine years in a plastic urn on the dresser in her bedroom and that is enough. Her lockdown began as he left and grief is sluggishly, ponderously releasing her into a different kind of freedom, new values and light. We are now able to talk without a chasm of unfamiliarity for I was always my daddy's girl. Much happier helping him under the bonnet of a car than only being allowed in the kitchen to dry the washing-up. We have time to read each other's faces. The virus has made this more poignant by her acceptance of the need to master the tricks of FaceTime in her eighty-first year. She is mentally emerging from her self-imposed monastic existence whilst ironically pinned physically to her house by the Government.

We talk of flowers, shrubs and trees in her garden. My dad's final canvas and where she feels her bond with him most. She tells me she can hear him admonishing her about planting methodology or techniques for pruning. 'George, what are you doing with the magnolia! I just give everything a good haircut,' she says.

I came to be a child of the hustle and bustle. My eyes were greeted by dirt and desolation. My ears pounded by the cacophony of building works and faster, sleeker vehicles. My nose was polluted by exhaust fumes and rank late-night takeaways. But all the time I looked for sparkly ice flowers and daffodils and found the wonder in the whorls of dandelions. The blackbirds and sparrows would sing me to sleep from the lime tree at the bottom of the garden and, although blasted throughout life with hay fever and asthma, I could still relish the smell of cut grass and honeysuckle breezes. Dad kept his childhood alive by taking the family on occasional Sunday jaunts into the nearest countryside from our London home, and I lived for these treats of reality and escapism from the greyness.

My body, due to the circumstances of life, is in a city right now. And I may have been shut even further within four walls. But my mind and soul are firmly established in the garden. One fine day I will return as a whole to Mother Nature and I will not look back.

On Reflection, Love is All That Matters

John Richards, UK

'Love is a many-splendoured thing'
Paul Francis Webster

Reaching the ripe old age of seventy-three is one thing. You become aware of the ticking clock. And stop planning very far in advance. But you don't really see the end of your life looming. There is still time ...

Until Covid hit. Then, all of a sudden, still the same person, still with the same expectations, the future shrank. By walking outside, by sharing contact with your family, your children, your loved ones, you could, in effect, be risking death within a few weeks or months. Suddenly the theory became reality.

It was, I think, rather like being diagnosed with a terminal illness. Except it was an illness you could in some way control. Stay home, stay safe, protect. And then you might survive the wave.

But at a price.

As it happened, I found myself separated from my entire family and most of my close friends. OK, the family was already scattered globally and I could have only imagined making contact sometime during the rest of my life. But now the rest of my life was threatened by my love for my family.

To enjoy and express that love I had to take risks. Not just with my own life but with theirs. If I left the sanctuary of my isolated farm in the mountains of southern Spain, I might carry the virus to whomever I visited. The expression of my love and concern might actually kill someone I loved.

Or, of course, me. Which again impinged. I am already concerned about the impact of my death on my younger children. It will not be easy for them to lose the Dad they love, the Dad with whom they spent the first years of their lives in 24/7 contact. The Dad as a bit of an old fart who loved the opportunity to savour the experience of life with babies, toddlers, young beings when, in the past, he had perhaps foolishly rushed though that time of life when love is all that matters. On both sides.

I had to face the reality that I might never see my children and grandchildren ever again. That all the pent-up, unexpressed love might never be expressed. That I would never be able to say sorry for my errors, my selfishness, in person. And receive absolution. Or indeed give it.

That was an awful prospect when it hit, when I was forced to accept the reality of Covid. And remains so. Sure, technology allows me to maintain a certain degree of contact with those I miss and miss me. But it is shallow, stressful and confusing. What do you say when faced with an image on a screen rather than a person across a dinner-table or on a beach or in the surf? Or jumping in the pool. Or bouncing on a trampoline.

There is nothing to talk about. Except perhaps schoolwork. Tasks. No spontaneity, no serendipity, nothing to trigger communication. I send messages to my eight-year-old son. He doesn't reply. I ask why, he says he doesn't know what to say. Me neither if the roles were reversed.

I live, it seems, in an environment where love has vanished. Where it cannot be expressed sensibly. Nostalgia replaces love perhaps, a fondness, even love of the past that cannot be lost because it is the past. The participants are already dead. I am the only living memory.

I find surprising solace in sharing those memories with those of similar age who are in the same boat, more or less. Details matter and trigger memories and then more details and more memories. Almost my entire life has been recreated, remembered, in fine detail as I suppose I seek a way to acknowledge, enjoy, the love that eased my path.

I finally begin to understand what 'love' is. That it is the gentle shared enjoyments of a moment, a memory, with no strings attached, no need to explain. To find someone who shared the fun I did, yet separately. An unspoken bond.

There are so many small incidents I thought I had forgotten, yet, as I recall more, I treasure them. And then find that strangers, albeit from a similar shared background, not only share similar memories but enhance them by adding detail. The names of primary-school teachers and classmates seemingly forgotten but only lost in the mists of memory. Ghosts if you like. Shared emotions towards the bigger things in life.

I guess it is something of a paradox to find oneself reaching a better understanding of love at a time when there is little opportunity to express, share or receive it. To be in a loving environment. Which takes me back to an essay I once wrote in support of an application to work with disturbed teenage boys in a residential environment. The title was 'Love in a therapeutic community', and I described how a friend of mine used love to control behaviour in his nightclub. A nightclub frequented by disparate groups between whom there was often friction. My friend quietly enrolled many of the men and boys he considered members of the 'club community', gentle giant security volunteers.

When the DJ, on a raised dais, spotted any signs of trouble in the crowd he would blow a whistle. The supporters would move to its focus and by sheer weight of numbers prevent combatants from moving. They would then gently lead them to the door and ask them to leave. They would be banned for a period but the entire procedure was carried out in the spirit of care, concern and friendship, not confrontation. An expression of love which, in almost every case, made a powerful impact on those affected.

It is the sense of living in a caring, affectionate community, even a loving one, that allows its population to relax, feel safe and enjoy the freedom it offers. One hopes that the cooperation and care that the arrival of Covid has generated continues; this common threat but one bearing no guns or bombs, may have created an awareness of the value of a caring community. It may have awakened people to what has been lost since 'loads of money' became the mantra. And may encourage society to seek to maintain and reinforce the impact of that understanding as rebuilding takes place.

Melting Pot
Rebecca Heloise Faro, Spain

Weary of this heaviness
startled by its intensity
fierce feelings
of unrest
sit smothered by obedience
shapes smashing out
smiles hidden
inside masked truths
fear leaking
like an ever-increasing puddle
The milk has been spilled
the chaos pirouettes
through our lives
the discomfort flails
at our throats
leaving metal-tasting spittle
Dissolving
we're dissolving
a distant memory
chimes in our hearts
reminding us
to grieve
as our losses

lean into our soul
we enter
into the melting pot
together
thawing out
as we liquefy our thoughts
reaching down
so we can see all
that's unbalanced
in the swell of the deep
When we rise again
and we will
like the phoenix
we can conjure up
a fresh untamed vision
embedded in our originality
as an unborn child
holds all the hope for new growth
our fragmented past
will gather like broken shells
nourishing the land
through its long untethered journey
back to the source

Our Shrinking World
Louise Gabriel, UK

'Every Story is Us'
Jalaluddin Rumi

Our borders are closed, our hatches battened, guiltily doing as we're told, in the naughty corner. A banal small intervention in a much bigger picture. Reduced days unfold; with mind-blowing decisions about what to watch or to eat and calls from outside, from family, from friends. TV got boring: we started sorting out our little piece of this planet, drawers and cupboards of scurried-away debris, buried treasures, 'Oh that's where that was!' Meanwhile, outside, the pile-up car smash of a worldwide crisis unfolds, multiple tragedies, panic and untold kindnesses. We will sing out of our windows like Italians!

C is for Commitment

I'm not sure how long we've been here, but here we are. Together. The thing is, as I've told you, the thing is, I love you. If I had to be locked down with anyone, it would be you - lucky that! How wrong they were!

The days have yawned, stretched and constricted. Is it summer yet?

Each day I blink, then turning see you, partly obscured by the pillow you use to block the worst of my snoring. A coffee kiss before your essential work and my mostly homebound teaching. Reunited after a shorter day, we are garden-bound, together.

D is for Daddy

There are two of you. One dead, one living. Both in my heart. I am blessed.

Each of you love me, not using tenses here, love is timeless. Your familiar smiles encourage my days, moustaches and beards tilting in recognition.

No comparisons, not fair, good men, good fathers, my love is big enough for both of you, always ...

Except one is Dad and one is Daddy. Can you tell them apart? Can you tear them apart from my heartstrings?

I held you while you died.

I bring you distanced necessities and have a chat.

I love you both, lots.

F is for FaceTime

FaceTime, Skype, WhatsApp, whatever! Phone placed, just so, balanced on top of the beaded bird in the plant pot, when this video call connects, you won't be gazing at my double chin!

Are you ready for your close-up? Oh! You've taken me to the toilet and farted! How rude!

Not you Mom, Janice, my faraway love! All our conversations are distanced, by fire, plague and what next? Frogs? We're used to not hugging, these days, smile and wave!

I think I would've slipped my bearings, without this, without all of you. Hearts break differently, minds too. Mine too. Keep calling.

H is for Happy Lockdown Birthday

It's not parked out the back, still haven't got that Bentley for you! This failure of a daughter you'd rather have than some car, even that one. I'd turn over any derelict engine, for you. Cracked green leather, our damp cold Saturdays with the promise of a roaring fire and a good film later.

There is nothing you can't do with your clever fingers, an imagination that hurts my eyes, mending all the broken things I give you.

Here and now, writing yet more words for you ... but coming to your doorstep later, presents, wine and me! Happy Birthday Daddy!

J is for Johnny

Another birthday, not a big one, that was last year. Oh My Love, the crow was full of moths, it had to go! This strange birthday began with a slideshow, good books and a promise of a sun lounger non-existent in the shops.

A party of five, but you look handsome in your birthday getup, as always. Damn! I forgot the cake!

We danced later, blinds drawn, no crows or ice cream.

This lockdown only means more of you and me, swimmingly, willingly, exploring nuances we had forgotten or not yet found. Months or more weeks, either way, we're lucky.

L is for Love

The oily swirl of vodka meets tonic about to be sipped, the phone vibrates ... delay, then delight! Love oozing through synapses, bouncing off satellites, a call from any place the heart stretches to.

There is a girl out there, building a life, despite corona. She's four hours away, normally ...

There's a son, a man now, at a greater distance, as far as the moon?

Both our mothers in other countries!

There's a father, two streets away, that moon thing, again ...

Missed friends ...

At home, waiting for dispatches from these foreign correspondents, the vodka makes an uneasy alliance with yesterday's lemon.

M is for Mummy

You drop me a message to tell me you've sent an email. You don't like to talk on the phone, but mention you've missed my voice, whenever I call.

My mother, my conundrum ...

I always tell you, eventually: a wee in the garden, the dead bat I was keeping, another broken heart.

There're times I'm surprised I can't turn and tell you everything! The sea between us has stretched to a Covid ocean I can't wait to cross.

I remember a little blue jug, some powdered milk, a tiny spoon just big enough for my hand and always you x

Awakenings
Pamela Marianna Lassalle, UK

'Our task must be to free ourselves by widening our circle of compassion to embrace all living creatures and the whole of nature and its beauty.'
Albert Einstein

Isolation

Time to reflect on me,

Who am I, why am I, how am I

What is the bigger picture?

Community, village, town, county, country, region, world, collective consciousness, other worlds, parallel dimensions, universe?

Where have I come from? Where am I going? What do I want to do? How do I do it?

Moving through emotions that can't be placed

Knowing that LOVE is fundamental to all the healing.

Realising humanity needs each other.

Compassion is fundamental

Kindliness helps everything

Acknowledgement of all experience

Understanding the term; no judgement

We are one

Nature survives ...

Gosh! The Quiet

Opens my eyes to nature ...
Nature in its intimate details, its awesome beauty, of all its new life as spring breaks into summer.
New creations in all directions, singing, painting, dancing, cooking fabulous creations out of old newly found ingredients, sharing and planting ...
Hey, it's so satisfying eating your own vegetables all summer long!
Lettuce was especially good this year and I'm so proud to see my leeks have survived.
My beautiful lovely gorgeous Family united, Thanking God, the Life Force for being able to care.
Long walks, long chats, nobody but nature to see us swimming naked in the British sea!
Anger storms brewing as heat rises in disagreement.
Demands on shielding, self-isolating, wanting to see friends, near physical fights.
Is claustrophobia setting in?
Step outside, clapping in the streets at 8pm on a Thursday evening.
WOW, such an electric atmosphere!
We were hungry for:
Change
Prayer, healing circles, synagogues, churches, mosques, spiritual halls
Compassion
Understanding
Thankfulness
Gratitude
Acknowledgement
Sharing
Caring
Communication far and wide
United, we are the experience of love in the time of Covid

Lockdown in Aotearoa: Kindness and Creativity

Cindy Baxter, New Zealand

'This is my simple religion. No need for temples. No need for complicated philosophy. Your own mind, your own heart is the temple. Your philosophy is simple kindness.'
Dalai Lama XIV

'Stay Home, Save Lives', the motorway signs told me. I was driving home from Auckland airport after dropping off my friend Karli, who was heading down south to her family. It was seven hours before New Zealand went into a full lockdown on 25 March 2020.

I'd been expecting Karli to stay with me. But she'd made a last-minute decision after managing to organise a car, to drive the three hours to her family, just in case she'd picked up the virus on her way through.

I'd also been at the airport the evening before, with my Brazilian friend Dani and her daughter, who had also been considering staying with me, but who ultimately decided to be closer to town in case they could get a flight home.

An hour later I walked into the house, to an enthusiastic greeting from my Border collie, Pearl … and silence. I burst into tears, tears of relief: the previous days had been stressful with all the people in my house struggling to make difficult decisions, and me frantically wiping down surfaces, trying to socially distance from my guests, thinking what if they'd brought the virus home?

Now they'd all gone and I was on my own.

I took Pearl down to the beach with its black sands and huge waves, surrounded by bush-clad hills dotted with houses. Only 900 people live in Piha, a tiny community west of Auckland, on the wild west coast at the edge of a 16,000 hectare forest. I felt safe. I know almost everyone here. And everyone knows Pearl.

As I walked back home along my quiet tree-lined street in the evening sunshine, the neighbours were all outside: was I OK? they said, did I have enough food? please let them know if I needed anything.

Later, I turned on the television and there was our lovely Prime Minister, Jacinda Ardern, whose main message echoed the signs on the motorway, but she added her own – and very important – mantra: be kind. For kindness is where she comes from, how she operates, and this was at the heart of her message.

Five days earlier she'd made an extraordinary broadcast piece to the country, explaining the government would be implementing a four-level strategy for dealing with the virus: we were at level two. Three days later she'd given us the deadline she'd prepped us for: a level-four lockdown at midnight Wednesday. We couldn't drive except for going to the supermarket, we had to stay home, were allowed out for exercise, but only locally, and this would save lives. Be kind.

Every day at 1pm, Jacinda and our Director General of Health, Ashley Bloomfield, livestreamed a press conference and the entire country tuned in. Calmly and clearly, Jacinda set out the decisions her government had made that day, and Ashley gave us the updates on the virus and case numbers. The communications were so incredibly clear. The Ashley Bloomfield fan club started almost instantly for this quietly spoken man. Jacinda's was already firmly in place.

We were to keep to our 'bubble' – the people in our household. Don't 'burst' our bubble by getting close to anyone else. It was a perfect piece of communication, so elegant, and so clear. Those on their own could find a 'bubble buddy' if they felt isolated. A government wage and benefit package was passed in a few days, and money was swiftly paid, literally within days of applying.

The clarity around the communications, backed by a huge advertising campaign, meant we knew what was what: it made me feel safe, informed and protected; with the calm, strong – and kind – leadership emanating from Jacinda – and Ashley, we also had our role, as the 'team of five million'. When hundreds of people called the police to turn in people breaking the rules, Jacinda gently chided us, reminding us this was the government's role, and we'd be best to focus on looking after each other. And on being kind.

Every window in every house had a teddy bear in it for the kids. Random acts of (distanced) kindness were happening every day as people supported each other.

My morning walks with Pearl, down to the beach or through the forest, which normally take an hour, stretched to more than two hours as I'd stop and chat with people; my entire community seemed to be out and about. There was plenty of space to talk across the road from each other. Pearl was a bit miffed that nobody was allowed to pat her.

Everyone was checking in: was I OK on my own, how was I doing …? The love of my community was beautiful, and caring. We all agreed that our beachside paradise was probably the best place in the world to be in a lockdown.

Social media was in overdrive, with horror stories pouring in from Spain and Italy. It was scary.

But then came the mandalas: two gorgeous Piha friends, Debs and Megan, started a Facebook page called the 'LOCKDOWN MANDALA CHALLENGE – finding beauty in the everyday'.

For the last thirteen years, my work as a medicine woman, community leader, naturopath, entrepreneur and mother of four has completely engulfed me. While birthing my own children, I have also birthed a community and a small business. As a medicine woman, I have taken hundreds of people through death and rebirth. My tribe extends far and wide, my spiritual children spread around the planet. I have been sitting in ceremony almost every two weeks for a decade and a half. The transformation has been profound and the love I have experienced even deeper. But the work and demands on my time have also been intense and while sharing love with others, I often forgot to take the time to love myself.

My creative process drove me to the edge of burnout. Despite living off-grid and trying to live the most simple and natural life possible, the sheer effort of daily life and the dedication to the healing work kept me busy around the clock.

When I left on a family holiday at the end of the year, I was exhausted and empty. I was going to Brazil to fill my cup, get some rest and rejuvenation, but a camping trip around the country with a family of seven doesn't allow for much relaxation. There were still daily chores and the challenges of travelling in a foreign country. Even having fun seemed like hard work, when all my body and soul craved was to spend some time alone and reconnect with myself. At the end of our trip, I still felt exhausted and was anxious about returning to work. Our flights back to Spain were scheduled to arrive on the first day of the lockdown. We decided not to board the plane and quarantined ourselves with some friends in a small country house on the outskirts of Sao Paulo.

We lived in limbo for two months. Gone were the hours spent in front of the computer answering emails and planning the upcoming work season. Time as I knew it had stopped. The future was uncertain and it was my first opportunity since becoming a responsible adult to truly live in the moment. Though these months were not without their challenges, they have been my most nourishing months since becoming a mother. This rare opportunity to slow down, spend quality time with my family, forget work and retreat from the outside world gave me the precious gift of time.

Throughout the lockdown, in moments of uncertainty and worry, I would reach for my Tarot pack to ask for guidance and regularly drew the card 'Wishes Fulfilled'. It was hard for me to believe that my wishes could be fulfilled as the world around me was collapsing. It is only in retrospect that I realise that my main wish for so many years was to have 'more time' and it was being granted. For the past few years, almost every hour of the day was accounted for and now suddenly I had nothing pencilled into my agenda. In my usual active fashion, I began to fill up my time, though promising myself to do only what my heart desired in each moment. Each day, I took the time to nurture my body, my mind, my heart and my soul.

My mornings began with yoga, meditation, visualisation and a Tarot reading. This was followed by a swim in the pool, grooming and a superfood smoothie in the sunshine. I enjoyed quality time with my children: home-schooling, games, preparing lunch together and evening meditation and prayer around the fire. I fed my creativity with gardening, making music, listening to inspirational speakers, reading and making love.

I had been trying to start a weekly yoga practice for years, but somehow never found the motivation or the time. From the first day of quarantine, I did a one-and-a-half-hour practice and maintained this during the rest of my stay in Brazil. After one week, I felt more relaxed than I had in years. What previously would have required discipline was suddenly effortless. It was such a gift to take this time to nurture myself and listen to my rhythms in a way that modern life had prevented me from doing.

Each moment I spent taking care of myself, I was remembering how to love myself. With it came the realisation that I had such a hard time receiving help and love from others, because I hadn't been giving it to myself. I was reminded of the time, pre-motherhood, when I lived under a tree in deep connection with nature. A time when I left the path that had been paved for me to follow my heart. It had been the first time in my life that I learned to respect and take care of my body, and in that process I healed many of my traumas and learned how to love and accept myself. Over the years, the self-care dropped away and with it went the self-love. During the quarantine, as I began to love myself a little more each day, traumas and fears also resurfaced but were quickly healed and released.

The lockdown ended and I found myself back in Spain. Life began to pick up its pace and old patterns re-emerged as work began to take up most of my time. I had to give up my leisurely morning practice and focus on the tasks at hand. However, I have managed to do it with more awareness that I need to find balance between giving to others and giving to myself. Some days, I have forgotten to love myself, but mostly, I find the time to give myself a little love each day, whether it is a ten-minute morning meditation, a foot soak before bed, or a mug of hot chocolate as I hide away under a fig tree. Love is a journey, not a destination, and each day I take another step along the path.

Something Lost, Something Found
Thuranie Aruliah, UK

*'Around us, life bursts forth with miracles –
a glass of water, a ray of sunshine, a leaf, a caterpillar,
a flower, laughter, raindrops. If you live in awareness,
it is easy to see miracles everywhere.'*
Thich Nhat Hahn

Our life as a couple has revolved, as for most, around a love of family, friends and for us in particular, the creative arts. Within a few short days in March, all this was ripped away. For David, his work in a theatre ceased as shows were cancelled. Our regular, life-enhancing jaunts to the ballet, opera, theatre, galleries and museums, all gone. Our weekend explorations of quiet, ancient country churches were frustrated by locked doors. We couldn't even indulge our love of turning up treasures in charity shops.

How quickly the recent past became a lost, Golden Age!

In the absence of live cricket, David resorted to old recordings, and so quickly had he adjusted to the new norm of social distancing that he was shocked to see stadiums thronged with fans. I travelled to work on empty trains and strode through the deserted concourses of King's Cross Station, pigeons, not commuters, thronging the pavements outside. Once teeming London had become a ghost town.

But spring 2020 brought brilliant sunshine and unusual warmth. Nature flourished in our small garden, which we had leisure and the urge to take in hand after some neglected years. With the lawn tamed and weeding done, we spent hours sitting outside, rediscovering our love of reading. I embarked on a project to read all twelve Poldark novels by the autumn (accomplished!).

David read more widely and whilst sitting with our books, we rejoiced in little visitors – our resident robins nested again after a disastrous attempt last year (the Night of the Cat), and brought their speckled fledglings to meet us and practice pecking for grubs. Sparrows bred four successive, incessantly squawking broods under the eaves over the course of the summer. (Boy, were those babies hungry!) The swifts arrived in early May and screamed their joy above our heads. A confused tawny owl crashed his way into a forsythia bush and fixed us with his midnight stare in the mid-afternoon. And insects: butterflies – red admirals, commas, the ubiquitous large whites; a rose chafer beetle glinting iridescent jewelled green; buff-bottomed bees, to whom we sang the alternative Queen song, 'Buff-bottomed bees, you make the buzzing world go round'.

The plants flourished. Gold and palest pink fragrant roses, azure agapanthus, fuchsias in every shade of, well, fuchsia, tropical candy-coloured lantana, and we harvested our first tomatoes, grown from seeds collected by my late father – a gift of love from beyond the grave.

We loved time together indoors, too, cooking new dishes and old favourites, packing 'takeaways' for my aged mother and sipping on a gin and tonic – or three. Live-streamed broadcasts from the Royal Opera House fed our yearning for the live performances we missed – and then, in August, the return of the Proms at the Albert Hall. Where once we stood crammed amongst other Promenaders, shamrock-shaped spotlights filled the dark amphitheatre and well-spaced musicians shared their love and the joy of performance.

How our work routines changed. David participated in a council initiative to distribute food parcels to those shielding or in need. This illuminating eye-opener into hardship and isolation, and the opportunity to be part of a team supporting the community, was a life-saver; he felt he was doing his bit.

For me, as a receptionist in a busy GP surgery, Covid brought a sudden emptying of the waiting room. No more chats with regular patients, the automatic doors locked, opened only by the waving of my 'magic wand' – a large cardboard star wrapped in silver tin-foil and attached to a long pole, which I waved at the electronic sensor to open the doors for anyone who needed to enter. It made the patients smile, and added a little fun to our stressed lives.

And so the year moves on and autumn brings a muted return to a changed normality. We suffer stress, uncertainty and nights of strange, disturbing Covid-dreams of loss and confusion; but our loved ones survive, the garden changes from green to gold, and once again we can step outside to meet friends and visit museums in a safe space. Our lives may never be what they were, but the important thought that we hold on to when we feel moments of struggle is that the natural world is lovely, little things can bring the greatest joy, and if we have each other, and those we love are safe, then we have everything.

Bearing Witness
Elizabeth Hill, UK

In the time of coronavirus
my daughter gave birth.
The midwives stayed past their hours
to safely deliver her.
I cannot visit,
hold my daughter tight
But I can wait, knowing
there will be time.
On the phone,
her first account flows out of her;
A mother is also born.
She speaks fast
wanting to get it out;
There will be more to come,
and other people to hear;
As much time as she needs
until she is healed.
A few days later
another voice
reaches me on the radio;
The story of a dying.
This woman also speaks fast,
this woman,
grieving.
As though she might not have

Enough
Airtime.
She speaks clearly,
her voice wavering just a little
as she describes her husband's worsening symptoms.
She remembers for us
the compassion of the frontline staff in hospital;
Someone doing extra time cleaning equipment;
their smile.
And how she begged, towards the end,
for her and her children to come and say
Goodbye.
Not to be able to hold his hand, to hold him close.
The important words could still be spoken,
those of love.
The weatherman who follows her account
leaves a fraction of a second of silence
before he speaks.
As for me,
tears come.
I sit on my balcony,
My face bare
To the sun's warmth.
And,
months on,
I remember.

A Secret Garden
Topy Jewell, UK

'Imagination is the only weapon in the war against reality.'
Lewis Carroll

(9 April radio, rewritten at midsummer)
Imagine you had to invent a game that took up the greatest possible amount of space for the fewest number of people; a game that inflicted as much damage as possible on the ecosystem, while making it as dangerous as possible for others to use that space. That game would look a lot like golf. During lockdown the golf course on the hill above our house was shut. Shut to golfers, so we could invade and occupy the green for our daily exercise.

We discovered a hilltop and views across the South Downs we had not seen before. A Bronze Age burial mound marked on the map was somewhere on the crest but difficult to decipher amongst the mounds and excavations of the golf course. We romanticised about a cluster of thorn trees with a magical presence, where the mower had left the grass rough and long. We started fantasising that the largest bunker carved into the hillside could be turned into an infinity pool, and another into an amphitheatre, recreational facilities that could be used by everyone.

One evening we walked up after supper to watch the sun set and saw the full moon rise on the opposite side of the hilltop. We had sort of just happened upon it, and in that weird time of self-isolating, not being able to hug our children or hang out with friends it felt like a special moment, secretly gifted to us by the golf course.

The True Meaning of Life
José Florenza, Spain

'We are visitors on this planet. We are here for ninety or one hundred years. During this period, we must try to do something good, something useful with our lives. If you can contribute to other people's happiness, you will find the true goal, the meaning of life.'
Dalai Lama XIV

I live in the beautiful nature of the Sierra Nevada, the highest mountain range in Europe after the Alps. I offer guided hikes for people interested in exploring this stunning and unique region, its flora, fauna and white Moorish villages.

With the onset of lockdown, I found myself with plenty of time to take in more of the beauty of my surroundings and my love and appreciation for nature continues to grow.

If it's about love, the pandemic has brought people together. I am very lucky to have such wonderful neighbours. We've helped each other as much as we could during this strange times with love, patience, helping hands and listening ears.

During this lockdown, I also met a very nice woman who needed help and a special friendship was born out of this meeting. It gave me a good feeling to be able to help her, and in so doing earning her gratitude.

My wish is that we can once again do what we want, when we plan to do it, without the inhuman restrictions imposed as a result of the pandemic.

The Blessing or the Curse
Bridie Jackson, Spain

'*Love* and compassion are necessities, not luxuries.
Without them, humanity cannot survive.'
Dalai Lama XIV

The blessing or the curse? Surely a blessing for me.

Corona started with shared family breakfasts every day, home-school play, recipes long considered, cooked; chi kung at sunrise and poi at sunset. It was a time of calm and catch up, a space that let us breathe fully again.

Then huge challenges met; my pay reduced, my hours of work lost, my value questioned, my self-worth bruised. Questions like 'Was it all just a bit too comfortable? Is this what we needed to push us back into reality?'

I love a crossroads. I love change. I love riding the metaphorical wave. I tuned in to my gut instinct. My husband presents all options, the facts and figures, the side of rationale. I feel as he talks. The truth is shouting deeply within me. More than ever the crisis I see happening around me, in the world, the crisis that is humanity is roaring so loudly I cannot ignore it. I have been gifted this crossroads. I can choose to continue on a path I don´t love any more or I can follow my heart and trust that everything will be all right. The sickness in my plexus when I think away from my heart is overwhelming. In contrast the lift and lightness I feel when I listen to my heart …

Husband agrees I must follow my deeper calling, now is the time. Surely this is what this moment in history is trying to teach us? When rationale takes the side of the heart, I know it must be true. Like the yin and yang meeting in harmony.

So, I find myself living my truth, following my heart, which has become our heart. I quit my job. I have taken up my heart's desire of years ago; I have founded a non-profit organisation that connects refugees to language teachers for one-to-on 1:1 lessons online, Language Linkers. We flex to the needs of refugees, we stretch to reach their requirements, we share our hearts and are gifted their trust and friendship. I have never felt so complete.

Such first-world troubles we have – pay reductions, shops closed, friends unseen, parties cancelled, schoolwork online, holidays lost.

Displaced people all across the world have no need of such worries. Their lives were threatened long before corona. Their families wiped out, their politicians corrupted long before corona. Fleeing gave them different worries; finding food for the children, coats to keep out the rain, a path free of police or traffickers, plastic and cardboard scraps to sleep under or on are the thoughts that occupy their minds. They've little time to consider the effects of lockdowns, the risks of catching corona.

In our home, it's true some things have quickly reverted back to the old ways but there is a pink warmth within our walls, a sense of fulfilment and satisfaction, a feeling that we have more than enough. Our priorities are different, expectations lower, demands sidelined, plans shelved and simple happiness the goal. We are more present, more united, more whole. The love of humanity, the love to love and living to love have become our new normal. A blessing indeed.

Music Is My Medicine
Cara Jane Murphy, UK

'One good thing about music – when it hits you, you feel no pain.'
Bob Marley

Where does one begin to tell a story when the ending is still so unclear? Perhaps, with an adventure. Today is Thursday 16 July 2020. This is the UK, and I am at London Heathrow airport, about to board a plane to Croatia, to sing at a festival. Something that only a few weeks ago I didn't believe would be possible for a very long time, if ever. This was because four months earlier, on Tuesday 24 March 2020, amidst the declaration of a global health pandemic, the UK government announced that England would be entering a national lockdown and isolation (many other nations had already done so) in a bid to try and tackle the spread of the Covid-19 virus. Never before, as a nation or in generations, had we been torn apart from our loved ones and put into such a state of national alert.

I had been listening quite closely to both the national and world news in the months leading up to the UK lockdown, after hearing about how the virus had swept through China in January 2020 and then up through Europe, so I knew what was coming.

I am a musician, I have always processed the world around me with music, through songwriting and singing, and I have been blessed in my life to share my passion with people in the festival fields, venues, city squares and town markets. I am lucky enough to wear a couple of musical hats. I am privileged to sing for UK/Global Dub pioneers, Zion Train, a role I have stepped into in the last two years. This was a dream come true, as I had been a big fan of the band since I was in my teens. My world in music has opened up since joining Zion Train and has already allowed me to travel out into the wider world to share my songline with other people from other cultures; for that, I am truly grateful.

I also have a solo acoustic creation in 'Cara Means Friend'; with this, I have played some of the best-loved venues and festivals the UK has to offer. Also, to keep my toes in the creative pool and to stay connected with people, in between gigs and festivals, I busk the cities and towns of the UK.

I have tried to make music my life mission and up until the lockdown I was reaching this goal with some success. Music has always been my constant, the thing that I turn to in moments of sadness, despair, love and joy, music is my therapy and my medicine, it is the thing that allows me to translate the world around me. So when I realised that the freedom to express this part of myself and my ability to share my creativity was to be stripped away indefinitely, I had to think about how I was going to keep adding to the creative pool.

I believe that through songwriting I am able to process this world and the spectrum of emotions that come with it. My hope in doing so is firstly, to understand myself and my life experiences a little better and secondly, to offer those listening a route to process and validate some of their own emotions and observations. I know that music is the thing that connects us to ourselves and to each other.

Music is the creation that lets us know we are not alone. For this reason, I knew it was important for me to keep music firmly by my side during the lockdown, like a trusty old friend I could turn to on dark days and a playmate on the joyous days. I decided I would set myself a music mission, to livestream *A Song a Day, at Midday, Everyday*, from my *Cara Means Friend* Facebook page. Primarily to keep my creative hand in and my heart and head right (routine is very helpful in a lockdown situation) but also hopefully, to create a meeting place and routine for people who might be in lockdown on their own.

On Monday 23 March 2020, the day before we were officially told to go into isolation and lockdown, I did my first ever lockdown livestream, set out my intention and invited people to come along every day at midday for a cuppa and a song – and they did! Every day, more people would come along and connect, not just with me but with each other. The positive response was so strong and posts were being shared left, right and centre, prompting more wonderful people to come along. I quickly realised that what was being created was a community, a familiar place to be in an unfamiliar situation.

Livestreaming is a very different beast to performing live to an audience. There is another level of nervousness that comes with it. In performance, as a musician, a big part of what I do is to read the energy of a space and the people within it. I believe that music is an energetic exchange between the music, the musician and the listener, so not to have the live input of energy from the listener is unnerving. I had to visualise the listener, in order to connect to that energy. From the very first day of livestreaming, the positive comments and connections became apparent and this inspired me to continue. As the days passed, I became a little more confident in talking to people and trying to process some of what we were facing as a species. The *Song a Day, at Midday, Everyday* sessions were becoming a live lockdown music diary.

Now I must introduce you to my partner, Ian. We were blessed to have found each other last year (2019) at the Strawberry Fair festival, both of us doing the thing that we love … music! I was playing at the festival as *Cara Means Friend* and Ian was playing bass with his band, The Blunders. We very quickly fell in love and from that point on have rarely left each other's side.

Up until the lockdown, even with our mutual love for music we had never jammed or played music together. Both of us realised that we had no gigs or festivals booked; our entire 2020 had been cancelled due to the virus. At this point we turned to each other creatively and began playing music together. This was a beautiful manifestation in the uncertainty of lockdown. We realised that we really enjoyed creating together and it helped us both to cope with the loss of our other creative outlets.

It became apparent as the weeks passed and the national and global death toll increased that life as we knew it might not return for a very long time, if ever. For us as musicians, the pubs and venues had been shut, the festivals were cancelled and we were told it was a risk to gather, as we would increase the spread of the virus. Life moved online.

I had been asked to come and play an online festival for a programme called *With Music Through the Lockdown*, hosted by Michi Kvin from Spain. Both Ian and I played the festival (our first live performance together), livestreaming from the UK. It was the first of many over a three-month period of full lockdown. Ian also played many of the midday sessions with me, providing some beautiful bass lines.

We also had our elderly neighbour, Lily, recite her poems over the garden wall on Tuesdays and Thursdays. I even livestreamed the *Illuminate* album launch, which was my first release, with Zion Train. Neil Perch (my creative brother and founder of Zion Train) sent me the tracks online from Germany and I sang them in a bedroom in the UK, to people across the globe, live (a beautiful, surreal moment, of virtual connection).

We always took time to set the scene for livestreams either in the garden or in the bedroom studio that we had set up for lockdown. We would dress up as if we were going to a real-life festival, in a bid to lift both our own and our viewers' spirits, a nod to the freedoms we were able to enjoy just months ago. It's helped with the feeling of loss that we feel for our music scene at the moment. As I write this, four months after we entered lockdown in the UK and even with many restrictions having been lifted, we still have no clue as to when the music venues and festivals will be able to reopen.

On 10 June, three months after lockdown was introduced, Prime Minister Boris Johnson lifted some restrictions and reopened non-essential shops. It was an indication that some things were about to start moving in the UK, some people were returning to work and I believed this to be the time to wind the midday sessions down. Knowing it had served its purpose to me, in keeping me focused and structured with my music and hoping that it had served a purpose in connecting people through music, when we were unable to connect in real life. On 15 June, I played my last midday livestream, signing off from lockdown, with seventy-two midday sessions under my belt and a whole new set of unexpected, beautiful friends, who continue to support *Cara Means Friend*, and what I am doing now.

On 17 June, a week after the towns and high streets were reopened, I returned to busk the busk for the first time in three months. The towns are slightly different places now; some businesses have gone under through the financial burden of Covid-19 and some shops stand unused, people are less likely to be carrying cash, preferring, in this 'New Normal', to go contactless, but there is enough footfall to bring some music to the streets. Among a sea of masked shoppers, this is the only place in the UK where I am able to play music in public at the moment. For this reason, when I play nowadays, I play with more passion and purpose than I ever did before.

These writings have taken me a few days to compile. Ian calls them my 'lockdown memoirs'. Here I am on 24 July 2020, after a few days back in the UK and an adventure that began at an airport en route to Croatia. For just a few days, we experienced a life that resembled the one we knew before, here in the UK.

In Croatia, where they locked down more quickly as a nation, they had far fewer numbers of Covid-19 cases and fatalities than here in the UK, so things were much more relaxed there. In Croatia on 17 July 2020, I sang on a stage with Zion Train, there were lights, there were sound systems and there were smiling, dancing people, full of love and hope. This, for now, is what I take from my experience of lockdown, in the wake of a global pandemic and the navigation of this new way of life: there will and must always be LOVE and HOPE.

For the Love of Flowers
Joanna Corcoran Wunsch, UK

'If we could see the miracle of a single flower,
clearly our whole life would change'
Anonymous

After much thought at the end of last year I left my job to take a career break and a year out to travel, explore and learn. My first awareness of coronavirus was on the TV in my room at the Sigiriya Village Hotel on the first night after leaving a remote week-long yoga retreat. Cases were being reported in China, news about it was on every channel, but oddly it seemed a distant threat.

Upon my return to the UK news of lockdowns across Europe began and still this creeping invisible virus felt strangely surreal, as it kind of still does to this day. As it advanced it meant that all my travel plans were cancelled, all of the enriching and creative classes I was taking were being postponed until further notice. The only thing that remained was a flower-growing project I had started working on at a local farm. I had decided to get back into flowers, and was spending one day a week at Ashurst Organic Farm, joining the two flower growers. I discussed rekindling my floristry skills that I had rediscovered whilst making wedding bouquets and arrangements for a friend's festival-style wedding in September of the previous year. We talked about increasing the scale of the flowers grown on the farm, to extend the reach and provide more flowers for farmers' markets and veggie boxes.

So each Friday it was my routine to go and help on the farm, plan for a year of flowers, think about different and new flower varieties to grow, look into new areas to plant on the farm. In February we started sowing the seeds, and a few weeks later we were pricking out the seedlings. And then lockdown came.

It felt strange but the guidelines were clear: if you could continue to work whilst maintaining a distance it was OK to do so, and I did. At first it felt very odd getting in my car to drive out to the farm, the roads were empty and it felt slightly wrong or questionable, but it was fine and not breaking any rules.

I was learning all the time, from the experience of the organic farmers and plant and permaculture experts, and I was gradually feeling more comfortable. After sowing, the seeds would germinate, and the seedlings were grown on in the polytunnel, nice and warm and snug. And so it went, each Friday out to the farm I would go; other than my family, the organic farmers Pete and Collette and botanist and gardener Kate were the only real-life people I saw. All at a distance and all outside. It was a marker of the weeks of lockdown going by: Zoom quiz with friends on Wednesday, clapping for the NHS on Thursday, and the farm on Friday.

As the seedlings grew into small plants, we would watch the weather, so very wet at the beginning of the year, with the threat of frost prevailing until mid-May. We worked making more growing spaces. Increasing the number of permaculture beds in the orchard, Pete cultivated a new strip to plant in, in the lower field.

At last it was time to start planting out. We planted a cultivated bed, covered to suppress weeds and retain water, such little plants, quite hard to imagine how they would grow into a full cutting-flower garden. Flowers went into the permaculture beds and another row emerged, reclaimed from nettles, bindweed and comfrey. The weather became dry, the wind blew, drying the soil further, and nights were chilly. But the flowers grew.

At the same time, I was still thinking about the idea of running a floristry service alongside the organic flower growing. We talked and decided how it might work; Ashurst Organics sell posies to their veg-box customers and at markets. My floristry would have to be something quite different. I had planned on promoting it to people organising weddings or events, but now with Covid-19 everything was on hold, businesses and venues were closed.

I'm not a natural at promoting and marketing, but it needed to be done. I needed a business name and my daughter came up with the idea of Joanna's

Flowers. It had a good ring, it suggested a small personal business, an individual service, local, friendly and down to earth – perfect for me.

Then June came, and the flowers really started to take off, with early varieties coming into flower. It was time to do it. I sorted out my social media accounts, which I had been dabbling in and posting the occasional photo on. I bought a domain name and settled down to teach myself how to use an online website-building tool, and eventually I got there. I'm still tweaking it, I still need to learn about what a blog is and why. But through this process my vision got clearer, I knew what I wanted to do and what my focus is.

Joanna's Flowers is about sustainable and natural floristry, using only materials that can be composted, recycled or reused. It's about using organic flowers that are locally grown and seasonal. As events for 2020 may not be possible, I am starting a delivery service of cut-flower bouquets and bunches. I deliver on Fridays but this might change as the season develops. As businesses open there may be opportunities there. I am sticking to my floristry style for now, I love naturalistic floral arrangements myself, and I am exploring to discover if others love them too.

I value the friendships with the people I see each week. It's really important for me to feel as though we communicate and that every decision is made carefully; that the balance between my floristry endeavour and the ongoing work of the team at the farm complement one another. I am extremely grateful for having the opportunity to explore, learn and develop this in a really beautiful place with kind and caring people. If it hadn't been for lockdown, I might not have had the focus needed to take this forward, so I am thankful for that.

When I announced Joanna's Flowers to my friends, I had such an overwhelmingly positive response. If nothing else I reconnected with so many lovely friends from my years living in New Mexico and working at Greenpeace before that. I am getting orders coming in now, which is wonderful, and who knows where this will take me as lockdown eases.

Beauty Everywhere
Lorena Marchetti, Italy

*'The best and most beautiful things in the world
cannot be seen or even touched.
They must be felt with the heart'*
Helen Keller

A personal story from Lorena in San Silvestro, Italy:
Love and respect of yourself means you can dedicate more love to others, so a big change for me was to give up smoking. Just a few days after lockdown, which was 4 March 2020 here in my part of Italy, I decided to go ahead with a long overdue change. I thought, 'How can I smoke if people are suffering from a respiratory disease?' Being at home helped a lot, no excuses for the bad mood swings of the first few days and if anyone is thinking of giving up this worked for me. Every time I felt like smoking a cigarette, I did something else, whatever I felt like; going out in the garden, some little house job to distract my attention, or nothing at all, and just meditated in silence until the urge passed.

But the biggest love in Corona Times turned out to be love of nature and the garden, nurturing our own land and appreciating even more the colours and sounds of nature. We live in the country about seven kilometres from the nearest town, so it is often quite quiet, but during lockdown it was silent. A beautiful silence, no aeroplanes, no traffic, no man-made excess. It seems like stating the obvious, but it was scientifically documented that during lockdown pollution decreased and the Earth reclaimed some of its space, refreshed its rivers and air.

We also had more time to spend outdoors and a huge evolution was to triple the size of our veggie plot. Again, this was something we have always wanted to do, but because of work never had enough time to dedicate to a bigger plot. It was really good fun and a great satisfaction. Now in July we have such a lot of choice of veggies we rarely buy any. What's more, we can give freely to family and friends, there's plenty for everyone!

Our love for nature continues with our day trips. We have decided not to go travelling this year but we are going on a series of day trips to nearby places. We have discovered paths in the woods with small waterfalls, clifftop paths leading down to quiet beaches, and amazing scenery in the nearby mountains. Nature never ceases to amaze, refresh and fill you with wonder.

I think love for humanity and love for the Earth are two of the biggest driving forces, and knowing that everything is connected; when you dedicate love to another person you are giving energy to the whole of humanity. When you respect the Earth, you are creating and working in the right direction.

An Earthly Love Story
Belen Alvarez Marin, Spain

*'And forget not that the earth delights to feel your bare feet
and the winds to play with your hair'*
Kahlil Gibran

My name is Belen and I live blessedly at the foot of the Sierra Nevada mountains, in Granada, in the village where I came to raise my children and put down roots after years of travelling. I am a mother, lover, artisan, poet, farmer and self-taught herbalist (among many other things) with a great passion for the study and collection of medicinal plants in the wild, their uses and preparations.

Spring is the time of the year when I find myself busiest going out to the mountains and fields to look for medicinal plants, but I will never forget the spring of the year 2020, when we were forbidden to leave our homes for more than two moons, and Nature rested at ease. And it rained a lot during this confinement! The fields began to burst with life waiting for my return with my basket and scissors.

At home, we don't read the news much, and I haven't had a television for many years, so I must say that 'the quarantine' and the obligation to confine us caught me almost by surprise. It has been something intense, worrying and at the same time nourishing. It started abruptly, confusingly, and little by little it became a blessing, an opportunity for true rest, to be at home, amongst family, without an agenda or plans, and in a creative and loving attitude.

I was confined with my partner and lover Sergio, his nine-year-old son and my eight-year-old son, while my other seventeen-year-old son was going back and forth from his father's house to ours, defying the emergency laws. We are a 'Patchwork' family, and there is no confinement that can handle us!

We feel privileged and give thanks to Life, for our comfortable house, a terrace overlooking the mountains of the Sierra de Lujar, food and water in abundance, health, and creative and resilient minds. Sergio and I were able to channel our energy into home-schooling our young children and joining in their play, cooking with love and without rushing, and finding time to clean and arrange things at home. Also, we now had the time and energy to work on a special project – our Huerta*!

We have a small area of land behind our rental house in the middle of the village. It had been abandoned and weed-strewn for years. Now it called for our attention and soon became our only way to get out of the house (apart from throwing out the garbage and going to do some necessary shopping). We would be in direct contact with the land, mother Earth, Nature and its rhythms, and the wonderful art of horticulture. Sergio got his start on 19 March – Father's Day. He went down the street with a sickle, and around the block to that little piece of land he had longed for and ignored until now due to lack of time and motivation.

In a few weeks the Huerta '*El Picotazo*' became pretty, then beautiful, filling us with an indescribable love and admiration, as if it were our new baby. This little piece of cultivated land became a refuge, a justification to leave the house, a high vibration for our spirit. All this while a rain of news – of all kinds – fell constantly over the village and its people, over all this beloved Planet that was confined and deprived of free movement on so many levels.

The social networks were red-hot, the social tension was noticeable, so was the division of opinions. I therefore paid special attention to where I was putting my attention and my energy. I appreciated the fact that I had come to live in a village south of Granada in Andalucia, where fortunately many brilliant, questioning and disobedient minds also live. It is an incredible mixture of cultures, styles and languages, a birthplace of constant initiatives and projects. This diversity has resulted in some very rich and deep conversations about health, freedom, community and nurturing.

Like many others, I have noticed and appreciated the rest we have given to Nature and all its works. The planes were parked, the vehicles stopped driving, we stopped walking on beaches, up mountains and in parks. The pollution levels and noise levels dropped significantly in many areas. This has been, perhaps, the most positive thing about this whole stressful and painful pandemic period for many.

During lockdown, I realised more clearly than ever how lucky and privileged I am to be with my family and my community. From this awareness, life is asking me to support others, and to participate in local activism as much as possible. More than ever, life is asking me to take care of myself, to respect myself and to be grateful for every second of this beautiful life that has been given to me.

In the name of Love, and in a good spirit, I wish you a full life.

Huerta: in Spanish, a (vegetable) garden or orchard

The Milk of Human Kindness
Svetlana Vinogradova, Denmark

'Too often we underestimate the power of a touch, a smile, a kind word, a listening ear, an honest compliment, or the smallest act of caring, all of which have the potential to turn a life around.'
Leo Buscaglia

When I think about corona times, I realise that it's often referred to as crisis. No doubt, it has been and still is a tough period – taking lives, leaving people unemployed, bankrupting companies, crushing private and national economies. At the same time, I've experienced this period as a kind of enlightenment and self-realisation on a quite different level than I've been used to.

The first thing I was impressed by was solidarity among people – the wish to reach out, understand and help others. Many companies offered free services, artists gave free online concerts, universities offered free online courses and neighbours offered help with shopping.

Solidarity was also seen in the Danish government. It was the first time in my life when I saw all political parties in Folketinget having a complete consensus and acting unanimously. I was deeply touched by the Danish Prime Minister Mette Frederiksen. Even though I've never given my vote to her, I was impressed by her compassionate, caring, inclusive approach in handling this extreme situation and supporting the nation in such a constructive, generous, firm and at the same time warm-hearted way.

The most precious thing that I've experienced during corona was presence with my loved ones. Even staying apart, I've spent many beautiful hours with my children and with my friends. We met online – all dressed up – with our cameras on – eating dinner together, talking, sharing recipes, ideas, thoughts, experiences, drinking wine and playing games together. Staying apart has brought us so much together that also today we continue this lovely tradition meeting outside and in our homes.

Last but not least, I've discovered new feelings within me. I had time to reflect upon my life and my priorities. I understood that love is the highest priority. Knowing this I found out that it's not difficult to make priorities in my life. In fact, it is quite easy. I found harmony in me. I found even more compassion and inclusion in my heart. I've got a feeling that I want to embrace the whole world and give my love and positive energy to whoever needs it. And I'm so grateful for that!

My Neighbours
Marc Joyeux, Italy

'Our ability to reach unity in diversity will be the beauty and the test of our civilisation.'
Mahatma Gandhi

I don't know his name.
I don't know his wife's name.
I don't know his little boy's name.
I know he's Albanian.

When they came to look at their new home they parked illegally outside my house. I saw the kids running around the green, spacious garden to the left of the small block of flats. As I went out with my wife, I saw his worried frown. 'Say you're friends of ours if anyone asks,' I shouted over to him. From that moment we've always nodded. His wife has never spoken directly to me. The girls just stare and smile. The little boy smiles weakly.

At 6.30 am the father goes off to work on his scooter.
At 8.00 am the school bus churns round the streets and collects the girls.

The wife hangs out long lines of washing. White, red, green but all whites together, all reds, all greens, whole blocks of colours. The little boy trails after her. In Italy at the end of February schools close.
General lockdown begins slowly.

The government closes everything except supermarkets, chemists, banks and hospitals.

My work crashes and my wife begins online schooling.

No school bus, the bike path opposite is virtually empty, the streets too. Few cars. Masked drivers. Souls on missions.

Permits are the rage. Even to walk up to a radius of 200m from my home a signed permit is obligatory.

The government tightens the reins, no moving between cities or towns, no visiting close family.

TV news – numbers, numbers, numbers:

Infected.

In intensive care.

Deaths.

TV films, I kid you not, titles like *Virus*, *Sharkageddon*, *Contagion*, *Outbreak*, *World War Z*. Zombie films aplenty and *Twilight* reruns!

Lockdown began in the north of Italy but after 9 March the clampdown went south. Our day-to-day routine was very simple. Yoga, online working, washing hands, going shopping with masks and gloves. An armed security guy at the supermarket would make sure no couples came in together (my in-laws were stopped and separated!). Italian culture gone pear-shaped in the name of health. Then home, wash hands and be bamboozled as to what to do with the products we'd bought. Had we let the virus in? Manic times!

Strained hours turned into days. Days slowly grouped together to form weeks.

The stress of doing sweet FA.

The stress of a distinct possibility of infection.

The stress of old folk dying in their thousands.

Back to the Albanian family.

One Covid day I remarked to my wife, over lunch, that they were enjoying the good spring weather by having a picnic on a spread blanket. 'Lovely,' she replied, and we watched the family members play out their roles. It looked like a live cinema production!

Father, small, strong, balding; instructing the order of things.
Wife, a bit roly-poly, smiling silently.
One girl pretending to ignore everyone.
The other, younger sister keeping the little boy busy.
An idyllic scene in those heavy, virus-ridden, early days of lockdown.
The picnic show.
The father, repairing bikes or doing gardening chores, would stop and sit with his family to eat and chat. The girls would play volleyball with no net, keeping the ball in the air or doing gymnastic moves, cartwheels or stretching. The little boy had his red Ferrari electric kid's car to buzz about in. Then they would all stop and eat and chat. Staying unified, calm and seemingly very happy.
Nowhere to go after lunch.
No rush to do anything.
No scrapping amongst the kids. They would all share time with the smallest.
Days rolled on.

Apart from the family nothing moved in the street. I would go on my constitutional walkabout, permit in pocket, say hello and have a chat with the Albanian dad, then keep on walking to exercise. The government recommended daily exercise but individual exercise only. Most days my wife would worry about who I'd talked to and how close this contact had been. Not from jealousy, but from fear of contagion.

Once the Albanian father told me that no money was coming in. He was using his savings to put food on the table. 'What will the future bring?' we asked each other. I heard my name being called so I crossed the road and returned home. 'You were standing too close, try to remember!' my wife kept repeating as she disinfected the soles of my shoes. News just in had revealed that the virus could live for six hours on asphalt.

These were NOT normal times.

Today these visions of the Covid-19 lockdown in my street in the seaside town of Cesenatico, Italy have gone.
The Albanian father is back at work.
His wife fills the washing line.
The girls are lanky and tanned. The older one has a boyfriend who parks his red car opposite, and they gab on into the night.
The little boy fizzes with energy when he has his little friends round to play.
No picnics
No need
No lockdown.

Getting Out: Reflections during Lockdown

Zoe White, The Netherlands

As a society, we value people who are gregarious and fun, but throughout history we have sought out those who live in isolation for wisdom and guidance. Hermits, gurus, mystics, even artists and authors who are notoriously private about their personal lives – these individuals have long been objects of fascination.

'I'm all right as long as I can get out.'

This was my mother's regular refrain some ten years ago when she was still a sprightly ninety-year old. When she said this, I used to wonder what would happen if and when a time came that she could not get out. Little did I ever imagine there would come a time when none of us could get out.

'Getting out', for my mother, meant her daily walk (with the aid of what she called her 'pusher') through the nearby park, to the local shop, where she bought her newspaper and milk and chatted with the woman at the cash desk. The route took her past some ancient horse chestnut trees, where, on crisp autumn mornings, she enjoyed picking up a few conkers to put in the corners of her rooms, firm in her belief that they would help keep spiders away. Each time she walked past those trees she wondered how long they'd been there and what they had seen in their long lives.

My mother has seen much. Now in her 102nd year she has lived through two world wars, the death of her husband and now a pandemic. With the help of regular visits from her two carers, she continues to live a fairly independent life at home. She says she is never lonely. She is not able to walk to the park as she once could, her milk and her newspaper are now delivered, and her way of 'getting out' has changed: 'I'm all right ...' she says now, '...as long as I have my newspaper.'

I admire my mother's courage, her capacity to enjoy her own company, and her ability to value the small pleasures which are left to her as her world steadily shrinks. By the time Corona came along she had already lived many years alone. Gradually, she had developed the skills and resources she needed to keep her going in isolation, while the rest of us, faced with sudden lockdown, had to scramble and surf and zoom to learn how to do it.

Who could have imagined, before Corona, how life could suddenly appear to close doors and shut windows on us, as, bewildered, shocked and afraid, we all suddenly became more aware of our mortality, our vulnerability, and just how much we had previously taken for granted the pleasure of simply being able to get out?

* * * * *

Recently I received a Facebook post from a very dear friend in her 80s who lives on another continent. Her world, like that of many people in residential care, became very much smaller, and more lonely during Corona. Already infrequent visits from family and friends were reduced to none. With the exception of minimal contact with care-home staff, she saw no one. Then she had a fall and was moved around to different hospitals for various treatments. She is now back home, receiving nursing care 24/7, and in constant pain.

This Facebook post contained a blurred photo which looked as though it had been taken by mistake, and a capital C. Just the letter C, followed by an inexplicable space. I stare at the photo, the C, and the empty space that follows, trying to make sense of it.

Some of her Facebook friends, doubtless unaware of her physical condition, have posted puzzled replies asking: What is this? What does it mean? Others, probably more aware of her circumstances, have responded with a weepy face, or a red heart.

This dear friend of mine is a person who has always inspired me. She has given her life to teaching; to passing on her passion for literature, her love for language and her delight in the subtleties and nuances of meaning. All of which makes the irony and pathos of this solitary 'C' more acute. And it touches me that even now, despite the pain in her joints, and the numbing, disorienting effects of drugs, she is still struggling to communicate.

I watch my finger hovering uncertainly between the weepy face and the red heart. And then I pull my finger back. There is something more in this unfinished Facebook post; something which must be more deeply seen. So I sit still, considering this C, and what it evokes in me.

C ..., she says, ... just have the courage to maintain your awareness here. Resist the temptation to scroll on down to other, more comfortable posts.

It is stark, this message.

C ... Remain here with your discomfort. This is the reality of now. Don't turn away, pretending you don't understand. Look at it. Honour this emptiness and search for the deeper perception.

This is, after all, what my friend has always stood for: the courage to honour what you know to be true, however uncomfortable, whatever the cost. So this is what I have to respect, despite my feelings of inadequacy and utter helplessness.

Slowly it begins to dawn on me that this aborted message is speaking more clearly than any more coherent post could. This 'C' is as naked and empty as a buddha's teaching; as bold and bewildering as a koan.

See, she says: This is the impossible, incomprehensible place where you can't get out; the place where you can't even get one short Facebook post out.

How to get out, when you can't get out?

How do you respond?

* * * * *

When the art galleries open again I take the opportunity to get out and visit the Rijks Museum before the tourists return. I book an early-morning slot and walk to the museum through the empty streets of Amsterdam, relishing the clear air and the calm water of the canals. Inside the museum I climb the stairs, deciding that I won't immediately make for the obvious Rembrandts and Vermeers. There's no rush after all, there are no crowds, I can take my time and just enjoy the luxury of ambling and seeing where my feet want to lead me.

Here!

The long, steady, resonant tick-tock of a grandfather clock draws me in to the eighteenth century. Enlightenment. Looking more closely at the clock I see a small glass panel at the top, behind which two model ships are rocking in time with each passing second, rising and plunging again into the waves. Tick. Tock. My pace slows as I fall under the spell of the peaceful, hypnotic sound.

I am entirely alone. Room after empty room welcomes me deeper into the silence.

Time is noticed. Time is noticed above an underlying quiet. This Quiet is present.

The waves draw me on and wash me up next to a Canaletto. Traces of other times are left. This is how Piazza San Marco used to look in eighteenth-century Venice; the great show and spectacle of the Piazza, conjured up with a few lines of pen on paper.

The clock chimes once. The time of peace.

I am struck by my own presence.

The chime hangs briefly in the air, trembles, then fades.

There is no one but me walking these rooms, but they are not empty. Who is here?

Am I the viewer, or am I the viewed?

Who is witnessing the passing of time in these empty halls?

The passing of this time. Now. The writing time.

Who is immersed here? Who is absorbed?

What to call it, where time is stilled; distilled?

Is it magic? Poetry?

We come and go as time ticks on, and we tell how it was to sail our ships on the high seas of Corona.

* * * * *

Libraries reopen.

(It's difficult to remember now that there was ever a time when we could do simple things like use lifts without stopping to consider the health risks and putting on face masks.)

As I'm going down, a man gets into the lift carrying a case which looks as though it might contain a musical instrument. In his other hand he's holding a white rose. He presses the '0' button for the ground floor.

'Have you been playing?' I ask him.

'I'm an illusionist,' he says. 'I just performed for the children.'

'Did it go well?' I ask.

'Yes, thank you.'

Then, after a pause, he turns to me. 'Here …' he says, offering me the rose.

I take the rose, thanking him.

We arrive at zero.

The doors open, and I get out.

* * * * *

www.thousandwingpress.com

A Rhyme for Our Time
Shujata Luptajan, Spain

Numbers are climbing
They're climbing all around
Stack them on the table
Stack them on the ground

We can't think those numbers
We can't think that high
We turn our eyes to heaven
But only see the sky

They've climbed up to my eyes now
I'm scared I'm going to drown
Ring a ring o' roses
And we'll all fall down

How many viruses
Dancing on a pin?
How many tiny holes
Where they get in?

Turn to your partner
Turn to your past
Tell your kids you love them
Tell them life goes by so fast

Curtsy to your partner
Turn around and bow
Now scrub your hands and rinse your hands
I'll show you how

With gloves on your hands
And a mask on your face
We're all surging forward
In the great human race

You're running for the president?
It's time to get in line
You're running to the future
You're running out of time

The road is full of people
How many can you see?
If I look out for you, babe,
Will you look out for me?

Some are fallen by the wayside
Some are on their knees
Will someone call an ambulance
To help them please?

Shut your eyes and open them
Shut your eyes and pray
But truth is staring back at you
It never goes away

Let's make a cake and share it
Let's bake it very soon
And mix in love like honey
Sliding off a spoon

Lock down, look down
Beneath our feet the ground
Has histories locked inside it
As the world goes round and round

We'll cut the cake and share the cake
And use up every crumb
We'll feast on love and laughter
And let the future come

Lock down, look up
Birds are flying free
As they cross the sky at evening
To their roost high in the tree

Lock down, look around
It's time to slow the pace
And halt the headlong scramble
Of the crazy human race

Then we'll raise a glass at sunset
And we'll raise our eyes at dawn
And we'll sing a song of sixpence
As the numbers all climb down

Live, Love, Eat
Amalia Yasmina Rasheed, Spain

'No matter how hard the world pushes me, within me there is something stronger, something better pushing back'
Albert Camus

Singing a year ago: Three little birds, saying 'Don´t worry about a thing!'

I embraced the love of dear family and angels. Yes, maybe I can slowly heal from my world having been turned upside down. Yet for everyone, the world got turned inside out as everything, everywhere, soon came to a halt.

What? Where? How? Why oh why? So many woes and no one really knows.

What was systematically and deeply hidden is now apparent; I am vulnerable. Safety mechanisms gone, I no longer can soldier on.

There is no shield or mask that can protect me from this silhouette of fear; between me and the vast valley ahead with its back to me, yet purposefully and persistently drawing my attention. Death behind, life ahead, and me in limbo between.

Flight or fight? Neither. At the limits of knowing, faith takes over from fear as I enter my space of Grace and spontaneously embrace the shadowy silhouette. It remains dark but still as if hushed by love and goodwill.

Yet, could it be a threat? Hide, create a distance, protect?

Drained and exhausted, I render up and ask for help. My eyes are drawn to a bunch of bananas, bursting and ripe. Literally going bananas, I laugh out loud!

Released from the strain of my thinking brain, I follow with love and bake a cake; the scent of cinnamon and cardamom brings me home.

Winter fades and spring bursts out in celebration in the midst of chaos. Sounds of distant traffic are transformed to the sound of the bees and birds in contrast to the palpable silence.

The neighbours, though distanced, grow closer. Eggs in exchange for vegetables, raspberry plants in exchange for sourdough starter passed down for generations.

There again it appears, the silhouette of fear. This time not in my path but on the side, distant as I reach out my hands. But what if? Should I stay, keep away, be on guard? This is hard.

So I turn to Grace and follow the answer of love; bake bread for all to share! There is calm, light and laughter in the air. I notice the silhouette fade and disappear.

But then back to my brain. I question and cannot function until pressed towards the door pushing open to the space of Grace, once again.

Moved with each small step, following an invitation to a challenge with meditation.

Blessed in confinement with my son, daughter and granddaughter taking refuge here away from the city. Sacred time of no distractions, embedded in this generously spacious ancient grove of olives and heavenly orange blossom.

It continues with Ramadan and my intention to fast is clearer and filled with prayer to embrace and breathe in life. While the drums of war divide with fear to rule, love permeates and persists.

Cherishing family and friends, near and far, with quality time for reflection.

My gait is lighter.

All is good.

Really?

Very good.

Too good?

It is true, so I pursue!

Out of the swamp onto solid but fertile ground and into joy, as burdens transform to air.

Baking, making and sharing love in celebration for Eid at the end of the fast, human relationships grow so much dearer than ever before. The flowers, vibrant colours of life … more than words.

Tears of deeply embedded grief gradually release and reveal an eternal smile.

And now, every morning for real, three little birds!

Perched on my doorstep, saying: Right?

Saying: Every little thing's gonna be all right!

Light and nourished, cradled in love and free just to be me.

'In the midst of hate, I found there was, within me, an invincible love. In the midst of tears, I found there was, within me, an invincible smile. In the midst of chaos, I found there was, within me, an invincible calm. I realised, through it all, that in the midst of winter I found there was, within me, an invincible summer. And that makes me happy. For it says that no matter how hard the world pushes against me, within me, there's something stronger, something better, pushing right back.' Albert Camus

Return to Self-Love
Veronika Poola, Spain

'Your capacity for loving another person depends entirely on your capacity for loving yourself, for taking care of yourself. Healing.'
Thich Nhat Hanh

For the last thirteen years, my work as a medicine woman, community leader, naturopath, entrepreneur and mother of four has completely engulfed me. While birthing my own children, I have also birthed a community and a small business. As a medicine woman, I have taken hundreds of people through death and rebirth. My tribe extends far and wide, my spiritual children spread around the planet. I have been sitting in ceremony almost every two weeks for a decade and a half. The transformation has been profound and the love I have experienced even deeper. But the work and demands on my time have also been intense and while sharing love with others, I often forgot to take the time to love myself.

My creative process drove me to the edge of burnout. Despite living off-grid and trying to live the most simple and natural life possible, the sheer effort of daily life and the dedication to the healing work kept me busy around the clock.

When I left on a family holiday at the end of the year, I was exhausted and empty. I was going to Brazil to fill my cup, get some rest and rejuvenation, but a camping trip around the country with a family of seven doesn't allow for much relaxation. There were still daily chores and the challenges of travelling in a foreign country. Even having fun seemed like hard work, when all my body and soul craved was to spend some time alone and reconnect with myself. At the end of our trip, I still felt exhausted and was anxious about returning to work. Our flights back to Spain were scheduled to arrive on the first day of the lockdown. We decided not to board the plane and quarantined ourselves with some friends in a small country house on the outskirts of Sao Paulo.

We lived in limbo for two months. Gone were the hours spent in front of the computer answering emails and planning the upcoming work season. Time as I knew it had stopped. The future was uncertain and it was my first opportunity since becoming a responsible adult to truly live in the moment. Though these months were not without their challenges, they have been my most nourishing months since becoming a mother. This rare opportunity to slow down, spend quality time with my family, forget work and retreat from the outside world gave me the precious gift of time.

Throughout the lockdown, in moments of uncertainty and worry, I would reach for my Tarot pack to ask for guidance and regularly drew the card 'Wishes Fulfilled'. It was hard for me to believe that my wishes could be fulfilled as the world around me was collapsing. It is only in retrospect that I realise that my main wish for so many years was to have 'more time' and it was being granted. For the past few years, almost every hour of the day was accounted for and now suddenly I had nothing pencilled into my agenda. In my usual active fashion, I began to fill up my time, though promising myself to do only what my heart desired in each moment. Each day, I took the time to nurture my body, my mind, my heart and my soul.

My mornings began with yoga, meditation, visualisation and a Tarot reading. This was followed by a swim in the pool, grooming and a superfood smoothie in the sunshine. I enjoyed quality time with my children: home-schooling, games, preparing lunch together and evening meditation and prayer around the fire. I fed my creativity with gardening, making music, listening to inspirational speakers, reading and making love.

I had been trying to start a weekly yoga practice for years, but somehow never found the motivation or the time. From the first day of quarantine, I did a one-and-a-half-hour practice and maintained this during the rest of my stay in Brazil. After one week, I felt more relaxed than I had in years. What previously would have required discipline was suddenly effortless. It was such a gift to take this time to nurture myself and listen to my rhythms in a way that modern life had prevented me from doing.

Each moment I spent taking care of myself, I was remembering how to love myself. With it came the realisation that I had such a hard time receiving help and love from others, because I hadn't been giving it to myself. I was reminded of the time, pre-motherhood, when I lived under a tree in deep connection with nature. A time when I left the path that had been paved for me to follow my heart. It had been the first time in my life that I learned to respect and take care of my body, and in that process I healed many of my traumas and learned how to love and accept myself. Over the years, the self-care dropped away and with it went the self-love. During the quarantine, as I began to love myself a little more each day, traumas and fears also resurfaced but were quickly healed and released.

The lockdown ended and I found myself back in Spain. Life began to pick up its pace and old patterns re-emerged as work began to take up most of my time. I had to give up my leisurely morning practice and focus on the tasks at hand. However, I have managed to do it with more awareness that I need to find balance between giving to others and giving to myself. Some days, I have forgotten to love myself, but mostly, I find the time to give myself a little love each day, whether it is a ten-minute morning meditation, a foot soak before bed, or a mug of hot chocolate as I hide away under a fig tree. Love is a journey, not a destination, and each day I take another step along the path.

The Gift of Deep Connection
Giovanna Barker, UK

'Clouds come floating into my life, no longer to carry rain or usher storm, but to add colour to my sunset sky'
Rabindranath Tagore

Essentially, I was the happiest I ever remember being. We were in transition, my teenage daughter and I. She was getting ready to leave home and meet the big wide world. These were precious days of unexpected time together that brought deep connection and simple abundance.

Looking back, it's easy to see the threads of beautiful connections woven through the layers of anxiety and uncertainty, uplifted by spring's increasing warmth and light.

I learnt many important lessons about how simple my needs are.

After the death of my mother a few months before, I had said yes to everything. I was away every weekend on work trips and conferences all over the country and the Isle of Man. I was exhausted! When lockdown stopped these trips suddenly, I felt responsible, as if I had manifested it, an extreme way to be able to say 'No' and not lose face. I was able to have deep rest and stay home.

This also meant that I got to spend quality time with my daughter. Our relationship has always been a good one, of respect and care. For several years her focus has been on being with her friends. Our time together was down to sharing meals and a few trips away each year. During lockdown, we bonded deeply. This time was a precious gift for both of us, which I consciously cherished every day.

We quickly got into a pattern of doing yoga together in the morning, sharing meals and walking our dog Ziggy in the late afternoons. In between I carried on working. We would create vegan feasts to share, in which she excelled. She became interested in foraging and permaculture. I see her now with a basket in hand collecting leaves and flowers for our meals from our forest garden. Lavatera leaves and fennel appear in salads and I see her in the bushes hunting out the red raspberry gems that last in the garden all the way into early winter.

Motherhood has been a journey, potent, raw, full-being experience. I once read being a parent is about constantly letting go from the birth, baby stage, toddler, then the first big milestone of going to school and now the biggest one as she physically will remove herself. It has sometimes been a relentless tsunami of dealing with behaviours and situations I have no strategies for yet. Once a stage is mastered, the next one arrives with its unique challenges, amidst the joys, of course.

From the time I was pregnant, I learnt to trust myself through the showering of contradictory advice. Now I am on the verge of an enormous, colossal, epic, letting go, as my daughter is on the verge of leaving home.

This deep love is said to be the strongest bond in the universe, the love of mother for child. I felt it from my own mother. I know sometimes she did not like me (teenage years!) but she always loved me. This deep love has been the saving foundation of my being as I roller-coastered emotionally through my teens and twenties. Just as well I had a child in my early thirties when I was much more internally peaceful and calm.

When my daughter became a teenager, I jokingly showed her the classic comedy sketch 'Kevin': how at the stroke of midnight on his thirteenth birthday he metamorphosed like a werewolf into a different state. She laughed and promised me she would be a 'nice' teenager! I believed her. She did try, and with amazing self-awareness in her adventurous adolescent years once stated grumpily 'I am sorry, Mum, I can't help it!'

During the lockdown I felt held every day by Mother Nature. The joy of my daily forage wherever I walked, in the fields, woods and especially in my garden were deeply nourishing at all levels. The plants and the birds were familiar friends, in tune with the ever-changing seasons. I felt my best self there as we became one being.

Amidst the joy, I spent the first weeks and months working through extreme anxiety around this for my daughter and all of us, wanting to know what I could do. I am still certain that the pandemic, continuing as I write, is one more symptom of our human disconnect from the natural systems.

My daughter in her mind has left now. I am excited for her and her coming adventures. I am concerned about me. My path is not clear. I will be on my own. I understand that this is my transition to a new life and I have started to be aware of some exciting possibilities.

In parallel, I see this time as the start of a great letting-go of outdated cultural norms as we hurtle towards a climate catastrophe and ecosystem breakdown. For me these mirror each other. Our culture is in an adolescent stage and that needs to move on to another stage – whether we are ready or not.

Love in the lockdown was a pause in the everyday hectic pattern of life. With it came the simplicity of life at home with its peaceful rhythms, the joy of being with my daughter, and being in our beautiful abundant, edible garden full of birds and life. The gift of a deep connection like this is precious indeed.

I will remember how simple my needs are.

Trust and Surrender
Sarah Tilley, UK

'Always say "yes" to the present moment ... surrender to what is. Say "yes" to life and see how life starts suddenly working for you rather than against you'
Eckhart Tolle

This is my story about trust and surrender.

About the agonising and unquenchable love between mother and child.

And how when time and circumstance intervene, the healing that comes brings a fresh story.

I was born into a life where love was conditional.

I was told to behave well or I would be returned to the children's home I had come from. I grew up with the injustice and unfairness of me, the child, having the role of making my mother happy.

Can you imagine the struggles a brain wired like that can wreak? The sort of confusion of existence it can lead a person into?

I haven't told many people this, but my ultimate goal in life is to have a happy family. I have a very literal image of Christmas around a roaring hearth that my family has travelled to from far and wide, a beautifully lit Christmas tree and the smell of cinnamon and pine in the air, of the room filled with nostalgia and contentment. That's my dream image of family love.

I grew up in a suburban home where both parents had lived through Second World War impoverishment. Both evacuated as children, they were sent away to the countryside without their parents, into bleak uncertainty and the dread of abandonment.

Where I grew up love was violent, communication was stonewalled and affection was non-existent. Hard work and non-materialism ruled.

With modern medicine we understand that trauma like this creates neural pathways of anxiety, and deep channels of PTSD (post-traumatic stress disorder), which are passed down through generations, shaping the same DNA through repeated patterns of behaviour, patterns of lack, and the amygdala brain in a constant state of flight or flight. Here, adrenaline and cortisol rule.

My life-long journey into unravelling and straightening out my relationship with love stems from the disassociation I conjured up as a child. My partner, my patients, the shopkeeper are all part of the practice, and I'm told the energy around me is calm and cosmic. From as early as ten years old I started reading about other people's lives. Dostoyevsky, Goethe, Anaïs Nin, Sartre, Hesse, philosophy and classic novels that gave me a peek into expression and romanticism.

My idyllic dream of Love is one I have gathered from films and books and fairy tales from all over the world.

Yet, nothing grows in a straight line. And there is one certainty, that our children are our greatest teachers.

Lockdown 2020, and this is the first time my daughter, my son and my partner of two and a half years will be living under the same roof.

Since 2015 when I asked my son to leave the house, he had vowed never to live with me again and never to live back in the family home. The vitriol between us was palpable, and it needed to change or die.

Divorce had fractured us as individuals and dispersed the family with its atomic bomb- like impact. It had clouded fifteen years of happy family stories and with no photographs to recall the good times, the fall-out became mistrust, disappointment, loneliness and isolation.

As each year passed, I could feel the grief between us all calcifying and gouging its own track of separation with which to take my family down, and it broke me in two.

As mothers we can't expect our children to love us. And it's purposeless to bend and mould ourselves to be the light in an adult child's life.

Just as we grew up and away, so do our children; the love, the bonds, are made in the fourth trimester and continue for seven years. Only.

Any personal growth of ours, or our traumas, are woven into the fabric, and the deed of raising the children is done.

Our children's lives move forward and away, towards opportunity and to the light, and it's only when they are gone that are they free to come back.

I'm nervous, as I prepare rooms and make trips to the supermarket, that the arguments and the PTSD of divorce will be too much. In my worrier-mind I'm concerned that my newish relationship will strain to bear the weight of disruption, and that my mother's guilt will spiral out of control.

It's accurate to say that love has become the thing I want to master in my lifetime.

In all its different hues, mother love, romantic love, family love, love for the community, platonic love, self-love and then spiritual love, I aim to be someone who has mastered the thing we all chase, that we all believe to be the ultimate cure.

In cold classrooms, trendy studios, yurts up dusty mountains and over Zoom, I guide individuals through the internal mind's eye into self-love.

To couples I teach that love is a verb, a set of skills, and most importantly the relationship we have with ourselves.

But here we are in May, each morning in the sunny garden in South London, drinking coffee, and encouraging each other's exercise.

As time unravels and days turn into months, we start to be able to be in the same room, we relax into a wartime habit of routine. Tentative conversations that have been buried by pain start to come out because if not now, when?

From one adult to another we talk about the truth of memory and how it plays games. We demystify mental illness in the wider family and tears are shed.

More than once I harden myself as I take the brunt of their childhood pain alone, as my own childhood buttons of shame and humiliation are pressed over and over; I know my job is to listen and acknowledge.

By July we start to appreciate each other's value, and we soften to each other's flaws. We follow rules of good communication; don't leave the room, don't raise your voice, don't argue when tired, focus on the point at hand.

More than once we have to be separated from a tailspin of angry words we didn't know had begun and that we'd forgotten the beginning of. And with each exchange there was a softening and tiredness. Let's move on to loving.

I believe each of us had an opportunity in lockdown to transform.

I learned that family love is sticking together through a storm. It's not just the fairy tale of Christmas but the reassurance after the vulnerability of a heated argument, and it's the apology for words that shouldn't have been said.

I learned that Love has a brave soul and a strong heart when it resides with abandonment. And the true love that weathers storms and thrives through separation, can, with time, deepen into unwavering tolerance for the ups and downs of life.

August, and for the first time in ten years we celebrate birthdays around the family table. These are the best birthdays ever, I'm told. Candlelit and in honour of a maturity that was suppressed and has now emerged, I embrace a gentleness that has descended and taken root. Love has transformed me and I believe its foundations are built on trust.

A Different Kind of Seeing
Robin Davies, Hong Kong

'I shut my eyes in order to see.'
Paul Gauguin

It took three years for my sight to fade into blindness seventeen years ago. Six of those years to come to terms with the situation, its limitations and vulnerabilities. My world changed completely, but I had time to prepare, adjust and accept.

The coronavirus took three months to turn from a news event into a worldwide pandemic. Then just a few months to bring many communities and economies almost to a halt.

The world had to deal with, in just months, the fundamental life changes that I had two decades to get to grips with. Everything is impacted; life, work, earnings, family, socialising, relationships, entertainment, even sports. Could my own experiences be helpful and provide some insight into this time of corona?

I thought back to the early days of being blind and a world almost without colour; blindness always associated with the colour black. Words such as blackout, black blinds, even dark rooms, no light with no sight, but I am not so sure. My eyes no longer function, both retinas destroyed, not sending signals through the optic nerves to the visual cortex. Like the Monty Python Dead Parrot sketch my eyes are gone, passed over, departed and deceased.

However, I still experience light and dark in my brain, my eyes move under my command, what I do 'see' inside my head subtly alters as I move or focus on a sound. What I see inside is not a uniform blackness; most days my inner vision sees a bright, white screen, moving or pulsing with smaller, mobile features. These shapes include multicoloured spots which alter shape and configuration, like an internal lava lamp. Occasionally it will switch to black, everything reversed, morphing from Michelangelo's clouds to Dante's Inferno, depressing me in the process.

For me, blindness is not just blackness or an absence of light and colour. Could the phrase 'Blinded by the light' speak to the same phenomena for the sighted? What we see in our visual cortex is created by the brain. Vision is learned, not instinctive like breathing or the heartbeat.

Dreams are different. I dream in colour, sound and vision, plus I can see perfectly! Now we need to dream of a corona-free future, with our world returned to a normality where we can live, love and progress. As this strange, quiet, distanced and isolated world embalms more and more of us, will dreaming of past life and possible futures become more prevalent?

I dream more since my sight ebbed away; it's the only place where I retain my vision. Landscapes brightly coloured, faces and emotions visible, the smallest detail to the furthest horizon clear. I love my dreams, all that light and colour, so much to see. The sky blue, the sun warm, with summer smells bursting into my nostrils. Squeezing eyelids tight shut I often fight to keep hold of my visions; when they are open – will it be a black or white day? A white day will let me keep my smile, the one I am certain has been there throughout my dream.

Swinging my feet out of bed, still smiling, I trail my fingers along the edge of the cupboard, on my way to the bathroom; Gulliver nuzzles my hand as I walk across the carpet, knowing my routine. Wanting to remind me that after answering my own needs I have to let him out to attend to his. The warm contact and his quiet contentment with our routine lifts my spirits and I know it will be a good day, a white day. Gulliver squeezes past my legs and bounds up the garden, a flash of my dream returns and I can see him, golden coat and feathered tail glinting in the morning sun.

Old dreams as I awake without my guide dog Gulliver, who now lives only in my memory. We miss him greatly and remember him with love and affection; I realise that, despite never seeing him, every sense in my body recalls him deeply. His low bark and soft breath, his claws clipping across the wooden floors, the smooth texture and fine grain of his thick coat, the warm long lick from his tongue, and the musky, dogginess of his scent, especially after a walk in the rain, or a swim in the Thames, all these were totally unique.

This deep memory makes me aware of how, in this time of corona, all our senses have been brought into focus. Our sight-obsessed world has begun to connect with its other neglected senses. I recall a statistic claiming that humans get over 70 per cent of input visually, leaving 30 per cent for sound, touch, taste and smell. The percentage appears high, but probable, in today's screen-fixated culture.

As our world quietened, slowed, disconnected, we gained time to become aware of these changes. The absence of aircraft overhead, little traffic noise, air tasting cleaner on our tongues, birdsong; the soundtrack of life and the clean scents of earth and flowers; sight no longer blanketing out our other subtle and evocative senses.

We need to retain and love this experience in the time of corona, as inevitably things will return to a new normal with sight once again assuming mastery. Try this experiment to examine this point:

Stand still, eyes closed, for four minutes. Discover the world around you, without sight. Choose somewhere full of normal activities. Focus on the sounds around you, listen hard and try to identify each one. People walking and talking as they pass, cars and other vehicles, city or country noises, weather sounds and the whole soundscape.

Reach out and touch something, a fabric, surface, wall, post or tree, turning as you do. Notice how different familiar objects and structures can feel if only identified by touch. Do the temperatures and perhaps sounds register in your mind? If you scrape, rub or tap them, what does the sound or vibration recall? Does describing touch bring up a different vocabulary?

Finally use the last minute to breathe in deeply, smell and taste the atmosphere. Recognise how both senses combine to help you identify what it contains, and how important memory is to the process. Smell and taste provide the quickest link to our memory banks. On opening your eyes reflect on the experience; will you pay closer attention to your other senses in future?

As a blind person I am often asked if my other senses have become enhanced, super senses? Of course not! None of my other senses have improved, and some will weaken as I age. What has changed is how much I rely on, focus and utilise them to replace the lost visual input. Sound, touch, taste and smell are the means by which I visualise, comprehend, navigate and interact with my world and the people around me.

In fact, there is now a growing awareness of the benefits of taking a break from the visual world, so prevalent and overwhelming today. Allowing us time to experience not only the unexpected benefits of focusing on our other four senses, but also a way to access our inner world of wellbeing and mindfulness.

Mindfulness, meditation and inner peace are buzzwords nowadays and many practitioners and teachers of these therapies require the visual sense to be paused, so that the 'noise' it generates in one's mind can be silenced. Perhaps blindness predisposes one for this latest way of achieving personal growth and inner harmony.

Some practitioners include instructions about reducing visual input as a way of clearing the mind and inner thoughts. For example:

Close your eyes and silence any thought.
Shut your eyes and focus on breathing.
Close your eyes, look inward to silence the mind.
With eyes closed, actively listen to sounds around you.

The last months have enabled me to try these exercises, but I don't have to work hard to shut out my vision of course!

Our lives and loves, in the time of corona, are different and challenging for everyone. I am still adjusting and adapting as the days, weeks and months pass. However, my blind life has thrown up a new experience too, despite seventeen years of blindness. It occurred on a June Saturday after a wonderful evening with friends, our first visitors after the easing of lockdown. I awoke the next morning feeling hungover and went back to bed. Got up later to an extraordinary world of vivid colours and movement. The screen behind my blind eyes transformed, instantly, magically, unexpectedly into a kaleidoscope of brightness and colour, without symmetry or pattern, more Salvador Dali than Bridget Reilly.

Was I still dreaming? Shaking my head, even tilting it back and forth the vision stayed there, even brighter and more energetic. I was not anxious, just fascinated. I felt unstable, disconnected from my body, everything was different. My normal practice of navigating by touch, familiarity and inner images was disrupted, disconcerted and distracted by the new visions in my head. Was it the food or drink last night, too little sleep, or had my eyes collapsed? No, all was OK, something else was happening. I sat on the edge of the bed and focused on what my brain was creating. I grinned, realising this is what many alternative therapists asked: 'Look into yourself to find inner truths and revelations,' an instruction my ever rational and practical mind had always resisted.

What was I seeing? Vivid colours swirling in a pool of bright greens; blues and yellows mostly, the colours on the surface of an oil slick, but catching the light differently with each movement. Not flat but effervescent activity, pulsating rhythmically and changing colour and tone. Above the pulsing colours was something else, difficult to describe. A moving network of line drawing, some natural objects, trees, people, buildings and animals, plus many non-identifiable items or outlines. Everything moved energetically, ghost outlines dancing crazily and appearing and disappearing magically. Far too much for my brain! I lay down again and slept some more.

Waking up later my usual white screen was safely back. The amazing colour and movement show had gone – will it ever return? I was grateful for the experience, but thankful for the return of normality.

This time of corona has made me grateful for all that I love, what I am, what I have and cherish. In particular:

Being alive right now with the health and mental ability to participate in life.
For my amazing partner, Chowee Leow, the love of my life.
For all who treat me as a capable individual, notwithstanding my blindness.
For our beautiful home, where we find peace, joy, respite and security.

For finances sufficient to provide for a good life and an unknown future.
For my country, despite its flaws and failings, where I prefer to live out my life.
For a society which accepts my life choices and allows me to live freely.

All this has enabled me to live calmly and to accept my blindness as a state of being, capable of loving and being loved. Also, to learn that being without vision can provide other insights and life lessons, for me one of the most significant being my state of Colour Blindness, which I have tried to encapsulate in a short poem.

A Colour-Blind World

Hands that caress and lips that kiss, feel no colour.
Words whispered to an ear or heart, carry no sound of colour.
Tongues exploring a mouth or body, taste no colour.
Scents arousing memories and yearnings bear no trace of colour.
Eyes shut, let your senses reveal the world's reality,
The blind truth, we are one colour, named Humanity!

'Where Do I Come From?'
Linda Sinclair, UK

'Whatever you can do, or dream you can, begin it.
Boldness has genius, power and magic in it.'
Johann Wolfgang von Goethe

This is a story of hope, some sadness, the sense of belonging and most of all, love. Alongside this story is also the message, never give up hope of finding what you may be looking for, even if it means some sadness thrown in the mix or some of it does not turn out quite as you expected or hoped. In this case, despite some sadness and initial disappointment, love was waiting at the end of this very long, but worthwhile journey ...

My partner Richard has spent most of his life wondering where he came from and who his biological father was. All he knew about his past were sketchy details from his mother. A brief romance in the early sixties culminated in his biological father disappearing when he heard of my partner's potential existence. They were young and naïve, so there was never any bitterness, anger or resentment towards either parent. These things happened, especially in the early sixties.

All Richard knew was that his father might be Italian, or possibly Greek. Even that could not be fully confirmed as there were obvious signs of embarrassment – even perhaps some shame – from his mother whenever the subject was broached. Not wishing to cause his mother, or even his wonderful new stepfather who eventually came into his life, any additional pain or anguish, the subject was eventually dropped.

So for nearly sixty years, my partner has continued with his life. The eldest of five, his half-siblings never really mentioned the curiosity that might have existed, from the obvious difference in skin colour alone. That said, my partner always felt deep down that some distance did exist between them – not when they were all very young, but as they grew older. One sibling in particular made painful comments to my partner when his stepfather died suddenly, saying he was not Richard's *real* father anyway. That comment alone led them to stop speaking for nearly five years. Until that point Richard was indeed deeply loved by his mother and the stepfather who had actually married his mother just before Richard was born.

Through his teenage years in particular my partner also experienced his own personal pain outside the family, involving racism, mainly from the ignorance of others. He also told me that during his childhood, he was sometimes embarrassed when walking with his family, on family holidays, for example. He said he would sometimes purposely fall behind the walking group so it was not too noticeable that he looked different from the rest of the family.

As time passed, I urged him to get some more information from his mother, before it was too late. My partner's interest was rekindled; he really wanted to find out where he came from, perhaps even to find his father and get to know him. Unfortunately, his mother was still not forthcoming.

It was actually the Ancestry genealogy website that ultimately paved the way to finding some of the answers my Richard had been looking for all those years. It led to a DNA test which ultimately led him to two half-brothers, who had absolutely no idea of his existence. One is forty years old, the other is fifty.

The sad news Richard was to learn was that his biological father had in fact died of a serious heart problem two years previously. Initially of course, on hearing this, Richard was devastated, as this meant he would never get to meet his father. What Richard did not know at the time though, was that his two Greek Cypriot brothers, who live and work in London, would welcome him with open arms and offer him the welcome, warmth and love Richard had always longed for from a family. They have still not been able to meet, due to Covid-19. However, the message exchanges between all three of them over social media are heart-warming to read. Those messages radiate that real and complete family connection Richard always longed for.

Seeing a picture of Richard's father for the first time, we saw a handsome young man staring back at us. This man looked *exactly* like Richard. We shed tears of sadness – and joy. It was overwhelming.

Yes, Covid continues to get in the way of meeting his brothers and his extended family. But he is fine about it. He has waited this long, so what's another few months? All good things are worth waiting for, aren't they? Love finds a way and conquers all in the end. A new chapter is about to begin in Richard's life at the age of sixty, a chapter that will hopefully be full of many good things. For him, the most important thing will be that feeling of belonging, no longer having to walk behind the family group because he feels he looks different. Now, at last, Richard knows EXACTLY where he comes from.

What a Time to Become a Granny!
Fiona Parker, UK

'When a child is born, so is a grandmother.'
Anonymous

Oh, the plans we made when my son and his partner told me they were having a baby!

Her family live in Lithuania, meaning she was counting on me for support and advice when she didn't know what to do, and I felt honoured to be asked to help. I arranged flexible annual leave from work so I could go up to London at the drop of a hat and stay with them when they needed me.

Little Leah was born in April, mid-lockdown, in a London hospital full of Covid cases. The plan to give birth in a midwife-led centre, as so many birth plans before, had to be abandoned, and labour was induced two weeks after the baby was due. Mum's temperature shot up inexplicably during the long difficult labour, leading to both her and Leah being given antibiotics intravenously.

My son looked happy but slightly bewildered holding his little girl in his arms for the first time, surrounded by machines and tubes, with no other family member to hold his hand and say, all will be well. He was not allowed back into the hospital after the birth and could only support his bruised and battered partner and daughter by phone.

Travel restrictions ruled out a trip to London, so I sent flowers and chocolates to express my socially distanced love and begin my virtual grannyhood. Meanwhile my son sent pictures and videos, which I'd watch over and over again.

I'd had a bottle of pink champagne on ice ready to toast the birth with family and friends, but that wasn't possible any more in a socially distanced world. It seemed a strange and slightly sad way to celebrate, all alone in my house. Thank God for the internet! I opened the bottle at the same time as the other granny opened a bottle a thousand miles away in Lithuania and we toasted the new baby together via Zoom.

We were both worried about mum and baby, with no real explanation about the long and difficult birth. Old mums like to go over the difficulties of labour and childbirth in minute detail with new mums and tell all the horror stories that we didn't dare to tell before the birth. The grannies shared stories with each other instead and speculated on what could have happened.

My granddaughter and I eventually met for the first time in June. With a Cheshire cat smile I sent the first photo of us together to friends and family, hoping that I wasn't being irresponsible by driving to London and bringing back potential virus carriers in the car. Luckily, the June heatwave meant we were able to keep windows open and spend most of the time in the garden, as little Leah got her first taste of the glorious Devon countryside and spent time with her aunty who was expecting Leah's cousin.

Little Leah reacts to me with smiles and giggles on the phone: the main way she has interacted with everyone except her mum and dad since she was born. Is this going to be our main way of communicating from now on? I hope not. I want to hold her and play with her like grannies used to do.

It's now September and my second grandchild has just been born. Yesterday I wet the baby's head together with his other granny. Baby Charlie is part of my family 'social bubble' so I'm going to hold him and kiss him every chance I get. My close family now consists of four parents, one grandparent and two babies. The new 'rule of six' means that in theory we can't all be together, unless we move to Wales. We'll see how that pans out. Time to search for a Welsh holiday let!

I Dream of Being What I Was

Joanna Crowson, Spain

'To be alive in this beautiful, self-organizing universe – to participate in the dance of life with senses to perceive it, lungs that breathe it, organs that draw nourishment from it – is a wonder beyond words.'
Joanna Macy

My first grandchild, Hannah, was born on 4 August 2019. I took one look at that tiny vulnerable baby and my heart swelled with tenderness, with love and fury, and with a resolute firmness that took me by surprise. For most of my adult life, I have been involved in environmental activism in one way or another; also I live in an eco-home we built ourselves that is off-grid and based on permaculture principles. But I suddenly felt like I was on the front line of imminent danger, and that I couldn't face my death without feeling I'd done everything I could to guarantee a decent future for Hannah.

I felt a fierce responsibility for a child that I didn't have to rear – leaving me free to fight in her name. I had been watching Extinction Rebellion with interest from a distance, and felt a real connection to the movement's demands, to its creativity, its non-violence and to its call for the creation of regenerative cultures. So I spoke to two close friends, Caroline and Andrew, and we got down to work to bring at least some aspects of the rebellion to our community.

In August 2019 we formed *XR La Janda* – our local chapter – in a rural area of Spain, about as far south as you can get and still be in Europe. We started giving 'Road to Extinction' talks in the autumn. In December we formed *La Janda por el Climato* to bring local collectives together to work on the same issues. We got motions passed to declare the Climate Emergency in two of our councils in early

March 2020, as well as a motion to implement *Vejer Sin Plásticos*, a campaign to reduce plastic use.

We were working full steam ahead toward a big demo for World Water Day at the end of March. Here, we planned to mark a dotted blue line through the coastal town of Barbate showing the levels of flooding predicted for 2050. We also had funding and volunteers in place to make a short video about a drained wetland, a one-day festival of regenerative culture, and a weekend of actions to defend biodiversity, culminating in the creation of a Life Cairn. The plan was to take a welcome break in July and hang out on the beach to recover while preparing for the next wave of action. In short, XR La Janda was really starting to get going when Covid-19 erupted onto the scene.

So the break came sooner than we'd planned, and was absolute – demo cancelled, everything else postponed until further notice, lots of time to think as we entered one of the strictest lockdowns in Europe. The leaflets for the demo arrived and went under the bed, the spray paint and flags went into the shed, and I used the sudden gift of time to make the ten Red Brigade costumes we needed for the video, as well as finishing off the costumes for the *Three Beings of La Janda* and working on the script. That done, I settled down to run lengths up and down our track, feeling grateful that I don't live in a flat, and that my track is long enough to be able to run up and down it without going totally mad.

In a way that was an act of love in itself – in an area with no cases of Covid-19, it felt a little mad to observe the lockdown so strictly. On the other hand, what of collective responsibility? And solidarity? There are no easy answers to this, everyone has to find their own way, but I opted to respect the spirit of the collective price to be paid to protect the health system nationally.

When the lockdown was lifted and groups were allowed to meet again in the outdoors, we went to the former Laguna de La Janda to film our video. This area used to be one of Europe's largest and most important wetlands, until it was drained during the dictatorship and the land leased to the wealthy Domecq family. At its full extent, the wetland covered as much as 50 km^2 and was a key point on the annual migratory route through the Strait of Gibraltar. It was a unique ecosystem and had been an oasis of biodiversity since the time of the last glaciation, confirmed by the many caves featuring cave art starring numerous animals.

The Laguna is a beautiful site where land and water still merge during rainy times with a soundtrack created by water, the winds rushing through the Strait and the rustle of birds and vegetation. Today, the ancient wetland is a green desert, managed purely for profit. It is still home to large bird populations including some important, rare species; protected in other places, here they take advantage of any channel or hiding place where there is water to nest, with no protected status whatsoever.

Wetlands are some of the planet's most fragile, most biodiverse and most threatened spaces. They protect the coasts from extreme weather events, forming a shield for the 60 per cent of humanity that lives and works along the coast. They reduce floods, mitigate droughts, absorb and store carbon. And Covid-19 is a timely reminder that when we destroy nature, we destroy the systems that support human life, exposing our communities to the increased spread of pathogens. In rural areas the work to mitigate the climate and ecological emergency we are facing must involve protecting what remains, while rebuilding healthy, resilient and biodiverse ecosystems from which nature can resurge. The title of our video is I Dream of Being What I Was, and this recognises a simple truth about nature – it will collaborate in its recovery if we can get to it in time. Link to the video: https://youtu.be/qIVDzR3sZ0s

The on-location filming with our group of volunteers was a moving experience. We met and gathered in silence, enjoying the feeling of being out in a wide-open space with a group of people, after so long in reduced spaces with just our family or housemates. After a short moment connecting with the lost Laguna and what it might want to say through us, we opened our eyes to look up and found a group of glossy ibis flying low overhead. It felt like a magical welcome. Filming can feel a little absurd, repeating things over and over while trying to look natural – but we had very little time, so in fact everything we did was fairly spontaneous and improvised, and no doubt all the better for it.

The Red Brigade spread out, creating points of colour in the land, like drops of blood in nature, or grouped together creating impactful images. *Ibis Eremita* (bald ibis) became a natural leader, *Lentisco* (mastic tree) often went still and almost unnoticed and *Ciervo* (stag) naturally stood apart, like a sceptical, wary observer of protest. For us in XR La Janda, the Red Brigade is an act of love and an act of beauty. Internationally the movement was started by the Invisible Circus during the nineties to protest against the war in Iraq, and it joined Extinction Rebellion in April 2019. It represents the blood shared by all species – what unites us and makes us one. For me, its presence in any demo or protest represents an act of poetic activism that aims to impact on the feelings of participants and observers.

As the Red Brigade comes together, we try to act as one, we connect to our surroundings, and from our silence we move very slowly and express emotions such as love, joy, sadness, grief, anger, fury and so on, in response to the climate and ecological emergency. We often seem to provoke a feeling of strangeness, and that feels important, because it's actually very strange that we have normalised such huge levels of destruction. Our action is simple, uncomplicated – we just try to be present and perceive feelings, so that others can feel again. We represent the silent voice of the living world – the presence of nature defending itself.

And the pandemic continues to make itself felt. What do you do when the traditional format of mass protest becomes impossible and yet danger looms? Because the window of opportunity is closing, and more and more biodiversity is lost, emissions continue to rise, and the danger is that the current economic fallout from the health crisis will drown out the bigger future problem and we will miss our chance. Here in Andalusia, the right-wing regional government is using the economic situation as an excuse to push through massive deregulation of land protection. It's being challenged, but if the government is successful, we will witness an increase in the speed of environmental destruction not seen for twenty years.

Covid-19 is a disruption, an uncomfortable reminder of what the natural world can throw at us; a huge rock thrown into the pond of 'normal life', creating ripples and making waves that move outwards in every direction. In Spain everyone talks about the 'new normal', but there is no safe new normal waiting for us. If there's one thing climate science has made clear, it's that other disruptions are on the horizon.

In Spain, the pandemic stopped us in our tracks, and we must use the time and space to reboot. We can't stand by and wait for governments to accept the truth and rebuild in the direction we need, so within the limitations placed on gathering, we are using the Red Brigade to create moments of connection to the Earth, moments of artful protest, moments of sublime, poetic beauty that arise from our love and our fury. Perhaps they are meaningless acts of random and ephemeral beauty, but I see they provoke and I know they have impact.

The pandemic and the resulting lockdown gave us some space and some silence, and this is vital for the creation of change. Likewise, the silence of the Red Brigade is an opportunity to those in costume – the mind stills, there is no justification; there are no words, no explanations, no argument. There is just presence. And I receive this stillness of the mind as love from nature.

Love comes into the experience in other ways too – both giving and receiving. We lovingly help each other to stay in role, to not get distracted, and to not feel hurt, annoyed or criticised when one of our fellow rebels calls us back to presence, or reminds us to slow down. We offer our sweat as we move fully robed under the sun.

We lovingly offer our time, and our doubt and uncertainty as we improvise within an action. We recognise that when we leave space, nature acts through us and what is created is so much more than we planned; and we receive this as loving participation from the animate Earth. For me, this shamanic element is what carries us beyond even the artful beauty of love and fury, into the territory of hope – for Hannah, for humanity and for the living planet.

Going Back to Normal?
Kim Henry, USA

'Today our very survival depends on our ability to stay awake, to adjust to new ideas, to remain vigilant and to face the challenge of change.'
Martin Luther King Jr

Going back to Normal?

As painful as this is ... no thank you.

It was never normal to me that governments profit from selling weapons and then we belittle our brothers and sisters running from falling bombs, scrambling off tiny boats with their children in their arms.

It was never normal to me to keep animals in cages and squeeze thousands of them into darkened spaces, left standing in their own shit and pumped with chemicals, so that we can eat their dead flesh.

It was never normal to me that we allow big pharma to put a price on living and to patent a cure, or that we poison the earth to grow the food that is supposed to nourish us.

It was never normal to me that we live by the fabricated existence of money to the point where people starve while others gorge, millions of lives lived in misery and fear, because they cannot access enough or they can access too much of this made-up thing.

We are the only animal that 'pays' to live on this earth.

It was never normal to me that we make the water toxic and believe justice has been served because those companies – just other humans who also have children and parents and sisters – pay a 'fine' with that made-up thing – ha! We cannot wash in it any more than we can drink it.

It was never normal to me that we define some love as right and other love as wrong.

It was never normal to me that just because I happened to arrive on this planet in a place we name the UK and not in a place we call Syria or Palestine or Libya, I am (was) somehow allowed to move more freely.

It was never normal to me that humans with differing pigmentation in their skin have to fight harder for respect or that humans with different body parts will be considered less just because.

It was never normal to me that we know, because we can be quite knowing at times, that there is no such thing as throwing something away and yet we continue to consume the plastic and the take-out cartons and the upgraded iPhones and the and the and the …

It was never normal to me that we hug the dogs and eat the cows, and that we point fingers at those who do it differently …

THERE IS NO DIFFERENCE – dog, fish, chicken … bat.

The never-normal-to-me list goes on and on and on.

I often wonder at us all, scurrying around this miraculous planet, somehow believing we are above it, or outside of it. That there would be no consequences to our actions.

Forgetting the fundamental truth that this earth, this tiny planet, this magical speck in just one arm of maybe millions, or billions of solar systems, will be just fine without us.

But that we depend on her for our very existence.

What kind of creature destroys that which it relies upon for life?

That which is so abundant and profound and connected and intelligent and cosmic.

My mind never could wrap itself around it all so back to my heart space I go … back to the hip-shakin' tunes, to the space-makin' movements, to the hug-holdin' of loved ones, to the child's sweet play, to the sun's blissful shining, to the moon's wild glow, to the delicious skin on skin, to the red, red wine and the songs of divine peace, and I wonder … I wonder and I hope, oh so very much … that our children may live a Very Different Normal.

Like a Rock
Anna Begas, Spain

'To the mind that is still the whole universe surrenders'
Lao Tzu

I live in the south of Spain, a single mum, with my two children aged three and nine.

A year ago I separated from the father of my youngest child, and the children and I moved to a house a bit further away from the community, in a very rocky place. It was the house that called to me most.

It has been a year in which I processed a lot of my personal issues. In which I processed a lot of the pain around loving a man who is struggling with the illness of addiction. A year in which I stood by and witnessed him spiralling further down to the point of rock-bottom. And time after time I could do nothing but surrender it all to a higher wisdom. A year in which I looked after myself and my children, the best I could. And a year in which I also learnt what it really means to love someone unconditionally.

Being a single mum is intense. It requires boundless discipline; it requires tapping into the inner strength you never knew you had. It was a challenge just to get the daily routine done. To keep the children well looked after and happy, to keep the money coming in, to keep my work flowing, while also dealing with the emotions around all the changes we went through.

And then lockdown came upon us some day in March 2020, and it lasted three months. Three months homebound with two children.

At first, both my children were ill, and especially my daughter took a while to get better. My phone was going crazy with messages about Covid symptoms, and she was showing all of them, including the breathing difficulties. We couldn't get her tested, so I didn't know whether this was Covid or another strong flu. Taking her healing in our own hands, we went to talk to the mullein plants here at the riverbed, to ask for help, and I made her a chest rub with mullein, plantain and garlic. Along with mega doses of vitamin C, suddenly she turned a corner. She started to cough up mucus, the fever went down, and her breathing normalised.

We celebrated, dancing through the living room, and my stress and tension finally dropped.

Soon after that, a very dear and important elder in my life died. He was a wise man and had been an important fatherly figure to me. And although he had announced his death already a year before, it still came unexpectedly, as he had been so strong and full of life. Now the virus had taken him so quickly and silently.

Meanwhile many WhatsApp and Facebook groups were filling the empty spaces with strong opinions, critical questions, doubts, anger and distrust. I live in a very alternative and rebellious community. There was no fear of Covid, but rather fear of conspiracies and corruption.

In these tender moments of grief and wonder, I could not connect to any of it. And I decided to step out of all the groups and discussions.

For me, the world just stopped.

Compared to other families in cities and towns in Spain, we were blessed. There was no police control in the area where we live, and so we could go out every day on our illegal clandestine adventures.

So far, I had rebelled against living in such a lonely rocky place. I had complained of the lack of children around. I felt that I needed more support, more community. And as tree planting had been my new love and passion, I felt I wanted trees. I longed for trees. I needed to calm my eyes and my heart with the colour green. The repetitive complaint in my head was 'where is the support when I need it'? Yet I knew in a deeper place inside myself, beyond my complaints and rebellions, that we were placed in this rocky area for a good reason. And the lockdown gave us time to discover our support in the landscape around us.

Day after day we explored the rocky rocks on the rocks. The ticking of the clock was replaced by the whispers and rumbles of our bodies, who told us when we needed to eat and when we needed to rest. We spent days picking thyme and rosemary. We made sandcastles next to the river. We created spiral art from different coloured stones. On rainy days we traversed our boredom to find our creativity. And together we managed many boundary tests, many emotions, many toddler rebellions, and pre-teenage moods.

I applied survival techniques when needed. Like YouTube movies for the children. And I became an expert in short and powerful meditations to find my way back to my guidance and my connection, on the toilet! As that was the only time and place where I could have a moment alone.

We also celebrated life with pancakes for breakfast, chocolate-cake picnics, collecting herbs for tea and medicines, and we crowned ourselves with flowers; which we called corona-flores, instead of coronavirus.

Because I now had time, I could really pass through the grief of my personal losses. And with that, through the pure joy and awe of being alive. Feeling the veil between life and death so thin, I felt more present than ever.

And in that space of presence, I started hearing the voices of the stones, the rocks, the mountain. The voices of the dear ones that passed away, taken by the virus. The voices of my spirit guides that became clearer; they kept guiding me away from all the outer noise, and into the silent mountain, or onto the rocky riverbed.

> And as there was nowhere else to look
> Spirit became visible
> And as there was no one to greet me
> Spirit guides became my companions
> And as there was no one to talk to
> I started to listen to the rocks
>
> They showed me
> How I am part of the whole

They taught me of ancient memory
Kept inside my cells

They taught me about digging deep
To find my own strength

They allowed me to crumble inside
While I still stood as a mountain

They taught me about standing strong
And knowing who I am

They said I have always been here
And they taught me how to walk
Without forgetting
that I have always been here

And in doing so they radiated back to me
the warmth of the sun
During the darkest nights

And now the quarantine has eased up a bit, but we seem to only be at the beginning of this big collective crisis. My newfound community of rocks shows me how to be stable and firm, during these very challenging and uncertain times.

These stones tell me that I too, am the mountain.

And I am grateful to be alive at these times of great transformation. I don't know what will come out of these times, but I know that I am ready. I am ready to connect to my soul's purpose. I know that all I need is already inside of me. And I walk through life, remembering who I am. So that I can take part in the writing of a new story. For my children. And for all of life on Earth.

Expecting the Unexpected
Cathy Stanton, UK

'And suddenly you know: it's time to start something new and trust the magic of beginnings.'
Meister Eckhart

For most people the major events of 2020 might seem like a bad dream, or a B-rated sci-fi movie with a totally confusing plot, far too many threads leading to literal dead ends and no sense of possible resolution. As a child of the fifties I was brought up to fear the threat of nuclear war and I did have many 'end of the world' dreams well into my teens – until the dreams transformed in the late sixties and early seventies into (sometimes drug-induced) fantasies of a new world order, where peace prevailed and we all learned to live in loving harmony with each other and nature. We sought 'love and light' and grew into adults with alternative lifestyles.

But I saw the reality of failing systems, environmental damage and the dire consequences of increasing global population. As a spiritual seeker I read Nostradamus and learnt about the Mayan calendar. Whilst hoping for peaceful transformation with the coming Age of Aquarius, like others I expected something BIG and BAD to happen. 2012 (the predicted world's end) came and went, but the signs were increasing, each new catastrophe further challenged us, each viral epidemic, environmental disaster, war, and failing governmental system added to the endless list of disasters and the sense that this could not go on, something had to give.

So I was waiting for and indeed, expecting something very big to happen. And here we are, with a 'pandemic' that is enabling governments, through fear, to control and lockdown their citizens to a degree that would have been totally unimaginable before the publishing of *1984*. The world as we knew it, ended.

From a spiritual perspective – where I stand as a healer and therapist working with the human energy field and dimensional energy – the shadow side of all that is happening on this amazing, wonderful planet is gradually being exposed for the light to shine on, uncover and ultimately dissolve the dirt. Many levels of corruption and mismanagement are being revealed and we have for the first time in our knowledge of the world's history the ability and opportunity to communicate everything to almost everyone on this planet! But communication is now at the very centre of the mess we find ourselves in, for who – or what – are we to believe?

With conspiracy theories muddling fact and fiction and lies being told at every level, often backed up by the media according to political or corporate agendas, it is no longer sensible to even try and discern truth in what we see or hear. So we have to listen to our own inner truth – this is the only place we will find a sense of peace. Now more than ever we need to go deep inside and open our hearts and listen to what that beat is saying in our innermost being. When we feel that inner truth we can seek out others whose hearts beat to that same rhythm and surround ourselves with a loving community of those who uplift us and support us in our sense of what is right.

Here is where listening to my heart got me …

My first instinct during the lockdown in England was to move out of central Brighton, an area that for some time I had felt was too edgy and not conducive to my work from home as a healer. This involved flat-hunting during lockdown, aided by my adult children. They had come down from London to support me in the care of my elderly father. The idea was they did my shopping and my father's shopping and I – who supposedly was avoiding contact with everyone – delivered the shopping to my father who lived a short drive away. The reality was that I had the true joy of having my children back home with me for the first time in years – and I delivered the heavy items to my maverick ninety-two year old father, who continued to shop for himself and walk miles when and where he wanted!

The truly unexpected aspect of the lockdown, however, was that I and my long-distance partner were forcibly separated for months. He has a cottage in

Wales in a remote village where he has lived for over thirty years, and we used to come and go, spending time in each other's abodes, enjoying the joint benefits of city life in coastal southern England, and the rural delights of Pembrokeshire – peace, fresh air and rain. He was not too keen on permanent city life and I am a bit of a sun-seeker. As an asthma sufferer and pensioner, it was sensible for my partner Paul to remain in the relative safety of village life. I was called by a sense of duty and love of family to stay close to my father and children.

So my heart led me from Kemptown to a delightful setting in Brighton marina, the sun shone, my daughter got a decent tan sunbathing on the patio, my dog Pickle thrived on long beach walks, and it was sometimes easy to shut out the reality of a world gone crazy. But my heart spoke again. Having lived in six different countries, given birth to my children in Sri Lanka, travelled to various parts of Africa and the Americas following my path, I remembered that I had always wanted to live in Spain. My first trip alone abroad was to Andalucia in Spain and I fell in love with the country and the energy of the people. I had given birth to my daughter dancing to the sounds of flamenco on my headphones! My feet were itching to tread on Spanish soil and I just knew I had to go.

Paul and I had done a recce in Spain just before Brexit in 2016. I found my perfect *cortijo* smallholding in Orgiva, Andalucia, but overnight the new exchange rate put the property out of my price range. It didn't come as a total surprise to Paul or my children when I announced I was moving to Spain. I didn't spend too long worrying about the thought I was leaving a sinking ship – after all, I am a citizen of Europe and the world having lived and worked in many different countries. Leaving my father and children was the biggest tug and one I am dealing with daily. Paul, love him, was persuaded to follow me and my heart.

The practicalities involved three short dashes to Spain, self-isolating back in Wales and hours on the internet looking for properties. The plan was to move early December with our three dogs – Paul had Pickle's two puppies; we had to get them vaccinated and [get?] pet passports, there was so much to do to beat the transition deadline if we were all to be able to move to Spain as Europeans! We were not alone though and discovered many Brits who were following this path to

Europe before the deadline. Then came the threat of further lockdowns and a rush decision to make a dash for Spain whilst we still could. Paul and the pups got out of Wales the night before lockdown and I changed our sailing to leave the week before the second lockdown began in England. No turning back!

We drove down through France and Spain in our old T4 VW camper van, Paul, me and the three dogs, thrown together by love and our circumstances, feeling like refugees, but knowing how much easier our passage was than it is for huge numbers of others – for whom it often really is a matter of life, or death.

We find ourselves in a Spanish lockdown, specific to regions and the high incidence of infection influenced by the large bustling city of Granada. It will be a while before I can pay my fifth visit to the fabulous romantic Alhambra palace, to show Paul one of the reasons I felt called by Spain and Andalucia.

We are surrounded by beautiful countryside and a sub-tropical micro-climate that nourishes me into a sense of wellbeing. I love it here, and my love for this land has brought me and my long-distance partner, plus Pickle and her two puppies, together – at least for the time being.

Love, Liberty and the Pursuit of Science
Charlie Griffiths, Spain

*'Nothing in life is to be feared, it is only to be understood.
ow is the time to understand more so that we may fear less'*
Marie Curie

We have been here so many times before. So easy to forget, so crucial to recall. War, hunger and disease have been the three monstrous recurring spectres haunting the lives of our ancestors. Hunger is still an avoidable and inexcusable curse in a wealthy world, but has dramatically diminished in the last century. Wars, too, though as repellently cruel as they have ever been, have tended to become less prevalent in recent years. And plagues and a legion of preventable illnesses have killed huge swathes with sickening and inexorable regularity. Until very recently, there seemed no hope of vanquishing these pestilential tyrants. And then, in 1797, Edward Jenner's discovery of a vaccine to combat smallpox ushered in an era of steady and beneficent medical advances, which, given vision and political will, are set to consign the great viral and bacterial killers of history to oblivion.

While cribbed, cabined and confined I have spent much time reflecting on these things. And on the role of pure luck, the remarkable and utterly fluky good fortune of my life; and on how the poverty of luck afflicts billions of my fellow creatures. Born at the close of the murderous carnage of World War Two, I have never known hunger or hopelessness, or been compelled by wars to kill other men and women. I have never been abused, neglected or unloved. I am inexpressibly grateful to all those who have gifted me this providential life.

And now I still find love around me and am never utterly alone or bereft of the milk of human affection. And yet I know that the unmerited great good fortune which has attended my life is missing, and needlessly missing, in the lives of so many of my nearly eight billion fellow humans.

Love cannot be easily legislated for or prescribed by society and politics. But some of the material and social conditions for it certainly can. Poor and sick and starving people, women forced by poverty and oppressive ideologies to bear many children in dire circumstances, are all less likely to be able to give their offspring or each other the love they need.

But liberty and humanitarian science are utterly different matters. They can be, and are, directly created by our social and political actions. Here are two proofs of this:

During my first sixty-five years of life I witnessed more lives saved by medical science than had been wantonly lost in the horrors of the two great wars, the genocides and all the other crimes against humanity that wars perpetrated in the twentieth century. Between 300 and 500 million people were rescued from horrible and premature deaths caused by smallpox, by one vaccine alone. And now we are in sight of the eradication of measles, polio and potentially all the viruses that have plagued us for so long. Black Lives Matter, and it is the very poorest people and children on the face of the Earth, most especially in sub-Saharan Africa, who desperately need saving from the scourge of preventable disease. The half a million senseless deaths from malaria, the 120,000 African children killed by measles each year ... these weigh like a nightmare on our consciences, and should weigh most awfully on the conscience of the science deniers and vaccine refusers who are contributing to this unspeakable suffering.

And liberty: there is more freedom in the world than ever before, despite the permanent threats it faces. Freedom of speech, of religion, freedom from slavery and want ... all have advanced most wonderfully in my lifetime ... though there is still a long and often desperate journey ahead.

Most people of my age in the wealthy world now owe a significant part of their longevity to medical science, to infrastructures which provide them with accessible health care, clean water and so on. It is these advances that make it possible to say that, since the Enlightenment of the eighteenth century, real progress in human health and happiness has become, for the very first time in the 150,000-year history of *Homo sapiens*, possible and, for most of us on the planet, real.

And now, as we reflect on the great river of history bearing us on and on, and in the midst of a global crisis of health and wellbeing, we have a unique and unparalleled chance to seize the progress of science and to divert the river towards welfare and hope. Never in the course of time has science been so absolutely central and publicised as crucial to our better futures. A huge international commitment to develop and administer vaccines could spell the end of virus-related deaths. And the newly polished prestige of scientific endeavour could deal an intensely needed blow to the quackery of science denial, and its associated charlatanisms of evolution, climate change and vaccine denial. These conspiracist fantasies pose perhaps the biggest threat ever to life and liberty and love on our planet.

But there must be a burning hope in the hearts of all of us well-wishing humanophiles that the world will emerge finally from the dark ages of myopic nationalism and puerile egotism, to an era when love, liberty and benign science will come into their own, and make our grandchildren celebrate with pride what great good has been achieved in their own lifetimes.

The grand sweep of our history has been a tale of unfreedom. Lack of liberty, no science, and a paucity of love. Everything that has most affected our lives has lain beyond our control. Our birth, our circumstances, our beliefs, our nutrition, our health.

For much of human life until the decline of intolerant religion began in the eighteenth century, even adults exercised their freedom to choose their beliefs on pain of torture and death. But, with the certainty of new pandemics assured, we have the chance to roll back some of these unfreedoms and, at the very least, prevent premature death from disease.

'Do no harm' should be replaced by 'Do proven good'. We all now know what this requires. Strong, affordable, accessible health-care systems in every country. Massive, coordinated research into vaccines and life-saving drugs, and huge educational programmes to confound the irrationalism of science denial. And a new zeal to implement the policies that have been proven by the lives they have saved (20 million children preserved from death by the measles vaccines alone since 2000).

Whatever the scale of the economic misery Covid may inflict, the world CAN easily afford these remarkably cheap, safe and effective measures. Indeed, the world cannot afford not to embrace them. Let us have faith that humanity and reason will prevail and that we are ready for the next viral onslaught, defended by love, liberty and the pursuit of science.

And let us also not forget the extraordinarily privileged time we live in. For the first time in our history we may well have a vaccine which protects us all, and will quite conceivably eradicate the virus completely, only a few years after the appearance of the pestilence. Science is not a cold companion. It is a warm, dependable and proven ally of humanity in our quest to care for one another. Grasp with gratitude the privileges that knowledge and freedom have bestowed on us. Seize the day, seize the chance!

And a Black Cloud Came

Darrie Payne

Translating Covidian
Arpy Shively, Spain

*'For last year's thoughts belong to last year's language,
and next year's words await another voice.'*
T.S. Eliot, Four Quartets

As Covid-19 reshapes our lives, a wave of new and repurposed words is helping us connect over shared experiences, fears and hopes. And it's more important than ever to choose our words, because the way we think, talk and act during this pandemic can make us part of the hurt – or part of the healing.

In the first New Year of a new decade, the unfamiliar words start to appear, a trickle becoming a wave. From China, from a *wet market* in Wuhan, the *contagion* spreads *human-to-human*. A *'novel coronavirus'* is born. Soon, the virus has travelled to Europe, with at least one *super-spreader* holidaying at an Austrian ski resort infecting dozens, who go on to infect hundreds more. Thousands more. Millions more.

The *epidemic* is now a *pandemic*. Italy is the first to announce a nationwide *lockdown*. Soon, a condition only used to control prison riots or mass shootings has become a household word. Spain best captures the mood, launching a *'State of Alarm'* that has lasted to this day.

With no sign of a *vaccine*, the world goes into *quarantine*. People in villages, towns and cities are ordered to *'stay at home'* and *'shelter in place'*. *Self-i-solate*. *Hands, face, space* as vital as *test, track, trace*. Without adequate supplies of *PPE*, health and care workers die disproportionately, especially those who are *BAME*. Globally, GDP and the economy are on the danger list. *Eat out to help out*, says UK chancellor of the exchequer, Rishi Sunak, inviting everyone to dinner. But his recipe for a *'V-shaped recovery'* contributes to a V-shaped *surge* in new infections. *Tiers 1, 2 and 3* mean job losses, especially in the arts and hospitality. We can't go anywhere but we can *Zoom* everywhere. In order to *'flatten the curve'*, we stay home, comfort eat and *'fatten the curve'* instead. In fact, some of us positively *bubble*.

Almost overnight, *masks, hand sanitiser* and *disinfectant* are the must-have accessories if you want to avoid being named, blamed and *socially shamed* as a *Covidiot*. Fortunate or *furloughed* workers can *WFH* (work from home), but many key workers or gig-economy workers don't have the luxury of *social distancing*. They are forced to join an unplanned mass experiment in *herd immunity*.

Everywhere, *curfews* curtail conviviality, so we stay home, *binge-watch* series on *Netflix,* pour ourselves another *quarantini*. *Pharmaceuticals* become household names: *dexamethasone, remdesivir,* and (deep breath) *hydroxychloroquine. Moderna, Astra Zeneca,* and *Pfizer/ BioNTech* vie for bronze, silver and gold in the race to erase the virus.

Clearly, Covid-19 must be the enemy. Science, medicine and our brave *health workers* (*clap* for them!) are the heroes, are the troops on the *front line*. *'We are at war,'* says French president Emmanuel Macron. *'Save India,'* says Prime Minister Narendra Modi. *'Save the NHS,'* says Boris Johnson, before succumbing to the virus himself. *'War-time president'* Donald Trump vows to *'liberate'* locked-down states from the invisible enemy, the *'China-virus'*. 'We will fight this virus with everything we have,' says UK Health Minister Matt Hancock.

In times of crisis, simple metaphors can help unite us against a common enemy. But warlike language can be at odds with how we need to face the pandemic. Wearing masks, staying home – these are not warlike actions, and those who comply with them are seen by those who do not as weak and fearful. Those who get sick look like *'losers'*. *Curfews, confinement to home* and policing of our private lives quickly override civil liberties – yet we must 'obey orders' because this is 'wartime'.

Of course, it's not that simple. *Covid-19* is not just a monster to be defeated and destroyed. It has swept over our societies like an avenging angel, shining a fierce light on the burden of inequality that has got heavier and heavier in the past decade. On the groups that suffer most, in developing and rich countries. On whose work is of real value when real life is at stake. It illuminates how society least rewards those who have done the most to keep life going this year. On how we are all truly connected, transmitting wellness and sickness through breath and touch, how *'none of us are safe until all of us are safe'*.

Leaders and the media should start to promote solidarity and civic responsibility; respect and empathy for each other. *Shared expertise*, not cut-throat competition, is producing vaccines. *Solutions* are global, not narrowly national.

Already, international movements are working together for justice and human rights. Their collective vision is of a world where people live in peace, conscious of their common humanity and shared responsibilities for each other, the planet and future generations. New leadership in the USA and elsewhere is publicly committed to re-engaging with Covid-19, climate change and injustice. Together they have stated their commitment to resolving conflict, challenging the terrible inequalities of our time, and promoting a more ethical leadership.

Covid-19 has shown us that no matter who or where we are, we are all connected by our breath, for better or worse. Words too are carried on the breath, and the words we choose to read, speak and act on can reshape our experience of an uncertain and sometimes fearful time. Let's stop *doomscrolling* for the latest disaster headlines. Let's read, look for and listen to the new language of hope; whisper it, text it, sing or shout: *connection, co-operation, kindness. Salvation.*

www.womanworks.org.uk

In the Light of Love
Antonio Perez, Spain

Life is beautiful when we erase every particle of fear from our minds
and maintain our essence with a touch of madness,
a little humour, and a lot of love to share.
Antonio Perez

When the Covid-19 invasion came, everyone panicked. This reaction quickly lowered the vibratory state of humanity, leaving the vast majority absorbed in an unconscious state of fear and uncertainty about the future. Meanwhile, other humans activated their consciousness and their hearts to counter this surge of chaos and despair.

For me, from the first moment I felt that the crisis was a call to universal consciousness and therefore demanded an instantaneous activation of the energy of love, the only and absolute creative energy. Genuine love is not sentimentality nor is it something that has to be thought about. These are just blind alleys that allow people to be deceived and manipulated by those who instil fear and confusion in the minds of what we call the collective mass or collective consciousness.

For my part, I feel that the reality that no one sees is more volatile and complicated to observe, but that it exists and is more real than any belief, ideology or religion created to steal the inner power that each individual possesses.

Covid-19 exists and is causing suffering, loss and chaos, but it can only be overcome if we each transcend our individual level of consciousness. To enable this, our lives and the lives of those we love must be protected from any source that projects fear and neglect, in order to prevent it from stunting and hindering our spiritual vision of life. Despite the dangers of living, we must always choose to live, and not just survive, burdened by fear and phobias. For this it is only necessary to feed our creative love and thus to banish the fear from our minds.

Ever since I was able to reason I have felt it this way, and now every day I see this more clearly. With the advent of Covid-19, the few doubts I still had have been dispelled. The human being as an earthly species has the greatest privileges and the best conditions to enjoy and create a better world. Yet this species is also the one that travels the world with the most ignorance, arrogance and stupidity. The average human being spends his life defending ideals and beliefs like an automaton, often without even stopping to reflect on what he defends or why.

I see this every day in terms of politics, religion, even soccer; people defend a certain party, ideology or team without even questioning their intention in doing so. People attack each other in order to defend 'their' party or favourite team. In doing so, they lose all their energy in vain. Meanwhile, these entities take away their followers' power, strength and conviction as individuals. They keep their grip on the money within society to continue manipulating it. Nobody sticks to the facts but only to their ideals, an absurd position that does not contribute anything benevolent to society.

I have always felt that seeking light is precisely that, illuminating with common sense and much love every corner of this world where darkness reigns. For this we must be honest – and honest with ourselves before anyone else. We must stop looking for war to defend ideals or beliefs that are not consistent with the facts in this moment. Being present involves the effort to be oneself, to cultivate a pure and clear mind as each day dawns. This is like the Sun, that is born anew every day and fills us with energy; no matter what happened yesterday, it warms us and gives us life.

When you work for your personal growth you cannot and should not accommodate the fears in your heart. Let them travel through your mind but do not shelter them within, even if they are huge; even if your legs say they don't want to carry on moving forward. Instead, obey your heart and let it direct your life. Living from the heart means loving all that exists, embracing those fears with all our love to melt them and transform them into our greatest strength. This way, we can create hearts as powerful and as radiant as the universe itself.

When people defend their own beliefs and ideologies, believing they are the most valid, they do nothing but create separation in humanity, destroying the potential for love. This is the ego at work. The soul travels by other paths: beauty is born in every action that is prompted by love. Hence, everything you say and do with love as your guiding principle will have a loving, beautiful and divine outcome. Your life will become the most interesting and beautiful documentary you could have imagined.

It was hard for me to understand certain facets of life, but since I was a child my soul knew what it wanted and what it came to this world for. So now I continue to carry out my role, allowing my soul to direct everything I say and do. The other day I realised that, just as the iris flower I have been growing had blossomed, my being had also bloomed with it, as I admired the velvet texture and colours of its petals. It was one more proof, one of many that I experience in everyday life; how life gives gifts and blessings every moment; how when something is cared for and treated with love, it flourishes with all its beauty. It is like this with everything and everyone, when you try to help others flourish, rather than allow them to wither.

If you cultivate your patience you will be able to see and feel deeply all the beauty that is around us. It is said that patience is the mother of science; I would add that it is the daughter of consciousness; patience determines the immensity and infinity of love and awareness that we are able to feel and treasure in our hearts, and thus the results that we reap in our journey through earthly life.

Life is as beautiful as the newly blossomed iris when we strive to give the best of our Being without conditions or limitations. Life is beautiful when we erase every particle of fear from our minds and maintain our essence with a touch of madness, a little humour and a lot of love to share. Otherwise life becomes boring and monotonous. We get trapped into a loop of fear and hopelessness that does not allow us to see or feel our love.

Our love must be like the rainbow, where we can never see the beginning or the end, but can only observe its beauty and feel its greatness. So choose to live in rainbow colours, vivid, crazy and fun. Make that attitude your great virtue and share it, without allowing yourself to be overwhelmed by criticism. Most of us who keep alive our spontaneity and joy in living tend to believe that others are sane and we are crazy. But if you have faith and believe in yourself, you will understand that that bit of madness that characterises you is the one that keeps you on your feet, trusting and radiating love, simply for the sake of love.

My Being always chooses to smile, love, and radiate warmth. This attitude nourishes me and keeps me alive. I try not to fall into the false sanity that others sell me. Sometimes I am weary because I can't reach hearts that remain closed and clinging to their fears, but I always go about my day with a smile and in good spirits. Above all, I live without losing the ability to love existence in its entirety.

*Please note, 'he' and 'his' as used here denote all human beings of any gender. Article translated from the original Spanish version.

Sending Out an SOS to the World
Shujata Luptajan, Spain

In these Covidious times many of us have found solace in the natural world; its beauty salves our souls, its fruits nourish our bodies, it provides our playground. Mother Nature: 'Age cannot wither her nor custom stale her infinite variety'. As we have reconnected, we recognise the loss we had experienced in our previous driven lives. We've noticed things. The ripening buds, the unfolding flowers, the visiting birds and bees, all have opened our eyes and refreshed our spirits. But we often forget that Mother Nature bears many children, some less welcome than others.

Mother Nature riding high
Waving branches in the sky,
Mother Nature in the grass
Bending softly as we pass.
Ticks cling on and pierce our skin
Mother Nature's getting in.
Pollen blows from flowers and trees
Mother Nature makes us sneeze.
Tiny unseen virus wild
Mother Nature's Covid child.
Her child is running loose and free,
To whom will be the victory?

Mother Nature is totally indifferent to who triumphs in the battle in which we are now engaged.

As I write I am remembering my dad, who died in 2002. He was a scientist who loved nature, poetry, philosophy, history, art, literature. During the war he researched penicillin. Literally millions of lives were saved by people like him, seeking with urgency, as we are doing now, a way of saving the thousands upon thousands of lives threatened by severe illness and infections like septicaemia. He nearly died of anaphylaxis as a result of his research. This was the second time that he had nearly died. The first time was from typhus when, as a twelve-year-old boy, he spent nine months in bed and lived on milk. Afterwards he could only crawl and had to learn to walk again. His story is the common one in previous generations where many millions have died as the result of now curable conditions.

Just after the Second World War the NHS was founded. Prior to that, when I was a tiny baby, the only way my mother could get me expensive antibiotics meant a choice between food or medicine. In the course of my lifetime our access to medicines and treatments has transformed human lives and we have become used to a life expectancy beyond the dreams of our ancestors. Yet sadly, even now, Our World in Data (Oxford University) gives a total of deaths in 2017 caused by vaccine-preventable diseases as over 1,500,000.

We are all struggling to be cheerful in these difficult times. I try to bear in mind what a walk in any English country churchyard tells me; that until very recently, less than the blink of an eye in human history, we were born to suffer heartrending loss through disease, and war, and poverty. In reading the gravestones the few bare facts say it all. I think too about *why* we have gravestones; that we remember those we love and honour them. For me, *Love in the Time of Corona* means showing respect for those who have died without recourse to modern medicine, and feeling immense gratitude for the changes we have experienced in recent times.

We already know that millions upon millions have been killed by the ravages of previous plagues, pandemics and diseases. The accounts bring tears to our eyes. Among them just a few from the endless roll-call:

William Shakespeare is honoured and remembered for his poetic gifts. But it is less known that his mother lost his two little elder sisters to plague when they were babes in arms, both dying before he was born in 1564. Then later his brother Gilbert and his son Hamnet were also victim to bubonic plague over subsequent years.

About a hundred years later Elizabeth Hancock was living in the little village of Eyam in Derbyshire. Plague was sweeping through, devastating the population and eventually leaving 200 dead. In the space of eight days Elizabeth dragged the bodies of her six children and her husband to bury them alone in a field, watched from a distance by terrified neighbours.

Charles Darwin's daughter Annie died in 1851 aged ten from scarlet fever or TB. He wrote 'We have lost the joy of our household, and the solace of our old age. Oh that she could now know how deeply, how tenderly we do still and ever shall love her dear joyous face.'

We remember the famous ones; Keats, who died of TB in 1821, Gustav Klimt and Egon Schiele, who died of Spanish flu in Vienna in 1918. Freddie Mercury to AIDS in 1991. We will of course never know how many geniuses we have lost to communicable disease throughout the world and throughout time. Infectious diseases do not respect status, fame or fortune. And the most unnoticed life lost is no less valuable. Most people who died vanished unremembered. However restricted we may feel now, we have so little to complain of compared with our predecessors.

But the times they are a-changing in the most extraordinary and miraculous way. The glorious and unified effort of the scientific community, supported by governments globally, in an unprecedented example of worldwide human cooperation, has produced vaccines within the space of one year. They have heard our Mayday.

'Science' means 'knowledge' and always was a path towards truth in ancient philosophy. Let us follow down the path with grateful awareness of what has been achieved to bring us to this point. With the concerted efforts of the global medical community we may yet survive to tackle the pressing concerns of climate change and species destruction ... if, that is, we have learnt something about love in all its breadth and generosity.

As Keats writes, 'The poetry of earth is never dead.'

From space it's a blue ball floating in blackness.
The hard core of iron is 5000 degrees and the size of the moon.
The inner and the outer core are 2900 kilometres below our feet.

It has a thick solid mantle wrapping the core.
Then there's the thin crust on which we stand.
It has mountains and forests, oceans and icecaps.
There are lemurs and ladybirds, and blackbirds and pelicans and doves.
There are pandas and mice and snails. Fishes and foxes.
Numberless species, some here, some gone.
But Earth has been overrun by one animal that is destroying it.
There are cities with lights that you can see from space.
There is crying and laughter, there is fighting and squabbling.
There are words and songs and dancing.
There is life and there is death.
There is you and there is me.
And there are viruses.

In fact, we depend on the approximately two kilos of bacteria in our microbiome. Millions of viruses and bacteria are cascading from the sky, hundreds of thousands of which an individual inhales every minute. The blind watchmaker Evolution has given us immunity to almost all. But *not* all.

In these times of Covid, with much time to reflect, we are acutely aware of how much love we need to safeguard ourselves and each other. And to safeguard our beautiful planet earth, remembering that Mother Nature is indifferent to the fate of humankind. In fact she may breathe a sigh of relief if some of her more troublesome children finally leave home, as many have done before, pushed out by their upstart siblings.

Most of us love life, spontaneously, vigorously, determined to survive and thrive in the face of challenges. We are bound to ask ourselves what loving life demands of us. For me Love means respect for truth, tolerance of temporary inconvenience, fortitude in the face of loss, and caring for others outside our immediate circle. Above all, now it means grasping enthusiastically and with gratitude the solutions that medical science offers in this time of worldwide uncertainty and anxiety.

As William Golding, who cites James Lovelock's original idea of *Mater Gaia* that all life is interconnected, said in his Nobel Prize acceptance speech, we live "in the blazing poetry of the fact, we are the children of the stars." We are made of stardust and will one day return to stardust. In the meantime, let us hope for a long life in the light of that old yellow dwarf in the sky, our sun. We have about eight billion years left before it dies. In the time ahead, if we survive as a species, we will harvest many unimagined fruits from the tree of knowledge. Let's keep the sun shining in our lives as we go forward together.

One Year On ...
How Much Longer Before It Ends?

Sue Edge

Confront the facts and situation as they are right now.
And retain faith that we will prevail in the end, however long it takes
Jim Collins

Today marks the one-year anniversary from when the World Health Organization declared a global pandemic. Back then I had no idea if the WHO was being over-cautious in their declaration or whether this was going to be serious? Most anniversaries of difficult events such as the loss of a job or loved one mark a stretch of time passing of remembrance, grief and adjustment. This year-on is different because we are still in the pandemic, we are still in a lockdown and life is still very different to normal. Social distancing has become a new-normal, as has not travelling far from home, nor booking holidays or getting our hair cut. Sometimes it feels like we are on an enormous merry-go-round where we go round in a loop of rising case numbers leading to restrictions followed by lockdown. While tucked away in our homes for months we finally get our case numbers down with a feeling of relief, only to then begin opening up and we repeat the whole process again.

One of the most challenging part of the pandemic is the emotional agility required to navigate the constant changes and fluctuations. Somehow we have to find a way to process opposite emotions on a very regular basis. Last week I was taking my daily walk by the sea feeling peaceful and uplifted listening to the bird song and waves lapping at the beach. Ten minutes later I saw a neighbour who

I'd not bumped into for weeks and engaged in a moving conversation about her loss of her elderly mother from Covid-19. She was one of 18 residents in a local care home who all died around Christmas during the peak of our second wave. As I walked on I felt touched and saddened by the enormity of the pandemic still around the world and right here close to home.

And alongside this on-going loss and illness worldwide, there is now the real potential impact of the vaccines. This Saturday I am driving my partner to the local drive-through at the GP surgery for his first dose. On the one hand, I am hopeful that the vaccine will slowly have an impact on the pandemic globally. But equally, I can't imagine a life that is back to normal perhaps by June 21st this year. Does anyone else try to picture what post-vaccinated UK will be like this summer? Will all social restrictions really be lifted, and if so will this be safe or will it prompt a third wave? The thought of people going mad with huge festivals, sporting events and unlimited parties, makes me want to remain a hermit! It feels too much too soon, even with the vaccine success.

How can I be cautious and hopeful all at the same time, I wonder? Is it even possible to swing between these two opposites? Recently I heard about the "Stockdale Paradox" which has been written about by Jim Collins in "Good to Great". Admiral Jim Stockdale was a US prisoner of war in Vietnam for eight years who survived and went on to live fully afterwards. When asked who didn't do so well in the camp, he explained, surprisingly, that it was the optimists. They kept thinking they would be out by Christmas and weren't, then by Easter and weren't. The disappointment each time caused immense heartache and suffering. So what was the alternative?

Stockdale survived these years by living more day-to-day in the present moment. He accepted the difficulties and the situation as it was each day, however brutal or challenging. But at the same time, he maintained a deep faith that he would prevail in the end, however long that took. By living with this paradox, he was able to cope. This principle also works well in other less extreme situations, and is even taught to potential business leaders. It is both hopeful and grounded at the same time.

Living through this pandemic for a year, I **have** become better at being more focused on the present moment. I am more appreciative of the small moments of pleasure each day and have managed to ride this emotional pandemic roller-coaster so far. Perhaps by reaching the end of a whole year of the pandemic today, my mind is less tolerant of just being in the present moment and wants to **really** know when it will end? Enough now, I say, enough. I am tired and weary of living in a pandemic for a whole year.

However, I am inspired by the Stockdale paradox, and remind myself that putting a random date in my diary that may well change, isn't going to make coping any easier. I may as well settle back into the day-to-day living with its ups and downs and come back to the present moment each time I try to jump six months ahead in my mind. And more importantly, find some deep strands of faith within me that we **will** survive this pandemic, and thrive once again.

http://keepingcalmincoronatimes.blogspot.com

Embracing Hope
Kalyani Sandrapragas, UK

*'Love recognises no barriers.
It jumps hurdles, leaps fences,
penetrates walls to arrive
at its destination full of hope'*
Maya Angelou

5 January 2021 – Covid infections and mortality rates have reached record numbers in the UK and Prime Minister Boris Johnson has declared a national lockdown.

1 **February 2021** – The worldwide figures reported for Covid infections and deaths, rise with a total of 103,577,230 cases and 2,239,013 deaths.

The infection and mortality rates in the UK have far exceeded the 'worst case scenario' anticipated by the government in March 2020. The total number of cases number about 3,817,176 and the total number of deaths 106,158. The lockdown is expected to continue to mid-March, though many anticipate strict restrictions to be in place until the summer. In the eyes of many, the handling of the pandemic has been less than satisfactory and the government has been criticised initially acting too late to reduce the spread of the virus.

Our worst nightmares were confirmed by the discovery of a new variant of Covid-19 in December 2020. Scientists investigating have confirmed that this variant has a number of mutations that make it more transmissible and may account for the record spikes in infections, as it is believed that it is 50 per cent more contagious than the original strain. More recently, new variants have emerged both in Brazil and South Africa.

The situation is also bleak in a number of EU nations as Covid cases surge, with stricter measures being imposed, ranging from tighter curfews to national lockdowns. As the pandemic spreads across the globe, it has left a trail of deaths in its wake. Mortality rates in Europe and North America outnumber those in Asia at the peak of the infection there. In Latin America, South America and the Caribbean, numbers are rising. New Zealand and Australia seem to have stemmed the infection rates and are, for now, enjoying a semblance of near normality, whilst countries like Taiwan, Singapore and Brunei have continued to control Covid-19 successfully since the first outbreak at the beginning of 2020.

22 February 2021 – As the coronavirus case rates and deaths continue to decline in the UK following stringent lockdown measures and a rapid vaccine rollout, the prime minister has announced his 'roadmap' for how restrictions will be gradually eased this summer. The reopening will be based on continuous assessments and reviews over the period outlined by the roadmap. People's hopes are rekindled, that at last we are entering a phase that marks the beginning of a return to 'near-normality'. With cautious optimism the nation prepares to step out of lockdown. *Hope springs eternal in the human breast.* Alexander Pope

23 March 2021 – The anniversary of the announcement of lockdown in the UK will be marked by a National Day of Reflection, with the backing of political leaders. More than 100 organisations are involved in the organisation of the event which has been initiated by the end-of-life charity Marie Curie, as a way for the public to remember those who have died.

The total number of deaths linked to the coronavirus in the UK on 23 March 2020, are variously reported as being between 335-465. A year later, according to figures published on the 13 March 2021, the latest figures state that there have now been 143,259 deaths.

Covid-19 has been likened to an invincible enemy, lurking at every corner, within and without, pervading our reality as it weaves its way through towns and cities, countries and continents, irrespective of borders. Pervasive and suffocating like particles of dust held suspended in the air. Lives suspended. Breath suspended.

Threatened by this 'invasion', as we pause for breath, even struggle for breath, we are reminded how powerless and insignificant we are when confronted by

Nature. *All things share the same breath – the beast, the tree, the man. The air shares its spirit with all the life it supports.* Chief Seattle.

Paradoxically we found ourselves locked-in by nature, having exercised dominance over the natural world, locking-in wildlife as we saw fit. Now we get a taste of our own medicine – oh the irony! Our twenty-first century existential crisis.

Despite the recent arrival of new vaccines and the hopes of millions that things will get better, it is now not known if they are effective against the new variants, and for that matter, future variants.

Nearly a year in, the pandemic continues to highlight the fact that the virus does not discriminate and that, behind the protective face covering and gloves, *#WeAreInThisTogether*. Essential goods and services take priority over luxury items and services, highlighting what a wasteful and consumerist society we were hitherto engaged in. For now, social distancing continues to be the norm and fear and uncertainty, with a sprinkling of hope, the prevailing mood.

It has been a long and arduous journey with no end in sight. A range of emotions felt in every household from panic and fear to trust and hope; those hopes and dreams we have nurtured and held close to our hearts being challenged once more. This is a time of reflection, as we remain locked-in, in both our *individual bubbles* and the *collective bubble* that hold us all together.

In order to look forward we sometimes need to look backwards, to understand better where we have arrived, and why. The pandemic however, reaffirms that we are all connected:

It is a portal, a gateway between one world and the next. We can choose to walk through it, dragging the carcasses of our prejudice and hatred, our avarice, our data banks, and dead ideas, our dead rivers and smoky skies behind us. Or we can walk through lightly, with little luggage, ready to imagine another world. And ready to fight for it. Arundhati Roy

As with all crises, the pandemic offers us an opportunity for growth and the hope of change. As human beings, hope is the one constant that has seen us through adversity. And despite our hopes being dashed on occasions, we are unwilling to relinquish hope. It gives us possibilities and enables us to continue on our path despite challenging circumstances. *It can make the present moment less difficult to bear.*

If we believe that tomorrow will be better, we can bear a hardship today. Thich Nhat Hanh

Hope enables us to surmount fear and embrace the unknown. It unites us on the same path as the rest of humanity, in the belief that things *will* get better. The expression *where there is life there is hope* aptly sums up our deep connection with hope, and as with love, hope fuels our longing for life. Like twins they go hand in hand. *Love is a springtime plant that perfumes everything with its hope, even the ruins to which it clings.* Gustave Flaubert

In her poem *Hope is a Thing with Feathers,* Emily Dickinson likens hope to a feathered bird that is permanently perched in the soul of every person. Whatever the weather or season the bird never ceases to sing.

> *Hope is the thing with feathers*
> *That perches in the soul –*
> *And sings the tune without the words –*
> *And never stops – at all –*
> * And sweetest – in the Gale – is heard –*
> *And sore must be the storm –*
> *That could abash the little Bird*
> *That kept so many warm –*
> * I've heard it in the chillest land –*
> *And on the strangest Sea –*
> *Yet – never – in Extremity,*
> *It asked a crumb – of me.*

Hope enables tomorrow to be a vision of happiness; that *there is* hope for the future, hope for unity and hope for peace. In sharing the voices of friends and family in this book, *my* hope is that the 'New Normal' encompasses all of Humanity and Mother Earth in one embrace.

In the depths of your hopes and desires lies your silent knowledge of the beyond; And like seeds dreaming beneath the snow your heart dreams of spring. Trust the dreams, for in them is hidden the gate to eternity. Kahlil Gibran

'This is the time to be slow
Lie low to the wall
Until the bitter weather passes.

Try, as best you can, not to let
The wire brush of doubt
Scrape from your heart
All sense of yourself
And your hesitant light.

If you remain generous,
Time will come good;
And you will find your feet
Again on fresh pastures of promise,
Where the air will be kind
And blushed with beginning.'

John O'Donohue – Excerpt from *'To Bless the Space Between Us'*

Your Covid Chronicle

These pages are here to record your own journey – your story

Fill your paper with the breathings of your heart
William Wordsworth